AWAKENING EDEN

Awakening Eden

J. MUTTI

If you purchased this book without a cover, you should be aware that this book may be stolen property and reported as "unsold and destroyed" to the publisher. In such case neither the author nor publisher has received any payment for this "stripped book".

This book is a work of fiction. Any reference to historical events, real places, or real people are used fictitiously. Other names, characters, places, and events are products of the author's imagination and any resemblance to actual events or places or persons, living or dead, is entirely coincidental.

Copyright © 2025 by J. Mutti
All rights reserved.

Genesis Publishing

No part of this publication may be reproduced in any manner whatsoever without the written permission of the author, except in the case of brief quotations embodied in critical articles and reviews.

For questions or more information, please contact the author at
jay.mutti@gmail.com

Cover Art and Design By: J. Mutti

First Printing, 2025
ISBN: 979-8-218-61429-4

Dedicated to all the closed doors—
Each one, unknowingly, opening a world of endless possibility and adventure.

| 1 |

Julie stood in the open doorway, between the garage and the tiled hallway leading towards the kitchen, her eyes fixed on the garage door as she watched it slowly close.

She had just said goodbye to her husband, Mike, who was leaving for another week on the road.

The space felt so empty, except for a stack of boxes against the far wall. The boxes were old and faded, containing a small history of her life before marriage, kids, and living on Cabot Lane.

In the middle of the garage was the stained halo left by her husband's car—a ring made by years of melting snow and drying rain. It was ironic that there would be such a large, lasting impression since Mike spent most of his time traveling.

For the last eight years, he had worked as the Regional Sales Manager for a local wholesale food supplier. He and his car were more often away, than parked at home. Nearby, two well-worn bicycles lay discarded in a pile for the winter.

Julie's life was so deeply rooted in habit and routine that the days quickly blurred together without distinction—each one rolling into the next in an endless loop of responsibilities. Before she knew it, a full week had passed since Mike had left last Monday.

Work only added to the haze. Projects piled up, deadlines loomed, and the weight of mounting stress settled heavily on her shoulders, demanding more of her focus and energy than ever before.

It was exhausting. But it was also easier—easier to lose herself in the cycle of busyness and repetition, easier to let the days slip by without stopping to think.

Because thinking led to questions.

And questions led to truths Julie wasn't sure she was ready to accept...

Her days were deliberately structured, built on a foundation of routine and predictability. For Julie, structure meant safety—safety she needed to keep moving forward.

Her morning began at 6:30 a.m., with her alarm signaling it was time to wake up. Once she shrugged off her drowsiness and rolled out of bed, she moved as if on autopilot, going through her morning routine—getting dressed, applying makeup, and fixing her hair—before heading downstairs to start a pot of coffee. Whether she had time to enjoy it was another matter entirely.

Like a finely tuned watch, the boys followed behind her, making their way to the bathrooms to get ready for the day as well.

The twins were almost 15 now. Chad always used the upstairs bathroom, while Tommy came downstairs to shower and get ready for the day.

Tommy's smile always brightened Julie's morning. He was the younger of the twins and she would always think of him as her baby boy, though he was far from being a baby now. Standing almost 5'6.", he was growing into a fine young man.

Most mornings, on his way to the bathroom, he would give his mother a happy smile and a cheerful, "Good morning, Mom!"

Chad, on the other hand, looked and acted a little more like his father. He was much less outgoing than Tommy—shorter, stockier and less athletic. Though Chad was a whole ten minutes older than Tommy, he was often jokingly referred to as the "little brother."

With the boys in the shower, Julie busied herself making and packing their lunches. She knew they wouldn't eat them, but still, it felt like her responsibility.

Even as they grew more independent, more self-reliant—especially with Mike gone so often—Julie struggled to let go of her role as *Mom*.

At 7:20 a.m. her phone alarm would buzz, letting her know it was time for her and the boys to leave. After a flurry of flying backpacks, jackets, and coats, the closing door sounded like the thud of a coffin. The house felt like an empty tomb and looked like the aftermath of a hurricane left behind by the two boys.

Each morning, Julie drove the same familiar roads, listening to her usual morning radio show as she stopped intermittently for traffic lights and school buses. She dropped the boys off at the high school before heading to work herself, just down the street. This was Julie's second year as a sixth-grade English teacher at Franklin Middle Academy.

Julie had dropped out of college at the start of her freshman year when she became pregnant with the boys. Mike insisted they get married right away, and they moved into a small apartment.

He took the first full-time job he could find that offered decent pay and medical insurance, landing a position as a material handler at the local wholesale warehouse.

For years, they struggled to make ends meet.

Over time, Mike climbed the corporate ladder, eventually earning a promotion to, Regional Sales Manager. The money he now made was enough for them to buy their modest house at the end of Cabot Lane, which had been their home ever since.

Seven years ago, with the boys nearing their teenage years, Julie decided to go back to school to fulfill her dream of becoming an English teacher. While the boys became more independent, she took advantage of the opportunity.

It took longer than she had hoped to complete her coursework and earn her degree, but it was worth it. She felt immense pride every morning when she saw her name on the classroom door: Room 10 - Mrs. Julie Tosh.

The air was brisk and sharp as she stepped out of her car that morning. This was her favorite time of year. By March, the students and teachers had established a good rapport and had settled into their own solid routines. Some of her classes were getting ready to move from basic grammar lessons to more complex topics like poetry.

The seasons were clearly changing. The old gray winter skies of Massachusetts were turning blue. The sun hung in the sky noticeably longer, and grass pushed through the clumps of melting snow. The world felt full of new possibilities.

Most mornings at school followed their own carefully crafted rhythm. Julie stopped by the main office to grab her mail before heading to the teacher's lounge, hoping for a second—but often her first—cup of coffee. Always pressed for time, she rarely socialized with the other teachers. The narrow window between dropping the twins off at school and making it to work on time left her perpetually on the edge of running late.

Her office stops were brief. She would say hello to Mrs. Reed, the school secretary, and check her mailbox. Julie rarely received much important mail—usually flyers, PTA notices, or her paycheck every Friday. But this morning, there was something different: a pink postcard in her mailbox. Julie reached in and pulled it out. On the front was a red rose, and on the back, it read:

"You Are Invited To Mrs. Waltz's Pure Eden Party! Friday Night, March 10, 8 P.M."

"What's that?" a voice asked over her shoulder.

Startled, Julie turned around.

It was Cole Anderson, one of the sixth-grade science teachers.

Cole was in his third year at Franklin. Unlike Julie, he had started teaching fresh out of college. Standing about 5'9." with an athletic build, his dark hair and brown eyes hinted at a Mediterranean descent. Cole had once mentioned he was adopted by the Andersons as a young boy and never knew his biological parents. The Andersons had always raised him as their own, so he never felt the need to pursue his heritage further.

Despite their age difference, Cole and Julie had become good friends over the last two years. They had bonded over the challenges of teaching and enjoyed a familiar, friendly chemistry that made work feel less like, well...work.

"I'm not sure," Julie said. "I've never heard of this before. Did you get one?"

"Uh, nope," Cole said, rifling through his mail.

Julie glanced at the postcard again. "I'll ask Barbara about it later today."

Barbara Waltz, the other sixth-grade English teacher, had become a trusted friend and mentor to Julie. However, she had never invited Julie to a party before.

"See you later, Cole," Julie said, realizing she was running late. She hurried down the hall, snatching a quick cup of coffee before heading to her classroom to greet her homeroom students.

The school was laid out like a giant "T." Down the middle was a long hallway that split left and right at the end. The first floor was primarily dedicated to the sixth grade, with two classrooms for each subject—one on the left and one on the right. The left side was known as the "A Wing," and the right side as the "B Wing."

The second and third floors housed the seventh and eighth grades, respectively, in much the same layout. The first floor also contained the gym, cafeteria, nurse's office, and two special education classrooms down the main hallway.

Julie's classroom was on the right, all the way at the end of the "A Wing" hallway—Room 10. This had become her home away from home. The classroom definitely wouldn't win any awards for décor. Julie wasn't much of a decorator, which was one of the reasons she preferred teaching middle school rather than elementary.

All the construction paper cutouts and primary colors were just too much for her. She was a much simpler person by design. A few well-placed inspirational quotes and some juvenile pieces of wall art for levity—that was Room 10.

Ring! The sound of the 8 O'clock bell signaled the start of homeroom.

As usual, the kids came barreling in like a freight train. The noise of laughter and excited chatter filled the room as the students found their seats.

"Good morning!" Julie greeted the class. "How was everyone's weekend?"

The class was too noisy to hear her.

"Good Morning!" Julie said louder, grabbing their attention.

"Before we break for first period, there are a few things I need to go over," she said. "First, there will be no After-School Program this Friday. If you usually stay after on Fridays, make sure you let someone at home know. Also, I need all of your field trip forms signed and returned by the end of the day next Monday. Again, EVERYTHING must be turned in by the end of the day on March 13th—both money and permission slips. I'll send out a reminder later this week to take home. It's going to be a fun trip, but if I don't have your permission slips, you cannot go! Does everyone understand?"

The bell quickly rang once again. The students grabbed their bags and books and, like a herd of cattle, shuffled toward the door.

Julie made her way to the doorway through the sea of middle schoolers. The hallway was where the school truly came to life, where its natural rhythm pulsed. She enjoyed observing the subtle interactions that took place "outside the classroom."

Generally, the students at Franklin were terrific kids. Serious incidents were rare, and disciplinary action usually consisted of lunch detention or a simple note home. Julie knew she had it pretty good here—the students were eager to learn, and the staff were nothing short of professional.

Monday's first period was Julie's prep time—her one chance during the day to make copies, review lesson plans, grade papers, and tackle the countless other responsibilities of a teacher.

But this morning, all she wanted to do was sit down and enjoy her coffee. It had been a long weekend of running errands with the boys and managing the countless domestic crises that came with managing a household. She just needed a moment to herself.

"Mrs. Tosh!" a voice called from the door.

Julie looked up to see Lisa and Alyssa standing in the doorway.

"Can we come in?" they asked. "We just want to talk to you about the paper."

Lisa and Alyssa were two of Julie's favorite students from the previous year. In sixth grade, they had both discovered a love for writing and excelled at it. Together, they had jokingly talked about becoming writers when they grew up and asked to start a school newspaper.

Barbara Waltz had explained to Julie that every few years, a group of students would take an interest in starting a paper. The project often fizzled out after the first issue. Being a new English teacher, Julie had been assigned as the paper's advisor when Lisa and Alyssa inquired about reviving it.

Lisa and Alyssa were inseparable, so Julie jokingly referred to them as "LA."

"Absolutely, girls!" Julie said. "What can I help you with?"

The girls explained that while they had a few articles done already, they were struggling to meet the minimum content needed for the issue.

"We've added the lunch menu to the back, which helped fill space, but we'd like a few more solid articles." Alyssa explained.

"Okay. I know about the ones you've already written, but what other ideas are you considering?" Julie asked.

"We heard there's going to be a school department meeting about the possibility of uniforms." Lisa suggested. "That could be a good article, but that's the only new idea we have."

"And Katie Dinn has a crush on Mr. Anderson!" Alyssa added with a giggle.

The girls exchanged mischievous smiles as Julie shook her head, chuckling.

"I think we'll leave Mr. Anderson out of this issue," she replied with a smirk.

"Hmm...?" Julie thought for a moment. "What about the sixth-grade field trip? I know you're both in seventh grade now, but if I can get you a seat on the bus, you could go and write about that. There's going to be so much to see and learn—you might even have enough for a few articles."

The field trip was one of Julie's new responsibilities this year too. The principal, Mr. Dryer, had tasked her with planning a trip that all the sixth-grade classes could use to enhance their curriculum.

After some research, Julie had decided on Old Patriot Village—a reconstructed colonial town complete with costumed actors, livestock, and demonstrations of early 19th-century life.

Putting together a successful trip wasn't just important to Julie—it was everything. For the last two years, she had battled relentless self-doubt, constantly questioning whether she truly belonged in the classroom. On paper, she was more than qualified—graduating with honors, earning her certifications—but deep down, she feared it was all an illusion. That at any moment, she might screw up, and someone would see right through her.

Being older than all her college classmates and the other new teachers only intensified the feeling that she didn't quite belong. She felt out of place, like an impostor in a world that had already moved ahead without her. But this trip—if she could pull it off—would be proof. Proof that she was capable. Proof that she deserved to be here. Proof that she hadn't been lying to herself all along.

"That sounds like a great idea!" Alyssa said excitedly. "What do you think, Lisa?"

"Sounds good to me!" Lisa agreed.

"Perfect! I'll talk to your teachers today and get you permission slips if they're okay with it," Julie said.

The girls were thrilled, and Julie felt a sense of accomplishment.

Two birds with one stone.

"Is there anything else I can help you with?" Julie asked. "You both need to get to class, and I'd really like to finish my coffee before the period ends."

"Not really! Thanks for your help, Mrs. T!" Lisa said with a smile as they left the room.

Julie decided to handle the field trip permissions immediately to avoid distractions later. She opened her laptop and composed a quick email to the seventh-grade teachers, explaining the girls' request and asking if they had any objections. With a *click*, the email was sent.

Pulling up her calendar, Julie reviewed her schedule for the rest of the month.

Nothing major besides the field trip. She breathed a sigh of relief.

Planning and coordinating the trip had been far more work than she'd anticipated. The endless behind-the-scenes details—policies, medical paperwork, logistics—had been overwhelming at times. But despite the challenges, she was growing more confident in her abilities every day.

She had handled nearly everything on her own, with little help or guidance, and now, piece by piece, it was all coming together. Only a few final details remained.

Her gaze shifted to the pink postcard sitting on her desk.

"Oh yeah!" Julie murmured, crinkling her face in curiosity as she picked up the card and read it again to herself.

She hovered her mouse cursor over the calendar box labeled Friday on her screen and added an entry:

"Party – Barbara, 8 PM."

Julie examined the postcard more intently, flipping it over and over in her hands.

Pure Eden Party? She wondered.

What's that?

Turning back to her computer, she opened her web browser and typed "Pure Eden Party." into the search bar. She waited as the page loaded. A list of links and descriptions appeared. At the top of the page, one description caught her eye:

"Pure Eden Party – Never Disappoints. A Perfect Girls' Night Out."

Oh, this looks like fun!

Julie clicked on the link for more information.

A website opened, displaying a menu, ad banners for shaving lotion, and a "Deals of the Day" section.

She scrolled down to a list labeled "Best Sellers":

- Vanilla Frosting Tingling Lube
- Whipped Cupcake Body Oil
- Love Story Shaving Cream

Beneath the list, a bold tagline read: "Pure Eden – The Leader in Women's Intimacy."

What? Julie gasped.

Is this a—

Julie couldn't believe it. It looked like Barbara had invited her to—of all things—a *Sex Toy Party*! As she scrolled further, the truth became glaringly obvious.

"Pleasure Awaits," the website proclaimed. Categories like "Self Care," "Vibrators," "Lubricants," and "His and Hers" lined the page.

Julie's heart raced as she quickly closed the browser window, her cheeks burning with embarrassment. She looked around the empty classroom, ensuring no one had wandered in unnoticed. Her pulse pounded in her ears.

Oh my God!

Oh no! I wonder if the IT people saw what I was looking at?

Julie didn't know much about computers, but she had heard rumors that IT staff could monitor what websites were accessed on the school's network. Her mind raced, imagining someone in the IT department laughing or gossiping about her accidental search.

"It'll be okay." she reassured herself aloud, though her voice sounded uncertain.

"I'm fine. It was just a web search."

"Nobody will know."

Her nerves settled slightly as she reminded herself that she was probably just being paranoid. Still, she was shocked—more than shocked—by the revelation.

Barbara? Julie's mind reeled.

Barbara was the last person she'd ever expect to host something like this!

Who else did she invite?

A flood of questions crashed through her thoughts.

Was this for real?
Who else knew about it?
And most importantly—
How was she supposed to respond?

Julie had never been to many parties before—and definitely never one like this. She'd never owned a sex toy or even seen one in real life.

What was Barbara thinking?

All Julie could focus on was how she was going to tell Barbara she couldn't go.

But why?

What excuse could she give?

Mike wouldn't like it—that was a given. He already disliked her going out, and a party like this would be completely out of the question.

Maybe she could just say she wasn't comfortable.

Or she could lie—say she already had plans.

Julie sighed, knowing she'd see Barbara at lunch and would have to come up with a convincing excuse by then.

For now, she still had a coffee to finish and work to do before the start of the next class.

| 2 |

The rest of the morning unfolded as smoothly as she had anticipated.

Julie spent the second and third periods trying to introduce her students to different styles of poetry.

But, no matter how hard she tried, she couldn't stop thinking about the invitation—about the party.

While explaining meter and prose to her students, her mind kept drifting, rehearsing how she would bring it up to Barbara. Over and over, she played out the conversation in her head, like a child memorizing lines for a school play.

But why was she so worked up about this?

It was just a party.

Deep down, she was actually glad to have been invited to something.

Nights and weekends at home had become painfully lonely and boring. With Mike on the road, the house was quiet in all the wrong ways. The boys were usually around, but not really present—Chad and Tommy spent most of their time holed up in their rooms, doing homework, watching TV or gaming online with friends.

Most nights, Julie found herself alone in the living room, grading papers, reading, and sipping from a too-full glass of wine, the soft hum of the television the only sound keeping her company.

Maybe that was why the invitation lingered in her thoughts.

Because for once, someone had thought to include her.

And that? That felt different.

It would be nice to go out for a change, she thought.

She caught herself daydreaming. "Uh, where was I?" she muttered, shaking her head to regain composure in front of her students.

"And so, that is what iambic pentameter is." she concluded. "For tonight's homework, I'd like you all to write your own poems using this model. Each poem only needs to be two verses long and can be about any topic you like. Any questions?"

The students exchanged glances, but before anyone could speak, the bell rang to signal the end of third period.

"Okay then! Have a great rest of the day!" Julie said.

Some students scrambled to their feet and bolted for the door, while others slowly packed their backpacks.

Julie sat at her desk, nodding and smiling at them as they filed out, but her mind was elsewhere, fixated on the impending conversation with Barbara.

When the last student left the classroom, Julie got up and started getting ready to make her way to the door. She stopped, picked up the pink postcard from her desk, and slipped it into her pocket. Grabbing her purse and jacket, she headed down the hall toward the cafeteria.

As she walked, Mr. Anderson stepped out of his classroom, closing the door behind him as he prepared to head to lunch. She caught his eye as he turned.

"Hey, Jules!" he called out. "How's it going?"

Julie was so distracted that she didn't even notice.

"Jules!" he said again, louder. "Hello!"

"Oh! Sorry!" Julie replied, snapping out of her thoughts. "I saw you, I just didn't hear you."

She smiled sheepishly. "Sorry about that. What's up?"

"Is everything okay?" Cole asked, concerned. "You seem… hmm… distracted?"

"Yeah, I'm good. Just a little scattered at the moment. It's nothing," she said, shaking her head and shoulders as if trying to shake off the tension.

"Mike must be coming home this week? You always seem flustered when he's scheduled to come back," Cole said, shrugging and raising his eyebrows.

"Oh, yeah, that's right! I almost forgot," Julie said. "That's probably it." she repeated, almost as if trying to convince herself.

"I feel like my head is everywhere right now. It just gets so hard sometimes, keeping everything organized—school, home, the boys, Mike's schedule, the field trip. I… yeah… I'm just…"

"…in need of a break!" Cole finished with a laugh. "Good thing you have a party on Friday. That should take your mind off things for a bit. I checked my mailbox, and I didn't get an invite, so—lucky you!"

Julie didn't dare tell Cole what she had seen online. So, as they walked down the hallway, she simply said she might not be able to go—especially with Mike coming home. She'd have to check with him first, and with everything else going on, it might just be too hectic.

They continued chatting as they walked toward the cafeteria.

3

Julie enjoyed being on cafeteria duty. It gave her a chance to see students from previous years and listen to the popular middle school gossip of the day.

Lunch was the one time, and the cafeteria the one place, where students felt free to truly be themselves, shedding the confines of the classroom.

Looking around, it was hard to believe this was the same school as the modern, polished hallways she had just left.

Over the years, Franklin's classrooms, front offices, gym, and halls had all been remodeled multiple times. But the cafeteria? It looked like it had been pulled straight out of a 1970s yearbook.

The awful orange laminate panels on the walls, the faded felt banners hanging from the ceiling (secured with everything from plastic ties to fishing line), and the gray-speckled square tiles on the floor gave the space an ancient, dingy appearance.

But, the students didn't care. For them, it was the middle school version of recess. Sixth graders still needed unstructured social time, while seventh and eighth graders found useful ways to take advantage of it.

Many of the boys used the time to catch up on homework they hadn't done the night before, while the girls eagerly shared the latest gossip and minor scandals.

Julie's job was simple—it had been explained to her as: "Just make sure nobody dies." Some days, however, that was easier said than done.

There were students with severe food allergies to monitor, the occasional conflict between kids that could escalate, and plenty of drama always waiting for an audience. And, of course, there was the ever-present risk of a student actually choking.

But as Julie scanned the room, everything seemed calm. Just the way she liked it. For the next 35 minutes, she could enjoy lighthearted interactions with the students as she casually walked around. Afterward, she would have a glorious 10 minutes to herself to eat lunch before tackling the last two periods of the day.

The bell rang, signaling the end of lunch, and students began clearing their trays and heading to the exit doors.

The teachers' lounge, tucked into a corner of the main cafeteria, wasn't much to look at either. It was a small rectangular room with painted block walls and a mishmash of collected décor accumulated over decades. Faded motivational posters adorned the walls, an ancient coffee maker sat with its stained carafes, and a full-size refrigerator bore a sternly printed sign: **"Please Empty The Fridge Every Friday!"** Old couches and chairs lined the walls, and a single large table dominated the center of the room.

For teachers without cafeteria duty, lunch was rarely a solitary experience. Everyone gathered around the table to share stories from the day, talk about their lives, and, occasionally, indulge in a bit of gossip. It was the only chance to have an adult conversation, which felt like a luxury by lunchtime.

Julie, however, wasn't fond of "talking shop" or chit-chat. She preferred to have a quick, quiet lunch of leftovers and coffee—a short 10-minute reprieve she always looked forward to.

But today, Julie wasn't focused on eating. Her mind was still on Barbara and the party she was hosting on Friday.

As Julie opened the door to the teachers' lounge, she saw everyone packing up, ready to return to their classrooms. Across the table, Barbara was zipping up her lunch bag.

"Excuse me, Mrs. Waltz?" Julie asked, lifting her chin slightly to get Barbara's attention. "Do you have a second? I have a quick question."

Barbara looked up and smiled warmly. "Of course, I do! And how many times do I need to tell you? Please, call me Barbara!"

Julie made it a habit to address other teachers formally, using "Mr." or "Mrs." There were still several whose first names she didn't know, and even if she did, she wasn't always confident she remembered them correctly. Out of professionalism—and to avoid the embarrassment of using the wrong name—she stuck to formal titles. The only exception was Mr. Anderson, and even then, never in front of students.

"What can I help you with, dear?" Barbara asked. "Is it about the field trip? I heard the kids are very excited! I think you really picked a winner." she added enthusiastically.

"No, that's not it," Julie said, fumbling slightly. "I have a question about this."

She reached into her pocket, pulling out the pink postcard. Her face betrayed a mix of confusion and apprehension as she handed it to Barbara.

Barbara's smile widened. "Oh, you got the invite! Great! It's going to be so much fun!" she exclaimed.

"Every year, I host this little party for the teachers and a few of my girlfriends. It's nothing crazy—just some food, drinks, and good conversation. A night for us girls, you know?" She winked playfully.

"Oh!" Julie replied. "I didn't know..."

"Last year, I was going to invite you, but I had to cancel. My husband, Harold, had back surgery and was laid up for eight weeks. By the time he recovered, it was already near the end of the school year, and Kevin McCarthy was talking about his End-of-School Bash. So, it was easier to put it off until this year." Barbara explained in one breath. "I'm so glad you can come this time! It'll be so much fun."

Julie didn't know what to say. Barbara sounded as though she had already accepted the RSVP on her behalf.

"I wasn't sure it would be... my type of party," Julie said hesitantly.

"Oh, don't worry!" Barbara reassured her. "It's just a fun night out. Like I said, food, drinks, and laughs. And tell me—don't you want to get out of that house full of boys sometimes?"

Julie didn't have to think hard about that question. Sometimes, she felt like she was losing her mind at home. She loved her kids and Mike, but the endless laundry, dishes, and smells of a house full of boys often felt overwhelming. Mike, a neat freak, insisted the house always be spotless, which added to the pressure.

"Oh my God, of course I do!" Julie admitted. "It's just... Mike is coming home in a few days. He'll probably want me to stay home. I'm not sure..."

"Oh, honey!" Barbara interjected. "It's one night. Once a year! I'm sure any good husband would understand. He can spend some time with those boys of yours for a change. They'd probably love it! It's a win-win," she said with a knowing smile.

Julie paused, considering Barbara's point.

Maybe she is onto something.

Maybe I do deserve a little fun, a night for myself.

"You know what? You win!" Julie said, smiling. "I think you're right. If you think I'll have a good time, I'll go. Thanks for the invite!"

Barbara beamed. "I need to get back to my charges," she said, glancing at her watch. "But if you have any questions, just let me know. I'm so glad you're coming!" With that, she quickly gathered her things and headed to her classroom.

For the rest of the day, Julie couldn't stop thinking about the party.

It would be nice to go out for a change.

It sounds like it could be fun.

Now, all she needed to do was figure out how she was going to make it all happen.

| 4 |

The remainder of the day passed in its typical fashion: two post-lunch classes, a short homeroom, and the final ring of the dismissal bell.

Mondays were also Julie's after-school days, where she stayed an extra hour to help any students who needed assistance with current topics or assignments. Today, no one had signed up to stay after, but that didn't mean a last-minute straggler wouldn't walk in.

Julie sat at her desk, waiting to see if anyone would pop by, but at 3:30 p.m. she was free to leave.

The boys usually took the bus home and would already be there by the time Julie arrived at the end of the day. But even with them home, the house often felt empty.

Lately, it seemed like they would come in, toss their things around, and head straight to their rooms. They spent most evenings upstairs doing homework, playing video games, watching TV, or using their computers.

When Julie walked through the door, the first sign of life was always an avalanche of belongings scattered throughout the house—backpacks, shoes, jackets, and whatever else had been carelessly shrugged off. The kitchen island was littered with food wrappers and containers, and dishes sat piled up in the sink.

Despite the mess and chaos, it was reassuring to know they were there. Julie often cleaned up after them with a strange sense of happiness and contentment.

They'll only be here a few more years, she reminded herself.

Soon enough, both boys would be out of the house—off to college and starting their own lives.

With that in mind, Julie always tried to make dinner a special time for the three of them—a chance for them to sit down, talk about their days, share funny stories, and catch up on life.

But even that tradition seemed to be slipping away. The boys were more interested in taking their food upstairs, staying online, and chatting with friends. It had become harder and harder to enforce the rituals she once found so important and comforting.

Planning meals had always been one of Julie's ways to manage the chaos. Having a set plan for dinner made evenings smoother when the boys were younger, and it was another routine she'd clung to over the years.

Monday nights were always pasta night—spaghetti, macaroni, something quick and easy after the first day back to work.

But lately, dinner had become less of a shared event. Julie would prepare the food, call the boys down to let them know it was ready, and leave it up to them whether they joined her at the table.

It was during these moments—alone in the dining room—that Julie truly wished Mike were home more often. At least then, she would have someone to talk to. But even that wasn't entirely true anymore. The distance between them had been growing for years.

Julie found herself growing more frustrated with Mike whenever he was home. Maybe it was resentment—resentment that she was always home, always the one responsible for the kids, the house, and everything in between—while he spent his days on the road, drifting from place to place, living in a carefree world of hotels and room service.

It wasn't that he didn't work hard—he did. But some days, it felt like she worked a lot harder.

Whenever she tried to express her feelings or frustrations, Mike would simply dismiss them, reminding her that she didn't *need* to work. If she was stressed, he'd say, it was her own doing—she was the one putting pressure on herself.

But Julie loved teaching. For the first time in her life, she felt like she was doing something for herself—something that mattered beyond laundry, dishes, and dry cleaning.

Still, it often felt like Mike didn't understand that, and Julie had no intention of bringing it up or explaining it to him anymore. It was easier to let it go than to rehash the same conversation.

Sitting at the dining room table, alone with her thoughts, Julie no longer needed to convince herself—she deserved to go out on Friday night. If anyone had earned a night off, it was her.

| 5 |

With dinner over, the boys fed, and the kitchen cleaned, Julie sat down on the couch to watch the news and enjoy a glass of wine. Right on schedule, her phone buzzed with a notification.

She noted the time—7:30 p.m. It was Mike's nightly *text check-in.*

She appreciated his messages and was grateful he took the time to ask how she was doing. But lately, every text only reminded her of how things used to be.

He used to call her when he was away. They would have long conversations about his day—where he went, what he did, who he talked to, and what was next on his agenda.

He'd tell her funny stories, vent about traffic and bad drivers, and then ask about her day.

Julie would share tales of middle school drama, the boys' antics, and the little moments that made her smile. Sometimes they'd talk late into the night, hanging up only because they both needed to get some sleep.

Now, all of that had been reduced to a few sterile lines of text. Julie sighed and picked up her phone.

MIKE: Hope you had a great day? Anything exciting going on?

How could she possibly summarize everything in a text?

She shook her head, tempted to just call him. She wanted to talk about the field trip, Barbara's party, and the thousand little things swirling in her mind. But she knew he wouldn't answer—he always said texting was *better* and *easier...*

Most evenings, he was out entertaining or "building relationships," as he put it, with area vendors or other sales representatives. He didn't like having to excuse himself to make or take a phone call from his *wife.*

"That was lame."

And holding a real conversation with her from a restaurant or bar? That was "*too hard.*"

If he was in his hotel, he was either *"too tired from driving"* or *"didn't have any conversation left in him"* after talking to people all day.

Either way, to him, texting was the best solution.

Julie had no doubt that he worked hard or that he put in long hours. But she also knew he enjoyed it—that he liked being on the road, meeting new people, going out, and living in that fast-paced world.

What she hated was how he used it as an excuse, making talking to her feel more like a nuisance than something he actually wanted to do.

So, as always, their conversation continued with its usual brevity.

JULIE: It was a typical Monday. Definitely have a busy week ahead, but nothing too crazy!

MIKE: I'm glad. Tell the boys I said Hi. And I should be home Wednesday night.

JULIE: I will. Can't wait to see you!

MIKE: Love you.

JULIE: Love you too.

Mike was coming home Wednesday, which meant Julie had two days to make everything perfect before he arrived. It wasn't as though she didn't keep the house clean while he was gone—quite the opposite. But their home was lived in, and that meant sinks, toilets, and showers that were regularly used, especially by two growing boys who had yet to master the art of cleanliness.

No matter how much Julie cleaned, the house always seemed to revert back to clutter the moment she thought she was done.

It didn't bother her too much—she'd grown up in a *lived-in* house. But Mike was particular. He expected the house to look like a museum, with everything in its place and absolutely no clutter.

Over the years, his obsession with order had sparked more than a few arguments. He'd gone on rampages over shoes left on the floor or an overflowing trash can.

Eventually, Julie decided it wasn't worth the fight. She simply made sure everything was spotless before he came home. She had already scheduled a deep clean for Tuesday night.

Once Mike left again on Monday, she and the boys would slip back into their usual routine.

Deep down, she knew it wasn't a battle she would ever win—nor an expectation she believed was realistic. She just did the best she could.

For now, though, all she had to worry about was tomorrow.

Julie opened her laptop and quickly composed a reminder flyer about the field trip permission slips and payments. It didn't need to be flashy—just clear and to the point. She emailed it to Mrs. Reed, along with a request to post the information on the school's Facebook page, website, and email blast.

She knew Mrs. Reed would handle it in the morning and have it circulating by the end of the day.

With that done, Julie graded a few papers to wrap up her work for the evening. Then, she leaned back, finished her glass of wine, and headed upstairs for a quick shower before calling it a night.

| 6 |

Mornings were all the same. A mix of madness and routine, and the school days were almost a mirror of the one before—classes, lunch, and more classes.

At breakfast, she reminded the boys that their dad would be coming home Wednesday night and that she could use their help cleaning. While they never outright refused, they certainly didn't enjoy it. They understood it was their mess too but silently agreed with Julie that the house wasn't really that bad.

Still, they knew enough about their dad's temper to realize it was better to help clean and keep things as neat as possible before he got home.

A whirlwind of routine carried Julie through the day—moments blending into one another—until, before she even had time to process it, Wednesday morning arrived.

Once again, she was surrounded by the boys scarfing down breakfast before heading out the door.

"Your dad is coming home tonight," she reminded them.

Chad and Tommy were well aware. They had stayed up late the night before, cleaning their rooms and helping Julie tidy the house to lighten today's workload.

"I just want to remind you to be home for dinner. And we'll be eating downstairs," she said, making sure to look directly at each of them to ensure they heard her.

Julie liked having dinner together as a family when Mike came home. It made the house feel more like a home and them more like a family—or so she believed.

"No problem, Mom!" Chad replied. "I'll be here. I've got nothing to do after school today."

Tommy nodded in agreement. "I'll be here too."

The boys loved their dad, but like Julie, they sometimes felt resentful about how much he was away. He rarely made it to basketball games or school events. He didn't play catch in the yard or take much interest in their hobbies. He also seldom called from the road or even sent a text.

And when he was home, he spent most of his time in front of the TV or at the golf course. He would say, "This is my only time off. Let me enjoy it, doing what I want to do," and leave it at that.

With breakfast done, Julie dropped the boys off at school and headed to Franklin Middle. She tried to focus on the day ahead, but her mind was divided—half worrying about Mike's return and half wondering how she would make it to the party on Friday night.

On the one hand, she knew she was a grown woman with every right and reason to go out. She had no concerns about leaving the boys home alone for the night either. But on the other, Mike could be unpredictable when it came to her going out. It wasn't that he worried about her safety—he didn't—he just didn't like the idea of her spending time with other people.

Whenever he was home, Mike expected her full attention. He didn't outright forbid her from going out, but he made it clear he didn't like it. And after years of subtle discouragement, Julie had found herself with almost no social life.

Aside from a few coworkers, she had no close friends, and she certainly didn't have anyone she spent time with regularly.

Dammit! Julie thought. *I deserve to go out and have fun too.*

The thought fueled her resolve as she drove to work. For the rest of the drive she pumped herself up for the inevitable conversation—and possible confrontation—with Mike about the party.

When she arrived at work, her thoughts were still racing. She couldn't stop thinking about Mike coming home or the party she both wanted to, and was nervous to attend. Sitting at her desk, she forced herself to focus on her teaching tasks for the day.

Once she settled in, her normal routine began to unfold and a calm set in. Julie loved the first few minutes at her desk in the morning—when she thought she wasn't running late. It was just enough quiet time to center herself before the bell rang and her students piled in. The room felt open, calm, and peaceful.

"Crap!" she blurted, realizing she had forgotten to stop by the office to check her mailbox or follow up with Mrs. Reed about the field trip flyers scheduled to go out that afternoon.

It wasn't that Julie expected anything important, but skipping any part of her usual routine was unlike her, and it left her feeling slightly off balance.

With a long inhale, she watched the clock tick to 8:00 a.m., exhaled, and listened as the bell rang.

Here we go, she thought.
Let's do this.

| 7 |

Julie handled first and second period with relative ease, even though her mind wasn't fully focused. Both classes were filled with sixth-grade students who had struggled on the state's standardized tests. Most of their time was spent on reading comprehension and grammar. A large portion of class was dedicated to reading short stories, discussing them as a group, and learning how to analyze and summarize them in writing.

Julie aimed to select stories that were both engaging and rich enough to inspire meaningful discussions.

Sometimes, her students surprised her, engaging in lively conversations that lasted the entire period. Julie loved those days—they left her feeling like she was truly getting through to them. It was fulfilling to see them grow as independent thinkers, expressing their ideas and standing by them.

But today was not one of those days. Instead, it felt like pulling teeth. Every response had to be coaxed out, and Julie found herself carefully steering their thoughts and opinions. The morning dragged on painfully.

By third period, she was relieved to have her prep time—a 45-minute window to catch up on class planning and other tasks. Today, her top priority was organizing paperwork for the upcoming field trip.

Although she had just sent out a reminder, most students had already turned in their permission slips and money. Still, Julie wanted to ensure nothing was left to chance. She also needed to finalize coordination with the school nurse regarding students' medications and health concerns listed on the forms, as well as confirm that there were enough chaperones.

With less than a week until the deadline for permission slips, Julie could feel her stress level rising. She wasn't sure she was ready to take on a project this big. Planning, coordinating, managing, and executing a successful trip for over 160 students felt overwhelming—far beyond her comfort zone.

So much to do, she thought, laying out her folder of paperwork on her desk.

Despite the workload, she reassured herself that most of it was finally under control.

She carefully went through each permission slip, marking a green check in the upper right-hand corner if it was complete, signed, and paid in full. Then, she cross-checked each student's name against her spreadsheet. Any incomplete forms were marked in red, with notes explaining what was missing.

The completed slips were bundled in groups with green paperclips, while the incomplete ones went into a red folder for Mrs. Reed to redistribute to students.

When Julie glanced at the clock, she realized it was almost lunchtime. She quickly shuffled the completed slips into a large manila envelope and placed it in her desk drawer. As the bell rang, signaling lunch, she got up and headed to the cafeteria.

Smiling, she walked down the hallway, lost in thought about how the rest of the day would unfold. She noticed Mr. Anderson leaving his classroom and called out, "Hey, Cole! I feel like I haven't seen you all day!" She laughed. "I was completely spaced out this morning!"

"Hey, Jules!" he replied with a smile. "Ugh, how is it already Wednesday?" He chuckled. "You know what they don't teach you in college? The days last forever, but the weeks fly by!"

Julie laughed as they walked together.

Cole began venting about his frustration with his students' science research projects. Earlier in the year, he had approved all their topics, sent home detailed instructions, and provided plenty of time for them to prepare. But when presentation day arrived, some projects had almost nothing to do with the approved topics—or with science at all.

"I mean, some kids just glued webpages to poster boards," he said, shaking his head. "Others completely ignored their topics. It was supposed to be a fun, easy assignment to boost their grades. But no! Sometimes, I feel like the easier I make it, the harder they push back."

"Tell me about it," Julie replied, holding up her red folder. "These are permission slips for the field trip—returned with no parent signatures. Everything else is there: the student's name, grade, homeroom, even the money. But no parent or guardian signatures! I mean, seriously, it's not a permission slip without permission!" She laughed.

Cole grinned. "I was thinking about what Dryer mentioned at the last faculty meeting last week. You know what we should do? We should team up on an assignment sometime," he said, his eyes lighting up.

"Think about it—I could give them a topic in science, like the planets or ecosystems, and you could help them write research papers on it. They'd get a grade for both science and English. I'd grade the presentations, and you'd grade the essays. Dryer would love it!"

"That's definitely something we can talk about," Julie said with a smile, wondering if it would mean more work for her than for him. "Maybe after the field trip."

"How's that going, by the way?" Cole asked. "Only a few more weeks to go?"

"So far, so good!" Julie answered enthusiastically. "It's going to be a great trip. The buses are booked, and I just need a final headcount for chaperones."

Cole gave her a supportive smile. "Let me know if you need more volunteers. I can get a sub for the day. I've never been to the Village before—it sounds like a fun trip."

"I'll keep that in mind—definitely!" Julie said, smiling as they reached the cafeteria doors.

It would be nice to have another teacher on the trip, she thought, though she knew she'd need Mr. Dryer's approval for that.

8

During lunch, Lisa and Alyssa stopped Julie to hand in their permission slips.

"We're all set to go," Alyssa said, handing Julie an envelope containing two permission slips and the required money. "This is going to be so much fun, and it'll make a great article for the paper."

"Thank you again for suggesting this, Mrs. T," Lisa added. "We really appreciate it."

"Well, thank you for getting this back to me so quickly!" Julie replied with a smile. "Just make sure you keep up on all the assignments you are going to miss. I don't want your teachers blaming *me*," she joked.

Julie was genuinely happy to see how excited the girls were about the field trip. Everything seemed to be falling into place. For a moment, she allowed herself to bask in a sense of accomplishment.

This was why she had wanted to become a teacher in the first place—and why she loved what she did. Teaching wasn't just about lesson plans and grading; it was about creating opportunities, fostering excitement, and inspiring growth in her students.

A surge of pride rushed over her. She remembered how nervous she had been when the responsibility of planning the field trip was assigned to her earlier in the year. But now, as everything was coming together, her confidence was soaring. She felt more secure in her role as a teacher and as a valued member of the school community.

After such a painfully slow start, the rest of the day passed in a blur. Before Julie realized it, the final bell had rung—it was time to head home.

She needed to stop at the store to pick up a few groceries for dinner before heading back. Mike typically didn't get in until after 4:00 p.m., so she had plenty of time to cook and tidy up if needed.

Chad and Tommy had promised to make sure everything was squared away when they got home from school, which gave her some peace of mind.

| 9 |

Mike wasn't into fancy foods—he was a meat-and-potatoes kind of guy. Julie didn't want to wrestle with an extravagant meal tonight, but she figured he'd appreciate it if it looked like she had put in some effort.

She decided to make her *famous* meatloaf.

She had found the recipe years ago in an old cookbook. It was a standard meatloaf recipe but with broccoli, onions, and cheese layered in the center. Julie always loved how it looked when sliced and how comforting it tasted. She usually paired it with mashed potatoes and a side of green beans or salad—simple, but with just enough effort to say, *Welcome home.*

When Julie arrived home, she was pleased to see the boys had followed through on their promise. Everything was as clean as it could be. Backpacks were put away, the living room was straightened, the stairs were clear of clutter, and the bathrooms sparkled—no toothpaste on the mirrors, no dirty clothes on the floor.

"Thank you!" Julie called from the bottom of the stairs. She heard mumbled acknowledgments—"Yup" and "Okay"—echo back at her from their rooms.

Julie unpacked the groceries and started prepping dinner. With a few hours until Mike's arrival, it was the perfect time to get everything ready.

This was a recipe Julie could make in her sleep. She worked quickly, her movements rhythmic—like a conductor directing a symphony. Ground beef, breadcrumbs, spices—it all came together effortlessly. She was in her own little world, lost in the act of cooking.

Before she knew it, everything was ready. The meatloaf rested in the warm oven, the mashed potatoes sat in a serving bowl covered with foil, and the salad was tossed and set to go. As Julie tidied up the kitchen, she heard the hum of the garage door opening.

Mike was home.

"Boys!" she called upstairs. "Your dad's home!"

She grabbed a dish towel and gave the kitchen island and sink a quick wipe just as Mike walked in through the side door.

"Hi, honey!" Julie greeted him. "Perfect timing! I just finished dinner. We can eat whenever you're ready."

Mike stood in the doorway, his shoulders slumped from hours of driving. His travel bag hung from one hand as his eyes scanned the kitchen.

"It looks good in here," he said, still surveying the room. "Dinner smells good, too. Let me put my stuff upstairs, and we can eat. I can't wait to just sit on the couch and relax."

"I thought we'd all sit at the table and eat," Julie replied. "I have everything set up."

"We'll see. Maybe you guys can eat there," Mike said quickly, his tone dismissive. "I just want to be comfortable."

"That's fine," Julie said, trying to keep her voice light. "We're all just glad you're home."

"Speaking of being home, where are the boys? And where are your rings?" he asked abruptly.

"Oh, shoot!" Julie said, still wiping her hands with the dish towel. "The boys are still upstairs—I don't know if they heard me say you were home. My rings are by the sink. I took them off while I was cooking. I'll put them back on in a second."

Mike had always been particular about Julie wearing her engagement and wedding rings. He insisted she have them on at all times—especially in public.

It wasn't that Julie disliked wearing rings…

It was just that she didn't like wearing *these* rings.

When they got married, Mike had rushed to buy rings for the wedding. He didn't want anyone seeing her with a small diamond or thinking he was cheap, so he chose the biggest, gaudiest, most elaborate set he could find and afford.

To Julie, they were simply *too much.*

Heavy. Clunky. Uncomfortable.

Wearing them every day felt impractical—more of a burden than a symbol.

Lately, she found herself only wearing them when Mike was home.

"Why don't you pop your head into the boys' rooms and let them know you're here? Dinner will be ready after you bring your bags upstairs," Julie suggested.

Mike nodded and headed upstairs, dropping his bag on the bed. He knocked on each of the boys' doors, poking his head in to let them know he was home. Chad and Tommy greeted him enthusiastically, quickly finishing what they were doing before heading downstairs to the dining room.

By the time they arrived, Julie had already plated dinner. Everything looked inviting. She sat at the table, waiting as the boys took their usual seats and Mike settled at the head of the table.

"I hope you like it," Julie said, watching him for a reaction.

"You think it's better than what I've been eating," Mike said sarcastically, chuckling.

Everyone began eating. Chad and Tommy practically inhaled their food, clearing their plates in minutes. Julie savored each bite, appreciating how well everything had turned out.

Mike, on the other hand, fidgeted in his chair, shifting as if he couldn't get comfortable.

Mike looked awkward sitting in the dining room chair. He was tall and broad but had never been particularly fit. For as long as Julie had known him, he had always carried more than a few extra pounds.

Years on the road, combined with his love of snacking, hadn't helped his weight either. He had tried going to the gym a few times but always claimed it didn't fit his schedule.

Beyond his height, his appearance was ordinary and simple—short, practical haircuts, khaki pants, and company shirts. Yet despite his unassuming look, he commanded a certain respect from Julie and the boys.

Still, he hadn't said much about the meal. Finally, he looked up and said, "I'm going to take this to the couch. I tried, but this chair is too hard. Maybe you should pick up some cushions or something."

"Do you think you could just sit for a bit?" Julie asked.

"Nah, I'm good. I can see you guys from the couch if you want to talk," he replied, gesturing toward the living room.

Mike gathered his plate and flatware, stood up, and pushed the chair back with his leg. "This is good, though," he added, as if to reassure her.

He settled onto the couch, set his plate on the coffee table, and reached for the TV remote. The news flickered on as he let out a loud, satisfied sigh.

"Can one of the boys bring me my glass?" he called out.

Chad, already finished with dinner, jumped up and brought Mike his drink. "Glad you're home, Dad!"

"Me too!" Mike replied with a wink. "Ahhh! It's so good to be home."

Julie stayed at the table with Tommy, appreciating his company.

"Thanks, Mom! This is really good. You did a great job," Tommy said, his sincerity clear.

Julie smiled in gratitude. "I tried," she said. "You finish up, and I'll clean up. I'm sure you have a lot to do."

As Julie cleaned the kitchen, she tried to keep a conversation going with Mike, but his attention was glued to the TV. She talked about school, the upcoming field trip, and what the boys had been up to, but his responses were limited to grunts, nods, or the occasional, "Oh, okay."

Finally, she sat down next to him on the couch, determined to keep the conversation flowing. "The only other thing is, I won't be home Friday night," she said casually. "I have a work thing, so I'll leave you guys dinner—or would you rather order pizza?"

That got Mike's attention. He turned to her, his expression suddenly sharp. "Oh, you won't be? What are you doing again?" he asked, his tone probing.

"It's a teachers' night... out... thing," Julie explained, hesitating slightly. "A few of us are getting together at Barbara's house for a small get-together. You remember Barbara? The other English teacher?"

"Oh," Mike said, his expression shifting. "I'm only home for a few days. Wouldn't you rather be here?"

"Yes, of course," Julie replied quickly, "but she already planned the date, and everyone else is going. I'd feel bad if I were the only one who didn't go. I work with her every day."

"Yeah? Well, you *live* here every day. Remember?" Mike shot back.

"You know how I feel about parties," he grumbled. "I just think you should stay home. It looks better for a teacher if you don't go out and stuff. But hey, I'm just trying to look out for you."

He lifted his hands in mock surrender. "You don't want people getting the wrong idea."

"I know," Julie said, trying to remain calm, "but Barbara only invited a few people. I'd hate to disappoint her. You get it, right?"

"Whatever," Mike barked. "I really don't care."

He let out a sharp, condescending breath. "It's fine. If you'd rather spend time there than with me. I can't make you. *You get it. Right?*"

Julie felt torn again, stuck between her wants and her obligations. On one hand, he had a point—he was only home for a few days before heading back on the road for another week. Maybe she *should* stay home.

But *damn it!* she thought. *I really want to go. I already told Barbara I was going. I deserve a night out too. I never get to do anything for myself.*

"I'll tell you what," she said, trying to strike a compromise. "I won't be out too late, and I'll make it up to you. How does that sound?"

Mike put his arm around her and leaned in closer, a sly smile on his face. "How about you make it up to me now?" he said, his voice low and teasing. "I've been working a lot, and I missed you," he added with a wink.

Julie forced a smile and winked back. "Why don't you finish watching TV while I go upstairs and get ready for bed?" she suggested. "I still have to get up early, take the kids to school, and go to work in the morning. I don't get to sleep in, remember?"

With that, she stood up and headed upstairs, leaving Mike to his television as she got ready for bed.

| 10 |

Like most things in her life, Julie had a routine she followed every night. Floss, brush, remove her makeup, wash her face, take a quick shower, then change into comfortable pajamas before sliding into bed. Tonight was no different.

Her routine had become instinctual, providing her with a sense of control and safety. She moved through it in a near-hypnotic state—so much so that she didn't even think about Mike being home until she walked into the bedroom and saw him lying in bed.

She glanced at the clock: **9:37 p.m.**

Julie plugged in her phone on the nightstand and couldn't help but think how nice it was to have Mike home. The bed felt so big and empty when she was alone. Having him there brought her a sense of comfort and reassurance.

But at the same time, she had grown used to sleeping alone. His tossing and snoring often made it difficult to get a good night's rest.

Mike, however, clearly wasn't interested in resting. The grin on his face gave that away.

Julie climbed into bed beside him and rolled over, draping an arm across his chest. "I'm glad you're home," she said softly, smiling.

"Me too," Mike replied, brushing a few stray hairs from her face. He leaned in and kissed her. "I've missed you."

His hand moved down her face and neck, then to her shoulder. Julie was reminded of how much bigger he was than her—how small she felt next to him. His hand continued down her arm and body, as she closed her eyes.

Julie wasn't naturally a physically affectionate person. Deep down, she never liked or felt comfortable being touched or hugged. But she tried to push those feelings aside, taking a deep breath and willing herself to relax.

Mike's hand slipped under her tank top as he kissed her neck. His cold fingers sent a jolt through her, but as her body warmed under the blankets, the shock faded. The friction of his touch grew warmer, and his movements more insistent.

"God, I missed you," he said as his hand slid past the waistband of her pajama pants, over her thigh, and down between her legs. Julie let out a quiet gasp, taking a deep breath to steady herself.

His large hand pressed between her thighs, urging them apart until his palm cupped her. His touch sent a conflicting rush through her—both stimulating and unwelcome. As he continued, she mirrored his movements, sliding her hand down the front of his boxers.

Physically, Mike had never been impressive. Besides being overweight, he was also not well-endowed—three inches at best when fully erect. Julie silently joked that his excitement was the equivalent of giving her a *thumbs-up*.

To make matters worse, Mike was prone to quick and early climaxing—sometimes so much so that they didn't even make it to actual sex.

Over the years, Julie had clung to hope—hope that things would change, that somehow, they would get better.

But it hadn't. Nothing had.

And now, she wasn't sure who suffered more from it—him or her.

Not that it really seemed to bother him.

Whenever it happened, he'd just laugh it off with a careless, "Oops. Sorry!" before rolling over and drifting off to sleep, as if it didn't matter at all.

As if *she* didn't matter at all.

Whenever Julie tried to bring it up, he'd dismiss her concerns with a smug, "You're just *that* good." If she pressed further, he'd get defensive, taking it as a personal attack.

Julie learned not to bother. Instead, she silently referred to him as her *little astronaut* because, in bed, he was *three, two, one—liftoff!* It was a private joke she'd never dared share.

As her fingers traced over him, she felt him already excited with anticipation. She couldn't help but laugh silently at how it felt under the covers—like a fleshy thumb.

Mike closed his eyes, enjoying her touch as her hand explored further.

"Oh, shit—get on top!" he said suddenly, his voice breathless.

Julie quickly pulled her hand away, slid one pant leg down, and climbed on top of him. This was the only position that worked well; in most others, he either slipped out or couldn't maintain enough depth.

She reached down to help guide him inside her. But, not being aroused and lacking any real desire, it took some effort, making the moment feel more forced and mechanical, than intimate and loving. As she lowered herself onto him, she felt the faintest nuance of penetration.

Julie had developed a private game for moments like this. She would move over him, while silently reciting the alphabet in her head, seeing how far she could get before he finished. His personal best was reaching *W* once, but most times, she only made it to *H, I*.

"Aghh!" Mike groaned, lifting his hips in a futile attempt to go deeper. His movements grew erratic, and she felt his body shake beneath her as he climaxed.

They didn't need to worry about contraception—complications during the twins' birth had necessitated a hysterectomy, so pregnancy wasn't a concern.

"Oh my God, baby!" Mike said, catching his breath. "You're fucking amazing."

Julie forced a small smile, knowing it wasn't really about her. "I'm glad you're home. Now, hopefully, you'll sleep well," she said, rolling off him and back onto her side of the bed.

She reached for her phone, ensuring it was plugged in and her alarm was set for the morning.

The clock read **9:43 p.m.**

| 11 |

The week was flying by. Before she knew it, Friday morning had arrived.

Julie woke up feeling excited to start her day. She rolled out of bed carefully, trying not to wake Mike, and quickly got dressed in the clothes she had laid out the night before.

He was still sound asleep as she made her way downstairs to prepare a quick breakfast, pack sandwiches, and start a pot of coffee.

Chad and Tommy were already downstairs, finishing up their breakfast.

"Good morning, guys," she said cheerfully. "Just so you know, I have a work thing tonight and won't be home for dinner. I told your dad we'd order a pizza, so there won't be much to clean up."

"Sounds good," mumbled Tommy, while Chad gave a silent nod in agreement.

"Car leaves in ten!" she called, grabbing a granola bar and her packed bag. "I can't be late today!"

Julie could hardly wait to get through the day—she was *so* excited about going to Barbara's tonight. It wasn't as though she'd never been to a party before, but it certainly *felt* like it.

She couldn't even remember the last time she had gone out for an evening alone.

Tonight is going to be my night, she thought, smiling to herself.

Traffic seemed lighter than usual—or at least it felt that way. Julie was so caught up in her own thoughts that she paid only half-attention to the road. Before she knew it, the boys were dropped off, and she was at school.

Her first stop was the office to check her mail. She had forgotten to check it on Wednesday, too preoccupied with Mike coming home, and yesterday, she had been running so behind that she didn't get a chance to check it either.

The staff mailboxes were arranged in a large wooden structure divided into square compartments, resembling a three-dimensional checkerboard. It was six boxes across and six boxes tall, each labeled with a room number and the teacher's name.

The boxes were placed at a height convenient for the average person, but at 5'2", Julie always struggled to reach the back of hers in the second-top row.

Standing on her toes, she reached into her mailbox, scooping out loose papers and letters. Some envelopes, however, seemed stuck at the bottom.

"Let me help you with that," came a familiar voice.

Julie turned to see Mr. Anderson stepping into the office.

"This is the only day I look forward to mail," he joked, reaching into his mailbox and pulling out a white envelope. "Payday!" he said with a grin.

Cole reached over and grabbed the remaining envelopes from Julie's box with ease. "And here's yours!" he said, handing her the envelope with her paycheck inside.

"Thanks! I've earned it!" Julie replied, matching his playful tone.

Cole smiled, gave her a wink, and bumped fists with her before heading out. Julie couldn't help but feel grateful for his presence at the school. While she got along with other teachers, Cole felt more like a true friend than just a colleague. He made Franklin a more enjoyable place for everyone.

With her mail in hand, Julie made her way to the teachers' lounge, determined to grab a cup of coffee. She had started a pot that morning but had been too rushed to pour herself a cup before leaving. At least she had remembered to grab her travel mug from the kitchen island.

As she walked, Julie sorted through her mail. Most of it was *school junk*—lunch calendars, policy reminders, notes from the PTA. But one envelope caught her attention, addressed to her from the Patriot Village offices.

An advertisement? she wondered. *Or maybe confirmation paperwork for the trip?* She made a mental note to look at it later, too focused on her coffee mission to stop now.

The teachers' lounge was a completely different scene in the morning compared to lunch. The calm, collected atmosphere of the afternoon was replaced with chaos and urgency. Teachers buzzed around like a swarm of bees, grabbing coffee, exchanging quick conversations, and rushing off to their classrooms.

Foam coffee cups lay tipped over on the table, tea bag wrappers and sugar packets littered the floor near the trash can, and the coffee pots were in constant rotation. Julie timed her approach like a mini-golfer waiting for an opening in a windmill.

"Gotcha!" she said triumphantly, pouring hot coffee into her oversized mug.

"Slow down there, darling!" Barbara called out teasingly. "Save some for the rest of us!" She held out her coffee cup with a grin.

"I was saving the last of it for you," Julie said playfully, filling Barbara's well-worn cup.

"That's a lot of coffee, Mrs. Tosh," Barbara teased in a mock-reprimanding tone.

"I need it if I'm going to survive your party tonight! I'm usually in bed by eight," Julie replied, feigning exasperation.

"Oh, dear, you really decided to come after all! I'm so glad," Barbara said, beaming. "You're going to have a great time. It's all about just getting together and having fun! I think you're really going to enjoy yourself. Gotta run, but I'll see you tonight!"

Like the other staff members, Barbara disappeared as quickly as she had arrived.

Julie took a much needed sip of her coffee, smiling to herself, and headed off to start her day.

| 12 |

With a sense of urgency, Julie hurried to Room 10. She dropped her purse and school bag onto the desk, sat down, and pulled out the envelope from Patriot Village. Opening it quickly, she skimmed the first paragraph:

"Dear Mrs. Tosh, ... changes ... policy ... chaperones ... immediately."

Wow, what's this? she thought.

Julie read the letter more carefully. It was short and to the point, informing her of a new chaperone-to-student ratio requirement. Due to larger class sizes, the Village now mandated one adult for every ten children to ensure groups stayed together and students remained safe.

"Every ten!?" Julie blurted out, a wave of stress washing over her.

She knew she had enough parent volunteers to cover every twenty students—but ten? She wasn't sure.

Okay, I can figure this out, she reassured herself. *I should be able to get enough volunteers.* She made a mental note to finalize the headcount by Tuesday. For now, there was nothing more she could do.

Julie slid the letter back into its envelope and tucked it into the desk drawer with the rest of the field trip paperwork.

The rest of the school day passed in a dizzying blur. The periods flew by, each one feeling like a round in a fast-paced boxing match, with the bell marking perfectly timed breaks.

By the last period, anticipation had built—for her students, her colleagues, and herself. Fridays always carried a unique energy.

When the final bell rang, Julie snapped out of her thoughts. She had been zoning out while sitting with her homeroom students, waiting for dismissal.

"Have a great weekend!" she called out as the students eagerly filed out of the room.

Okay! Julie thought, mentally running through her list. *I have time to stop at the store, pick up Mike's dry cleaning before they close, and get home to shower and change before ordering pizza.*

She completed her errands efficiently and returned home to find everything relatively calm. Mike was asleep on the couch with the TV still on, and the boys were upstairs. The house didn't need any immediate attention.

Now, it was time to figure out what to wear.

| 13 |

Julie hadn't thought to ask Barbara if there was a dress code, but she figured if there was, it would have been noted on the invitation.

Jeans? My beige cardigan? she wondered, rifling through her closet. Then inspiration struck. *Oh! I know!*

She decided on an outfit that struck a balance between cute and casual: black leggings and a red flannel button-down. It felt comfortable yet stylish—something that didn't scream *Mom! Over 30!*

Laying her outfit out on the bed, she hopped into the shower. As the warm water cascaded over her, Julie felt the stress of the day melt away.

Finally, she thought, closing her eyes and soaking in the peaceful moment.

"Hey! Are you alone in there?" Mike called from the bathroom door, his tone teasing.

"Ha! Of course I am!" Julie replied with a playful, sarcastic laugh.

"Then there's room for two!" Mike said, sliding the shower curtain open and stepping in.

"Seriously?" Julie's voice was a mix of disbelief and irritation. "I just need to take a quick shower and order the pizza before I leave."

"Yeah," Mike said with a grin, "but I figure I'll be asleep when you get home. And we still need to catch up on some..." He glanced down, winking suggestively.

"Oh my God, Mike! *Seriously?*" Julie rolled her eyes. "Right now?"

Julie already knew the answer. When Mike was home, it often felt like all he cared about was sitting on the couch, golf, or sex.

Mike leaned against the shower wall, his arousal apparent but unremarkable.

Julie sighed. *It really does look like a thumbs-up,* she thought, trying to suppress her frustration.

She didn't like the sight of Mike naked. She hated admitting it, but she simply didn't find him attractive.

His round, droopy face and nearly bald head reminded her of *Shrek*. His body was unshapely, his stomach spilling over his waist, nearly obscuring his unwelcome excitement. Together, it painted an unflattering picture that only deepened her resentment.

"It was supposed to be a quick shower!" she pleaded.

"It will be!" he insisted. "Come on, please?"

Julie sighed again, already resigned. "What do you want?" she asked, though the answer was obvious.

Mike glanced down at himself. Julie let out a defeated, "Ugh."

Turning away from him, she stepped back under the warm stream, letting the water cascade over her head and shoulders. Reaching behind her, her fingers brushed against him, finding him tense and waiting.

As she ran her fingers, she couldn't help but note the odd combination of soft and firm. She squeezed and pulled rhythmically, her movements mechanical.

Squeeze, pull, release. Squeeze, pull, release, she thought, counting silently in her head.

"Don't stop!" Mike groaned almost instantly, his hips beginning to thrust.

Julie felt his hand grip and tighten over hers, his movements urgent as he shuddered against the shower wall, his body trembling with release.

"Better now?" she asked, rinsing her hand under the water.

"That wasn't so hard, now, was it?" Mike replied with a smirk.

"Nope. It wasn't," Julie said flatly. "You were right—I owed you."

She turned back to the water, letting it continue to run over her, giving Mike ample time to dry off and leave.

She hated how he was sometimes—so dismissive, so self-centered, showing her little attention except when he wanted something. Usually sex. Yet, in other moments, he could seem so loving and kind.

He's so confusing, she thought bitterly.

Once Mike was gone, Julie finished her shower, dressed in her black leggings and red flannel shirt, and added a touch of makeup. She styled her hair into a messy ponytail, smiling at her reflection in the mirror.

Not bad for someone with two kids! Her slim, athletic build made her feel confident.

Let's do this! she thought, mentally hyping herself up. But as she checked the time, panic set in.

"Shit! It's already seven!" she yelled. "Boys! You'll need to order the pizza—I'm already running late."

Chad called back from the kitchen table. "A! You were upstairs forever. And B! We already took care of it. Tommy and I ate, and Dad's on the couch sleeping. You're good to go."

Julie sighed in relief. She glanced at her phone for directions—Barbara's house was about 45 minutes away, and she hated driving in the dark. But if she left now and took her time, she'd get there right at eight.

14

Julie backed out of the driveway, feeling eager and adventurous. The drive took her beyond the familiar streets of her town and into a neighboring city she had rarely visited.

Wow, she thought. *Barbara drives all this way every day?* Julie couldn't help but reflect on how her own relatively short commute sometimes felt endless.

"In 100 feet, turn left. Your destination will be on the right," the voice from her navigation system announced.

As Julie turned onto Barbara's street, it was obvious there was a party. Cars lined both sides of the road, broken only by the occasional driveway or fire hydrant.

"Your destination is on the right."

Julie glanced over her shoulder. *Okay, that's Barbara's house. Now, where to park?*

The density of cars lessened as she drove further down the street. Eventually, she found a spot not far from the house.

The March breeze was cool and crisp as she walked along the sidewalk, lit only by the soft glow of streetlights overhead. There was still a lingering chill from winter in the air.

Barbara's neighborhood consisted mostly of ranch-style houses, each neatly aligned with the next, creating a sense of uniformity. For Julie, accustomed to the cul-de-sac's soft curves and two-story homes, the linear streets felt foreign.

Barbara's house was similar to the others—long and low, with a set of steps leading to a front door Julie assumed was rarely used. The driveway stretched up the side of the house toward a detached garage. But a large lamppost in the front yard, with the house number hanging from it, made Barbara's home stand out.

Julie walked up the driveway, the sounds of laughter and conversation growing louder as she approached the side door. Through the window, she could see people holding drinks and chatting animatedly.

"Julie! Come in!" Barbara's voice called from inside. "The door's open!"

Julie opened the side door and stepped into the kitchen. Barbara's sense of style was immediately evident. The kitchen featured pristine white cabinets and dark gray granite countertops. Glass doors on the upper cabinets revealed neatly arranged plates and glasses, illuminated by soft lighting.

I could never pull this off with the boys, she thought.

Everything was immaculate, organized, and intentionally put together—a reflection of Barbara's personality. The deceptively modest exterior of the house belied its spacious and stylish interior.

A large island anchored the kitchen, adorned with name tag stickers, markers, a laminated sign, and a glass bowl filled with shiny objects.

Julie stepped further into the house, glancing around. She recognized a few familiar faces from school, but several of the guests were complete strangers to her.

It didn't take long for her to notice that everyone at the party was a woman. While not surprising, the realization felt strange. She was so accustomed to being surrounded by Mike and the boys that this all-female environment felt novel. Her eyes quickly scanned what everyone was wearing—not out of judgment, but out of curiosity and reassurance.

Julie had worried about being over- or underdressed, but seeing the variety of outfits put her at ease. Some women wore jeans and sweaters, while others had dressed up in stylish dresses with jewelry. Julie felt perfectly comfortable in her leggings and flannel.

"Julie!" Barbara called, waving to catch her attention. "You look so cute!"

Barbara beamed. "It's so fun to see everyone outside of work and to find out who we really are beneath all the *Mr. and Mrs. Teacher Talk.* You look absolutely adorable!"

Pointing with one hand while holding a drink in the other, Barbara gave instructions. "Go over to the table and make a name tag. Everyone needs a name tag. Then, make sure you read the paper on the island and sign the guest list. We've got a few minutes before we start, so grab a drink. The bar is open all night, but it's good to start early!"

Julie smiled at Barbara's energy and followed her instructions.

At the kitchen island, she wrote her name on a tag that read, *Hello, My Name Is:* and stuck it to her shirt. Stepping aside to let others grab their tags, she began reading the laminated sheet in the center of the island.

We are here to have fun and enjoy ourselves.
Please Drink Responsibly.
Place your car keys in the bowl and sign the guest list below.
Your keys will be returned to you later this evening when the party ends. If you do not leave your keys, you will owe the hostess $100.00.

What a cute and curious idea, Julie thought.

The bowl was already full of keys—some with quirky keychains, car starters, and other trinkets. Julie reached into her purse, pulled out her keys, and tossed them into the bowl. Then, she signed her name on the guest list beneath the laminated sheet.

"Good call," said a voice behind her.

Julie turned to see a familiar face but struggled to recall a name.

"Um... Mrs....?" she asked hesitantly.

"Miss Crane," the woman replied. "But tonight, I'm Melanie," she said, pointing to her name tag with a smile.

Melanie looked years younger than Julie. She was tall, with long red hair and pale, freckled skin. Her makeup—eyeliner and eyeshadow—was expertly applied, making Julie suddenly self-conscious about her own minimal effort.

"I teach Special Ed at Franklin, but I don't think we've ever actually talked," Melanie said.

"Right!" Julie replied. "I'm Mrs.—I mean, Julie. I knew I recognized you, but I don't think we've ever really spoken. I walk by your room in the mornings, but I'm always in a rush," she admitted awkwardly.

"It's crazy how so many of us work in the same building but barely know each other," Julie added, trying to steer the conversation.

"I know, right?" Melanie laughed. "I think that's why Barbara has these parties. They're a chance for us to forget about work for a bit and just be ourselves for a change. Well, and of course, there's her presentation," she added cryptically.

"Presentation?" Julie asked, puzzled.

"Yes! Just wait—you'll see," Melanie said excitedly. "This is only my second party."

She leaned in slightly. "The first time I came, I didn't realize the key thing was serious. When I tried to leave without asking for my keys, Barbara tried to charge me $100."

"No way!" Julie exclaimed, turning back to look at the guest list she had just signed. She read the top line: *Pledge to Have Fun and Be Safe.*

"She's sneaky, huh?" Melanie laughed. "Last time, she told me I either had to pay $100 or buy something from her catalog... I bought a bath salt set."

Melanie's tone softened. "She told me she started taking keys after her son was killed by a drunk driver. It became her way of making sure no one else makes the same mistake.

And she still does it—hoping that, maybe, another mother will never have to experience that kind of loss."

Julie felt a pang of sadness. "I had no idea. That's heartbreaking."

"Yeah," Melanie said. "I think that's part of why she loves hosting these parties. For her, it's not just about having fun—it's about keeping people safe. Bringing them together, making sure they look out for each other. And, well, the sales don't hurt," she added with a grin.

"Ladies! Ladies!" Barbara's voice rose above the chatter. "We're starting in a few minutes! Grab a drink and find a seat in the living room!"

| 15 |

Julie poured herself a large glass of wine and made her way from the kitchen into the living room.

Once again, she was surprised by how well-designed and spacious Barbara's home was. The living room was a large rectangular space with a fireplace centered along one wall. Comfortable couches lined the other three walls, each accompanied by a lamp in the corners. Above the fireplace hung a large flat-screen TV.

In front of the fireplace, Barbara had set up a folding table adorned with boxes, bags, and a tri-fold presentation board.

Folding chairs were arranged neatly in rows, providing ample seating for everyone. Julie took the first seat closest to the kitchen door—the furthest spot from the table.

Her attention turned to the TV, which displayed a slideshow of *Pure Eden* information. From her angle, it was hard to read, but she caught glimpses of slogans: *For Women, By Women.* and *Satisfaction Guaranteed.* There were even photos from what appeared to be past parties. Julie chuckled when she spotted a picture of a younger Barbara.

As other guests found their seats, the room buzzed with anticipation. Some women chose the folding chairs, while others stretched out on the long couches.

Ugh, I should have picked the couch, Julie thought with an amused smile.

"Is anyone sitting here?" came a familiar, lively voice.

Julie turned to see Melanie standing behind her, pointing at the chair directly behind her.

"I don't think so," Julie replied. "It's all yours."

Melanie placed her purse under the chair and sat down. Leaning close to Julie's ear, she whispered, "I don't really know anyone else here, so I'm hanging out with you. Okay?"

Julie laughed. "That's fine with me. Thanks!"

Barbara dimmed the lights in the living room, and the room quieted instantly. Conversations ceased as everyone turned their attention toward the table and TV. Barbara exuded a confidence that commanded respect, but her demeanor was warm and inviting.

"Ladies," Barbara began in a calm, gentle tone. "First, I want to welcome you all to my home and thank you for coming tonight. And hopefully, after you leave here, you'll be *cumming* every night!" she shouted.

The room erupted with laughter and cheers.

On the TV screen, the *Pure Eden* logo appeared, surrounded by images of sex toys.

"Now that we've had a little something to eat and drink, let me say this: we are here to have a *fun* time. I invited each of you personally because I value our friendships. I respect each of you as individuals and appreciate your unique stories."

"Tonight, this is a *judgment-free* space. I'm going to take some of you out of your comfort zones. We're going to talk about things many of you may have never discussed before. We'll laugh, joke, tease, and share—but above all, we will be *respectful.*"

"Nothing shared here tonight leaves this house. That's all I ask. We all have different experiences and comfort levels when it comes to sex. You never know what the woman next to you has been through. But one thing is certain: we are *all* women, and we *all* deserve frequent, satisfying, and *quality* sex."

A murmur of quiet agreement filled the room as Barbara continued.

"I've been a *Pure Eden* representative for fifteen years. I've seen, heard, and tried it all. There are no silly or embarrassing questions. Tonight, I hope to educate, inform, and enlighten you about your bodies and your sexuality."

"Now, let's get started!"

Barbara launched into her presentation. Slide after slide, product after product, she passionately detailed the *Pure Eden* catalog.

Julie wasn't sure what to make of it all. Barbara's enthusiasm was infectious, and the products ranged from oils and lubricants to bath products, skincare items, and lingerie—some of which featured peek-a-boo tops and crotchless panties.

Barbara's commentary was *hysterical.* She joked about pinching and chafing, keeping the room laughing and engaged.

"And *here* we go!" Barbara exclaimed with a flourish. "None of this matters if it doesn't help you *orgasm!* Because women deserve frequent and *quality* sex! Partners are *optional*—pleasure is *not!*"

The TV screen changed to a bold slide with bright red text:
HERE WE GO!
SEX TOYS.

The room erupted in cheers and laughter.

"Oh yeah! That's what *Mommy* came for!" a woman hollered from the back.

Barbara raised a hand to quiet the room.

"Ladies, serious question. How many of you have *never* had an orgasm—either by yourself or with a partner?"

The room fell silent. Women glanced at one another, hesitating.

"Come on," Barbara encouraged. "Who has never had an orgasm? Be *honest.*"

"I'm pretty sure I have." one woman said tentatively, breaking the tension.

Barbara shook her head with a knowing smile. "If you're not *absolutely* sure you have—then you haven't." She winked.

The woman raised her hand reluctantly as Barbara scanned the room.

"Who else? There's no reason to be ashamed. The world doesn't teach us that women are *supposed* to have orgasms. It's not something we're taught."

She rolled her eyes dramatically. "And *men!*" She let out an exaggerated sigh. "They can't even find the mustard in the fridge—how are they supposed to find the clitoris?"

The room *erupted* in laughter again.

Julie glanced around as more women slowly raised their hands.

I know I've had an orgasm, she thought.

But the more she thought about it, the less certain she became. Memories swirled in her mind as she tried to recall specific moments.

She remembered being a teenager, around thirteen or fourteen, when she first started to understand her body. She had experimented with masturbation, though it felt strange—both good and guilty. But, it wasn't something she did regularly.

Oh my God, yes! she suddenly remembered.

When she was sixteen, she had been infatuated with Scott Lawson, the lifeguard at the local pool. He was older, tanned, and confident—the epitome of a summer romance in her adolescent mind.

That summer had been one of self-discovery. Julie had gotten her first bikini and finally felt noticed by boys. Her first kiss had even happened at the pool—though not with Scott.

She vividly remembered running home after long days at the pool, consumed by fantasies of Scott. She would change out of her swimsuit, get comfortable on her bed, and let her imagination run wild.

And yes, she had *definitely* had an orgasm.

Julie smiled to herself at the memory.

Barbara's voice pulled her back to the present.

"Women aren't taught about their orgasms. We're barely even taught about *sex!* All we learn is how babies are made and how to be mothers. If you're lucky, someone explains your period before you get it, but most of us stumble onto orgasms by ourselves. Women *deserve* frequent and *quality* sex!"

Then, Barbara posed another question. "How many of you, who are with someone, have *never* had an orgasm with your current partner?"

Julie's stomach dropped. She didn't have to think about this one. She *knew* the answer.

She had *never, ever* had an orgasm with Mike.

And as she reflected on it, she realized something even sadder—she couldn't remember the last time she'd had an orgasm *at all.*

One by one, more women confidently raised their hands—this time with a sense of camaraderie, the room shifting from hesitation to growing support. Some even smiled and laughed, as though joining an exclusive club.

Julie's thoughts raced.

How had I never noticed this before? Or even thought about it?

It wasn't that she didn't like sex. But if she was honest with herself, she had to admit—Mike made sex... *not fun.*

For Julie, sex had become more of a chore than an act of intimacy or passion. Most of the time, it took longer to *prepare* for it than to actually *do* it. After the boys were born, whatever passion she had left seemed to evaporate. She was always busy, always exhausted. And when Mike was home, his selfish and demanding nature did nothing to set the mood. If anything, it pushed her further away.

Barbara's right! This isn't right. Or fair! Julie thought, anger simmering inside her.

Taking a deep breath, she looked around the room—then, boldly, she raised her hand.

"It sounds crazy, but... never," Julie admitted quietly, almost under her breath.

Her eyes widened as she glanced around the room, taking in the number of women with their hands in the air. She turned further and spotted Melanie, still seated, her hands down.

"Lucky you," Julie teased lightly.

"I *am!*" Melanie said with a wide grin. "And I *know* it! I'm never letting him go. You know, I can't even *begin* to tell you how absolutely *incredible* CJ is and how lucky I am... It's *unreal.* I'm so glad I found him."

Julie forced a smile.

Must be nice, she thought, feeling an unexpected pang of envy.

"Isn't it *sad?*" Barbara exclaimed, her voice cutting through the murmurs. "Why are we, as women, expected to carry children, birth them, raise them, *and* also suffer in the bedroom? *Sisters, tonight is our night!* Let me show you the best products I've ever tried, and I *guarantee* you'll love them!"

The room erupted into cheers. Drinks clinked, arms waved, and Barbara began displaying a dazzling array of products: dildos in various sizes and colors, discreet vibrators shaped like lipstick, anal beads, warming lotions, and even strap-ons.

Women laughed, asked questions, and shared their frustrations and advice.

One woman joked, "I've *never* wanted to divorce my vibrator!"

The room *howled* with laughter.

Julie found herself laughing along, though her mind was racing. She had never seriously considered the idea of sex toys. Between raising the boys and managing her home life, she had rarely thought about *herself* in that way.

The occasional hot bath and her regular glass of wine were the closest she came to self-care.

But now, Barbara made it all seem *normal*, even *exciting*.

Maybe it was the crowd mentality, or maybe it was the wine, but Julie found herself feeling more open-minded—and, for the first time in a long time, she was *having a great time.*

"Okay, okay, *okay!*" Barbara hushed the room, waving her hands to quiet the chatter. "I have *one* more product to show you. Ladies, this is *the one.* My personal favorite—*the OMG!*"

She held up a sleek, uniquely designed toy with a plastic handle and a small cone at the end.

"I'll be honest with you," Barbara began. "Sometimes the constant *buzzzzz* of a vibrator can be *too much.* You get numb, distracted. And let's face it—most of us can't climax from penetration alone. If you need *more* robust clitoral stimulation, this will be your *new best friend.*"

She turned the toy on, and a faint sound emitted from the cone.

"This, ladies, is *not* your average vibrator. It's a *clitoral stimulator* that uses *pulses of air*—not vibrations. No buzzing, no numbing, just directed, rhythmic pressure *exactly* where you need it. This soft funnel fits directly over the clit—with or without a little lube—and *poof!* Air pulses in just the right spot."

"There are *six settings*," she continued, "and *three* cone sizes. This baby will have you *knee-buckling* and *lip-biting* in *record time*. And because you're *not* numb, you can use it again almost *immediately*. The first time I tried it, I *literally* said, '*OMG!*'"

The women gasped and giggled as Barbara passed the toy around. Each woman took a turn feeling the gentle air pulses against her fingers.

"I'm *sold!*" one woman exclaimed from the front row, earning a round of laughter from the group.

Barbara beamed with pride. "Ladies, I hope you've had a *great* night so far. I've had an *absolute blast* with all of you. Remember, some of the stories and things shared tonight *must* stay here. As women, as *sisters*, we have to trust one another."

She gestured toward the table. "I also encourage you to take one of my business cards. If you decide to order anything, use my name and account number to get an extra *five percent* off your first order. And if you have any questions, *please* feel free to email me!"

Barbara suddenly threw her hands in the air. "Now, it's time for the *PRIZES!*" she yelled.

"Prizes?" Julie asked, turning to Melanie with a look of surprise.

"Yeah," Melanie said, grinning. "Barbara always does a few door prizes. I didn't win anything last time, but I'm *feeling lucky* tonight. It's one of the reasons I came back—Barbara *knows* how to make a party fun!"

They both laughed as the excitement in the room grew.

Julie couldn't help but feel that this night—unexpected as it was—was shaping up to be one she'd *never* forget.

| 16 |

Barbara must have slipped out of the room while Julie and Melanie were talking because she returned carrying the large glass bowl of keys. Setting it down on the table, she flashed a wide smile.

"All right, ladies, it's time for *prizes!* We have *three* amazing giveaways tonight. First—" she held up a decorative bag, "we've got a *self-care bundle!* It includes our new bath washes, bubbles, and scrub salts, plus some luxurious loofahs and a variety of body oils."

The group murmured approvingly as Barbara continued, "The second prize is this envelope containing a *$100 gift card* to use online for *anything* your heart desires.

"And last, but certainly not least—" she reached for a small bag, "we have what I like to call *'The Best Night Ever'* package. This includes a soothing bath bomb, the discreet yet powerful *Mighty Mite* vibrator, and, of course, our sensational *OMG! Toy.*"

Excitement rippled through the room as Barbara explained the rules.

"I'll be pulling keys from the bowl. If I draw *your* keys, you *win* the prize! But," she added with a playful smirk, "as I mentioned earlier, if you *didn't* put your keys in the bowl, you *owe me* $100—so no sneaking out without contributing!"

The group erupted in laughter.

"Let's get started!" Barbara plunged her hand into the bowl, swirling the keys dramatically.

"Sometimes keys come out stuck together," she said, grinning. "If that happens, the chain I'm holding *wins.* Ready?"

The room leaned in with anticipation as Barbara lifted a set of keys with a flower-shaped keychain.

"Whose are these?" she asked, holding them up.

"That's *me!*" a woman shouted from the back.

It took her a moment to rise from the couch, clearly unsteady after a few too many drinks. The group laughed as she stumbled toward the front.

"Carrie, my dear," Barbara said, half-smiling, half-serious, "I'm going to *hold onto* these keys for now. But here's your prize!"

She handed over the bag of bath products, and the room cheered as Carrie made her way back to her seat.

"For the *gift card!*" Barbara announced, dipping into the bowl again. She extracted another set of keys and squinted at the attached name tag.

"Melissa! Are these yours?"

"Right here!" Melissa called out, raising her hand.

Julie recognized her as a fellow teacher from Franklin—someone she didn't talk to often but always found pleasant.

The group applauded as Melissa came up to claim her envelope.

"Last but *not* least," Barbara said with a sly grin, "*The Best Night Ever* package!"

She dug deep into the bowl, swirling the keys dramatically.

"Okay, whose keys have this *blue carabiner clip?*"

Julie froze for a moment before realizing—*Those are mine!*

She raised her hand, laughing nervously as the room erupted in cheers. Grinning despite the sudden heat creeping up her neck, she made her way to the front.

"Congratulations, *Julie!*" Barbara exclaimed, handing her the bag. "You're going to *love* these." Then, with a wink, she added, "And I *can't wait* to hear what you think of the *OMG!*"

Julie laughed awkwardly, trying to play it cool. "Sure! I'll, uh, let you know," she said, clutching the bag and heading back to her seat.

She felt a mix of *embarrassment* and *exhilaration*—winning sex toys wasn't exactly on her bucket list, but the energy in the room was *contagious.*

Melanie leaned over, grinning. "You're so lucky! I'm jealous! You *have* to tell me how it is."

Julie laughed. "I think *you're* the lucky one. CJ sounds like he's worth more than *all* of this!"

Barbara's voice cut through the chatter. "Thank you *all* so much for coming tonight. I hope you had as much fun as I did! Remember, your keys will be on the kitchen island, and if you need a ride home, let me know. Stay as long as you need to.

"And *please,* before you leave, fold up your chair and put it against the wall—it'll make cleanup *so* much easier."

The group slowly began to disperse, chatting and laughing as they folded chairs and retrieved their keys.

Julie offered to help clean up, but Barbara waved her off. "Thank you, but I've got it covered. I'm *so* glad you came tonight, Julie! And to win a prize, too!"

Julie smiled. "Thanks for inviting me. You were right. I *really* had a great time."

Barbara pulled her into a warm hug. "I'm so glad you came. Now, get on home to that family of yours."

Despite the crisp, frosty air biting at their cheeks, Julie and Melanie kept their conversation flowing as they strolled along the sidewalk. Their laughter wove through the night—unhurried and easy.

"I *still* can't believe you won!" Melanie said, her voice rising with surprise.

"I *know!*" Julie giggled, still in shock herself. "I don't even know what I'm gonna do with these." She paused, holding up her bag of prizes.

"Mike won't want them in the house. He's already *bent out of shape* enough that I came to the party. I can't even *imagine* how mad he'd be if I brought them home."

"Well, if you don't want them, *I'll* take 'em!" Melanie teased with a grin. "But seriously, why does he even *need* to know?" she asked. "You *won* them. You should *keep* them."

Julie's tone shifted. "I'd feel *bad* hiding them from him. And who knows what he'd do if he ever *found* them. I just..."

"You *just* what?" Melanie interrupted, a note of sarcasm in her voice. "You won them. You should get to *keep* them. It's that *simple.* If he's *half* as bad as you say he is, you *deserve* them."

Julie smiled faintly. "It's just that... he's not like CJ. You wouldn't get it. He'd take it *personally,* and then he'd—"

"He'd have to *deal* with me!" Melanie cut in sharply. "You *are* taking those home, and that's *that*."

Julie hesitated, then her smile grew.

"I *won!*" she shouted, throwing her hands in the air in mock triumph.

Her voice rang out into the night, crisp and clear—like the sound of breaking glass.

"That's the *spirit!*" Melanie cheered, her encouragement lightening the mood.

"You are *so* lucky," Julie said, lowering her voice. "You have *no idea* how great you have it."

Still buoyed by the effects of Barbara's open bar, Melanie spun in a circle with her arms outstretched, laughing.

"I *am* lucky! SO damn *lucky!*" she cried, her joy filling the cold night air.

Then she stopped, leaning in close to Julie.

"I'm sorry, I can't complain," she said, her smile turning wicked. "Girl, what can I *say?* That man *knows* what he's doing. He's a *perfect angel* and the *sweetest gentleman* when we're out, but in the bedroom?"

Melanie's grin widened.

"Oh my *God*, Julie, he's an *absolute devil.* When he goes down on me—*fuck!*" She fanned herself theatrically before adding, "And that *dick!* That *fucking amazing dick!* He'd give *any* toy a run for its money!"

Julie burst into embarrassed laughter, her cheeks warming as she tried to deflect her own surprise.

"I'm *totally* jealous," she said, keeping her tone light and playful.

Melanie sighed dramatically.

"Ahh! Oh My God! I *want* him *now!*" she groaned, her eyes sparkling with mischief. She pulled out her phone, her fingers moving quickly over the screen.

"I'm calling him. He'd *better* be awake."

Julie watched as her friend's expression softened while she waited for the line to pick up.

"Hey, you. It's me," Melanie said, her voice suddenly lower, a little sweeter. "I know it's late, but... do you mind if I come over?"

Her smile grew as she listened.

"What? Great! I'll be right there!"

She hung up and turned to Julie, grinning.

"Well, sweetheart, I've got a date," she said, her voice practically a purr. "You enjoy your night. I'm definitely going to enjoy mine!"

Julie laughed again, feeling a little awkward, before waving Melanie off and continuing toward her car. The night air felt cooler now, but her heart was warm.

As she walked, she thought about how much fun she'd had. It was the most she'd laughed—and maybe the most *alive* she'd felt—in a long time.

At home, the house was quiet and dark. Julie carefully set down her keys, then tiptoed upstairs.

Mike's soft snores filled the bedroom.

She tucked the prize bag into the bottom drawer of her nightstand and smiled to herself.

Tonight had been more than just a party—it had been a reminder that she *deserved* joy, laughter, and maybe even a little adventure.

Sliding into bed, she exhaled deeply.

For the first time in a long time, Julie felt something she hadn't realized she was missing.

| 17 |

The next morning played out like every typical Saturday for Julie and the boys. The twins were part of a youth bowling league that met every Saturday at 10 a.m. at the local alley.

Julie woke up a little later than usual but still had enough time to make breakfast and get everything ready.

Mike came down to the kitchen a little after everyone else, still wearing his pajamas and looking like he had *just* woken up.

"Honey? I thought you were going to watch the boys bowl this morning," Julie asked, a hint of disappointment in her voice.

"Huh?" Mike mumbled. "Oh, that's *today*? Huh. Yeah, sure, I can go, I guess. What time?"

"We need to leave *now*," she said. "If the boys are going to have time for practice before the meet."

"Okay, you guys go. I'll meet you there after I take a shower," he said.

Julie hesitated. "Okay, so… *see you there?*" she asked, making sure they were on the same page.

Mike didn't respond. He just turned and walked away.

"All right, boys! Let's go!" Julie called out, and with that, they were off.

Meanwhile, Mike moped around the kitchen for a little while, rummaging for something to eat before heading back upstairs to take a shower.

When he reached the bedroom, he sat on the bed, grabbed the remote, and turned the TV on.

I'll just watch some news while I get ready, he thought.

The volume was so low that the news report was almost indistinguishable.

Julie liked to fall asleep with the TV on, but with the volume so low she could barely hear it.

Mike thumbed the volume button up.

No change.

He tried again.

Nothing.

"Ugh, damn batteries," Mike grumbled under his breath.

Even though he had lived in the house for years, he had no idea where Julie kept certain things. *Some* things, sure, but most of the house was organized by her.

What drawer would have batteries? he wondered.

He walked to Julie's side of the bed and pulled open the top drawer of her nightstand—that's where she usually kept the remote. He rummaged through it, moving things around. Hair ties, loose change, a sleep mask, a phone charger—*but no batteries.*

Whatever, he thought, tossing the remote onto the dresser. As he walked by, he turned off the TV manually and headed into the bathroom.

Julie and the boys made it on time for practice. The boys were doing well, and their teams were already quickly wrapping up their second of three games.

Where is Mike? she wondered.

He *said* he was coming to watch. She checked her phone.

It's already 11:15 a.m.

This game is almost done. And they only have one more after this. Where is he?

She dialed his number. It rang once, twice, three times.

"You've reached Mike Tosh..."

"Ugh! *Voicemail.*" Julie muttered, hanging up.

She dialed again.

Voicemail.

She forced a smile as she watched the boys bowl.

Why? she thought. *Why can't he ever follow through?*

The second game ended, and the third moved along quickly.

Julie enjoyed watching Chad and Tommy bowl. They weren't the greatest, but they did a solid job. Some days, they played better than others, but that didn't matter.

They had *fun.* They hung out with friends.

And they spent time *with her.*

"Hey, is this seat taken?"

She turned at the sound of the voice over her shoulder.

It was Mike.

"Sorry I'm late," Mike said, sitting down. "I sat down to watch the news for a second, then took a shower. The batteries were low in the remote, so I started looking for new ones. I didn't find any in your nightstand, so when you have a second, we need batteries."

Julie's eyes widened. "*My* nightstand? You went through *my* nightstand?"

"Yeah, but there weren't any batteries," Mike said again, as if that was all that mattered.

"Wait... so why are you *so* late?" Julie pressed, irritation creeping into her voice. "If you didn't find them and just took a shower, it's almost *noon* now. What else did you do?"

Mike sighed loudly. "Jesus, Jules! I took a *shower* and got dressed. Then I made something to eat and watched TV for a *minute.* I didn't realize it had gotten so late, and when I noticed, I came *straight* here.

"Seriously, what the *hell?* I'm *here,* aren't I?"

Julie struggled to process what he had just said, trying to piece together the timeline—and how selfish it all seemed.

"Well, they're *almost* finished. So you missed *most* of it," she snapped. "Can you do me a favor? When they're done, can you bring them home? I want to stop at the grocery store and grab something for dinner. Any suggestions?"

"Yeah, that's fine," Mike said with a shrug. "I was planning on checking out that new indoor driving range today, but I can drop them off first. Whatever you want to do for dinner is fine. I don't know. *Whatever, really.*"

"You're *going* to play golf today?" Julie asked, her irritation mounting. "I thought we were going to spend the rest of the day together. When are you leaving?"

"I have to leave Monday morning, so I wanted to get in some club time before then. And they're closed tomorrow."

"So you're just going to leave the boys at home and go golfing *all* afternoon?" Julie asked assertively. "Can we at least spend tomorrow as a family? *Hey,* why don't you take the boys to the range? They would *love* that."

"They'd just *get in the way.* They don't even *like* golf. It'd be better if I just go alone."

"Fine," Julie muttered. "But *tomorrow,* we spend the day together. Okay?"

"That's what I'm *talking* about," Mike said with a wink, shooting finger guns at Julie's chest. "Spending the *day* together!"

"That's *not* what I'm talking about," Julie replied flatly. "Don't be like that, *please.* There are people watching."

"Fuck, Jules. *Fine!*" he snapped.

The boys wrapped up bowling and excitedly showed their dad their scorecards, pointing out every strike and spare. Julie watched as the three of them laughed, smiled, and joked together.

"You guys are coming with *me,*" Mike said enthusiastically.

Julie glanced at Chad and Tommy. "I'll see you when I get home," she said. "I'm gonna run to the store real quick and then meet you back at the house."

"The house? I'm *not* taking them to the house," Mike said, sounding surprised.

Julie looked at him, confused. Hadn't they *just* talked about this?

"How would you guys like to go check out the new indoor driving range and whack a few balls around?" Mike asked the boys.

Julie's mouth *dropped.*

"Yeah!" Tommy exclaimed.

"Awesome!" Chad grinned.

Julie couldn't believe it. *Didn't he just say it would be better if he went alone when I suggested this?*

I can't win, she thought.

"Wow! Okay," she said out loud, forcing a neutral tone. "You guys have fun then. I'll be at the house when you get back."

Shopping gave Julie a place to cool off and *tame her nerves.* She found comfort in the quiet and the time alone.

Mike wasn't trying to be an ass, she told herself. *It's nice to see him doing something with the boys. Maybe I'm just overreacting. Maybe I'm being too sensitive?*

She pushed the shopping cart slowly through the grocery store aisles, letting her thoughts wander as she absentmindedly tossed items into the cart. She tried to focus on the mundane—what to make for dinner, whether they needed more milk, if Chad still liked the snacks he used to love.

But no matter how hard she tried to distract herself, her mind kept circling back—to *Mike and the boys* at the driving range.

She *wanted* to be happy that Mike had decided to take the boys along. That was *something,* wasn't it? He wasn't always so involved, and she *should* be grateful he was making the effort.

But she couldn't shake the frustration that it only happened *when it suited him.*

It was as though her suggestions were dismissed—until he could take credit for them.

Julie sighed and shook her head, trying to push away the negative thoughts.

Maybe it's just me? she wondered.

It's just me.

Back at home, Julie unpacked the groceries, putting everything in its place. The house was still *quiet,* and she found herself relishing the solitude.

She already knew that when the boys and Mike returned, the energy would shift—peace replaced by noise, demands, and chaos.

The sound of the garage door opening snapped Julie out of her thoughts.

Moments later, Mike and the boys tumbled into the house, laughing and chattering about their time at the driving range.

Tommy carried in Mike's golf bag while Chad excitedly told her about a long drive he had hit.

Mike smiled as he set his bag down. "They did *great!*" he said, his voice carrying a rare note of pride. "I think we might have a couple of future golfers on our hands."

Julie smiled back, *genuinely* happy to see the boys so animated.

"That's wonderful," she said. "I'm glad you all had fun."

Dinner that evening was *lighthearted,* with the boys recounting their adventures at the range and Mike chiming in with his own stories.

For a moment, it felt like everything was *just as it should be*—a family enjoying each other's company.

| 18 |

The rest of the weekend flew by, as weekends usually did.

On Sunday, everyone slept in, and Julie made a big breakfast for Mike and the boys. Sundays were usually slow and easy—a chance for her to catch up on schoolwork while Chad and Tommy focused on their homework.

After a lazy morning, Julie set up her makeshift office at the kitchen table. She combed through her grade books and lesson plans, fine-tuning schedules and assignments. She liked knowing everything was in order before Monday morning.

Meanwhile, Mike sat on the couch, engrossed in a documentary about how things were made, drifting in and out of sleep with intermittent snores.

At the top of Julie's list of concerns was whether she had *enough* chaperones for the upcoming field trip.

Reaching into her large school bag, she pulled out the folder with all the trip details.

Carefully, she crossed off names from the sixth-grade roster as she double-checked the permission slips, ensuring all the necessary information was filled out correctly.

Out of 160 sixth-grade students, a handful weren't attending due to not meeting the grade requirements. So far, she had collected about 120 permission slips.

Before Friday's policy change, she thought she only needed six chaperones, but now the required number had possibly more than doubled. She currently had ten parent volunteers who had agreed to go, which meant she needed to find at least two more.

Julie quickly drafted a short message for the school secretary, requesting her to post a call for volunteers on the school website, Facebook page, and email blast.

That should get a few more people involved, she hoped.

With that task done, there wasn't much more Julie could do at the moment. She closed her laptop, tidied up the table, placed her school bag by the door for the next morning, and wandered into the living room.

Mike was still on the couch, drifting in and out of sleep.

Feeling playful, Julie *launched* onto the other end of the couch with a burst of excitement.

"Whatcha doing?" she teased, her tone light.

The couch shifted violently under her weight.

"What the *fuck*?!" Mike snapped, jolting upright.

"Shit, Julie! I was *trying* to rest! What the *hell* are you doing?" he barked. "Seriously, what's *wrong* with you?"

Julie recoiled, caught off guard.

"Sorry!" she said, her voice tinged with surprise. "I just wanted to hang out with you… show you some attention. I didn't mean to upset you. I was *trying* to be fun."

"Well, you're *not*. You're being pretty *annoying*, actually. Can't I just *relax* on my last day home?" Mike grumbled. "Is that too much to ask?"

Annoyed and hurt, Julie stood up.

"Fine," she said curtly. "I'll just clean up and start dinner. Let me know if you need anything."

She walked back into the kitchen, muttering under her breath.

Fucking asshole, she thought, yanking open the dishwasher.

"Ugh!" she grunted, slamming a cupboard shut.

Before she knew it, the day had slipped away.

She spent most of the evening finishing house chores, doing laundry, and packing Mike's travel bags. By the time she was done, it was already late.

Julie laid out her clothes for the next morning while Mike sat in bed, eyes glued to the TV.

After brushing her teeth, removing her makeup, and taking a quick shower, she pulled on her favorite sweatpants and T-shirt.

The thought of a *good night's sleep* felt like a much-needed reprieve as she turned off the bathroom light and climbed into bed.

"Goodnight, babe," she said softly, resting a hand on Mike's shoulder.

"Can you turn the volume down a little?"

"I've got a *better* idea," Mike replied, reaching for the remote and turning off the TV altogether.

"Oh, you don't have to turn it *off*," Julie said. "I like to fall asleep to it—just *not that loud.*"

"We can turn it back on *after,*" Mike interrupted, rolling toward her and sliding his arm around her waist.

Julie stiffened.

"*After today?* You *really* think so?" Her tone shifted, edged with frustration. "You *really* pissed me off this afternoon. I was trying to show you some attention, and you just *yelled* at me! What makes you think I want to do *anything* tonight?"

"Oh my *God,*" Mike groaned. "Are you *serious?* That was *nothing!* I was *kidding*—it was a *joke,*" he argued.

"Come on, don't be like that. I have to leave tomorrow. You're *not* being fair," he whined.

"Just real quick?" he pleaded.

Julie's mind flashed back to Barbara's party—to the *candid* conversations about selfish partners, about what women *deserved* in the bedroom.

Barbara was right.

Women deserved *Attention, love and honest affection.*

But looking at Mike now, she felt *defeated.*

He would never *really* listen to her thoughts or feelings. He'd *twist* any criticism into a *personal attack.*

This was probably as *good* as it was ever going to get.

How did this become my life? she thought bitterly as Mike's hands roamed over her, pulling her closer.

"Come on, baby," he murmured.

"You know what I like."

"I like *you.*"

He slid his hand under her T-shirt and cupped her breast.

Julie let out a small gasp, his touch both *cold* and *uninviting.*

"You're right," she finally said, conceding to avoid another argument.

Mike continued to caress her breast as he moved closer, pressing his lips to her neck.

Julie took a deep breath, forcing herself to give in.

She tilted her head back, exposing more of her neck as he trailed kisses from her ear down to her collarbone. Closing her eyes, she *tried* to enjoy the sensation, *tried* to clear her mind.

Her hand slid across Mike's chest, wandering lower.

She felt his breathing shift as her hand moved down.

Wearing only his boxers, his arousal was evident.

She let her palm glide over him, feeling his firm response beneath her touch.

Despite herself, she *tried* to remain present in the moment.

As Mike's breathing grew heavier, his movements *slowed*.

The kisses *stopped*.

His hand rested limply on her chest while he groaned softly.

Julie slipped her hand beneath the waistband of his boxers, slowly making her way between his thighs.

Mike shifted onto his back, giving her easier access.

Adjusting her hand, she wrapped her fingers around him—barely enough to fill her grip.

A quiet breath hitched in his throat as she applied just enough pressure to elicit a reaction.

"Oh, *fuck!* Fuck, *yeah!*" Mike groaned.

"Oh my *God*, baby! I'm so close!" His breath hitched. "*Do it!*"

Julie quickly let go, slipping one leg out of her sweatpants.

In one fluid motion, she climbed on top of him, guiding him inside her.

Almost instantly, Mike let out a *muffled cry.*

"Ughhh! *Fuck!* FUCK!" he gasped, his body flexing and jerking beneath her.

His release was *quick and intense.*

"Fuck!" he said again, breathless. "You're the best. Oh my *God!'*

Sliding off him, Julie shifted to her side of the bed and pulled her pants back on.

"I know," she said flatly, avoiding his gaze.

"Love you, babe," Mike mumbled, pulling the blanket up and rolling away from her.

Julie lay still, staring at the ceiling, her thoughts *racing.*

What happened to Friday-night Julie?

The Julie who felt empowered, confident, in control.

This was the *opposite* of what she wanted—of what she deserved.

Her mind wandered back through the choices she had made—every *twist, every turn*—that had brought her to this moment.

She didn't *hate* her life. *Far from it.*

She loved her boys.

She felt proud of the home she and Mike had built together.

But that didn't stop the hollow ache that lingered inside her.

A feeling she couldn't quite name.

Disappointment?

Longing?

She didn't know.

All she knew was something was missing.

| 19 |

The next morning, Mike and Julie woke early and dressed in silence. He packed his car, pressed a quick kiss to her cheek, said goodbye to the boys, and was off for another week on the road.

Julie watched him go, feeling a twinge of envy. He could just leave—escape the endless responsibilities of their home, their children, and the weight of daily life. Another week of driving, chatting with vendors, sleeping in hotels, and dining out on the company's dime.

Of course, she wouldn't trade time with the boys or teaching at Franklin for anything, but the imbalance still stung.

After dropping the boys off at school, Julie headed to Franklin to begin another week. Her first stop was the main office to check in with Mrs. Reed, the secretary, and confirm that her email about recruiting more chaperones had been received. She also wanted to swing by Barbara's room to thank her again for the invite on Friday night.

As she walked through the hallway, she started recognizing faces from the party—and, with a small jolt, realized they now recognized her too. Though she didn't know many of their names, they smiled and nodded as she passed.

"Good morning, Julie! Hope you had a great weekend!" Melanie's warm, familiar voice rang out.

"Well, good morning, Miss Crane!" Julie said with a warm smile. "I absolutely love your outfit today!" She meant it.

Melanie was wearing a sleek black skirt with a vibrant purple top that made her red hair pop. Even with her hair pulled back in a ponytail, she looked effortlessly polished and full of energy.

"Thanks! You too," Melanie replied, beaming. "How was your weekend?"

"It was okay," Julie said. "I spent most of it with the boys and my husband, so that was nice. Plus, I'm almost done planning the field trip. So, I'd say it was productive!"

"Your husband the astronaut?" Melanie teased with a knowing smirk.

Julie froze. A flicker of panic shot through her as she scrambled to remember. Had she really called Mike her *little astronaut* at the party? And had she said it to *Melanie*?

"Shh!" She pressed a finger to her lips, laughing nervously. "But yes, the astronaut."

Melanie grinned. "Well, good luck with the trip. Let me know if you need any help!"

"Thanks, I'll keep that in mind," Julie said as she continued down the hall.

But as she walked, a creeping unease settled in. What else had she let slip at the party? With every smile and nod from a colleague, she found herself wondering—were they just being friendly, or did they *know* something? Maybe this party hadn't been such a great idea after all.

Julie made her way to the teacher's lounge for coffee before heading to Room 10. Once she reached her desk, she let out a heavy sigh and took a slow sip, savoring the rare moment of solitude before the day officially began.

Just then, Cole popped his head into her room, his usual bright energy cutting through the quiet like a spotlight.

"Good morning, Jules!" he said with a grin. "Just wanted to say I hope you have a great day!" And just like that, he was gone.

That was Cole Anderson—always brimming with enthusiasm, effortlessly upbeat. Julie couldn't help but feel a flicker of envy. While she found peace in quiet moments, Cole thrived on people and connection. He greeted *everyone*—from the office staff to the custodians—and they all adored him. His warmth was contagious, his easy charm making him a favorite at Franklin.

The school wouldn't be the same without him.

The morning flew by, and before Julie knew it, lunchtime had arrived. She locked her classroom and spotted Cole across the hall doing the same.

"Hey, Cole!" she called, catching his attention.

He turned with his trademark smile. Today, his polo shirt fit snugly across his broad shoulders, and for the first time, Julie noticed how strong his frame looked under the fluorescent lights.

Wow. She thought. *How had I never noticed before?*

"What's up?" Cole asked.

Shaking off the thought, Julie answered, her cheeks tinged with a slight blush.

"I was thinking about your idea for a collaborative project," Julie said. "We should definitely sit down sometime and make a concrete plan. I like the idea of the kids doing something beyond just straight-up 'English.'" She made air quotes. "If we could approach a topic from a science perspective, they could do the research in your class and then work on the writing portion in mine."

"That's exactly what I was thinking!" Cole said, his enthusiasm shining through. "How about this—I've got a crazy week ahead, and then next week is the field trip, so why don't we meet after that? We could brainstorm an end-of-year, multi-subject capstone project. Something to wrap things up with a bang."

Julie nodded, impressed by his foresight. "That sounds perfect. And hey, were you serious about chaperoning the field trip? I'm still short a couple of people, and I'd love to have you on board."

"Absolutely," Cole replied. "Just let me know. If most of the sixth grade is going, my schedule won't be packed that day. I'm sure we can work something out with the other teachers."

"Great! I'll let you know for sure this week," Julie said.

"Sounds like a plan." Cole gave her a friendly fist bump. "Ready for lunch?"

"Let's do this!" Julie grinned, falling into step beside him as they headed for the cafeteria.

Lunch duty felt more like a break than an assignment. The kids were generally well-behaved, and there wasn't much to do besides daydream or get lost in thought.

By the time Julie and Cole walked in, the cafeteria was already bustling. The hum of chatter blended with the rhythmic clatter of trays and utensils, filling the space with an easy, familiar energy.

Julie found herself watching Cole as he moved through the room, effortlessly weaving himself into the flow of the students.

He didn't *have* lunch duty, but that never seemed to matter. More often than not, he spent the entire period here anyway—making his rounds, greeting each table with an easy *"Hey, guys!"* and cracking jokes that sent the kids into fits of laughter.

It was like he was a grown-up kid himself—but one who understood responsibility. He carried himself with a rare mix of playfulness and purpose, never taking himself too seriously but always commanding respect.

Julie found herself thinking, *He's the kind of guy who would make a great dad.*

And the thought settled in her chest—heavy, lingering—in a way she wasn't entirely ready to unpack.

Even though she worked more closely with Cole than most of the other teachers, she didn't actually know much about him. She knew he had gone to UMass, started as a physics major, then switched to education in his junior year.

She knew he was incredibly smart, that the kids *loved* his class, and that he never seemed stressed, overwhelmed, or angry. *Ever.* But beyond that, her knowledge was surprisingly limited.

Of course, he knew she had two boys—their pictures were prominently displayed on her desk—and he knew she was married. But aside from these basics and the small tidbits shared in casual conversation, their interactions had never gone much deeper.

Maybe this project idea is a good thing, Julie thought. *Maybe I'll get to know him better.*

The ringing bell snapped Julie back to the present. It was her window to grab lunch and prepare for the rest of the day.

She made her way to the teachers' lounge, where she found Barbara still sitting at one of the tables.

"Hey, sweetheart!" Barbara called out. "How was your weekend?"

"It was good," Julie said with a smile. "I'm glad I ran into you—I just wanted to thank you again for inviting me Friday night. It was so much more fun than I expected, and I *really* needed a reason to get out of the house."

Barbara laughed. "My pleasure. No need to keep thanking me."

Then, motioning for Julie to step closer, she lowered her voice. "I do it because I care. Because if I don't, who will? I do it for all our sisters, and…" Barbara paused, drawing a steady breath. "I do it for women in your shoes—because I used to be there too."

She smiled warmly, then leaned back in her chair. In a much louder voice, she added with a grin, "And I do it because it's one hell of a fun time! Right?"

Julie grinned. "It definitely is! I can't wait for the next one!"

"That's my girl!" Barbara said, pushing back from the table. "Now, enjoy your lunch. This old lady has a bucket-load to do before the next bell."

Julie nodded, watching her go, a smile still lingering on her face.

What an amazing woman, she thought.

The rest of Julie's day passed in a blur. Before she knew it, she was sitting at her desk, waiting to see if any students would come for extra help. No one had signed up, but she liked to wait—just in case someone popped in at the last minute.

"Looks like you got stood up," Cole said, poking his head into her room for the second time that day.

"Ha!" Julie laughed. "I never thought of it that way before. There wasn't anyone scheduled, so technically, I never even had a date."

"I find that hard to believe!" Cole teased with a grin. "You, without a date? No way."

"Well, thanks," Julie said with a chuckle. Then, more quietly, she added, "Honestly, it feels like that sometimes. Most of the time, really. With Mike gone so much, I feel like a married single parent. Very rarely like *Mrs. Tosh.* And never like *Julie.*" She hesitated. "Sometimes being alone sucks."

Cole's smile softened into something more thoughtful. "I'm sorry," he said. "I can't entirely relate, but... I do know what it's like to feel alone."

Cole stepped further into Julie's classroom and pulled up a chair beside her desk. As he sat down, he took a deep breath, hesitating slightly, as if unsure whether to continue.

"I don't share this with many people," he began. "But you know how I've told you I never really knew my parents?" He exhaled, shaking his head. "Well… my brother did."

He paused, choosing his next words carefully. "Growing up, he was the one who told me how we ended up in the system." Cole took another deep breath.

"You see, my dad left right after my mom got pregnant with me. After I was born, she couldn't support both of us *and* her drug habit, so we were both put up for adoption and fostered by the Andersons."

He leaned forward slightly, his voice quieter now. "Dylan carried that sense of rejection with him his entire life—always wondering why *both* our parents had to leave. And always feeling like a burden to the Andersons. Even after we were adopted, he *still* felt… abandoned and unwanted."

Cole swallowed hard. "Eventually, it became too much for him. He turned to drinking and drugs, but no matter how hard he tried to escape it, the depression consumed him. He tried so hard. But…" He hesitated, his voice unsteady. "In the end… he took his own life."

Silence settled between them. Cole took a steadying breath before continuing.

"The Andersons will always be my Mom and Dad. They will always be my family. But at Dylan's funeral I realized… without him, in a way, I was alone too."

"That's when I made a promise to myself—that if I could, I'd never let another kid feel like that. I'd never let them feel unloved, unseen, or unnecessary."

His expression hardened, but there was warmth in his voice. "That's why I switched majors and became a teacher. I figured... if I could make just *one* kid feel like they belong, like *they* mattered—then I've made a difference."

He let out a small, self-aware chuckle. "Let's be real—most of these kids aren't going to need to know how molecules are made in ten years. But if they know they *matter*? If they know they have *value*? Then they'll *make it* another ten years."

Julie sat up straighter, her eyes wide. "Cole... I'm so sorry. I had no idea."

"It's okay," Cole said with a small nod. "It's been a few years now, and it's easier to talk about. And honestly, I've tried to make sure *some* kind of good has come from it."

He exhaled slowly before adding, "But... I would like to keep this just between us. You know?"

"Oh my God, of course!" Julie said quickly. "I would never."

Cole's stoic expression softened into a faint smile. "Thanks, Jules." He held up his signature fist bump before standing. "You're a great friend, you know that?" His smile grew warmer.

"I'm gonna head out. But if you ever need to talk, just remember—you're never alone. Okay?" His eyes held a quiet sincerity. "Now, have a great rest of your afternoon! See you tomorrow."

And just like that, he was gone—just as casually as he had walked in.

Julie sat at her desk, stunned by what he had just shared. *Wow.* That was... awful. She had never imagined the depth of the stories and experiences shaping the people around her.

On the drive home, she reflected on Barbara and her son. On Cole and his mom and brother. *How do I even have a reason to complain?* Maybe her life wasn't perfect, but that didn't mean it was *bad.*

She thought about the areas she *could* change—what she *could* improve. As she pulled into her driveway, she couldn't help but hope she might learn something from both Barbara and Cole.

| 20 |

The boys were already home when Julie pulled into the driveway.

As usual, they had come in before her, tossed their backpacks in the hallway, kicked off their shoes, and grabbed snacks—before either settling in front of the TV or disappearing upstairs to their rooms.

Julie opened the door and was immediately greeted by the mess.

It was both comforting and frustrating. The scattered backpacks and shoes reassured her that the boys were home, safe—but it was also a constant reminder that she was always the one left to clean up.

Still, she knew there wouldn't be too many days like this left. Within a year, both boys would probably have their licenses, and after that… who knew how often they'd actually be home?

With a sigh, Julie tossed her bag and jacket onto the kitchen island and glanced around. The house suddenly felt too big, the emptiness stretching around her. She could hear the faint sounds of the boys upstairs, but somehow, it still felt like she was completely alone.

What to make for dinner? Julie sighed. This was the part of the day she hated most—deciding what to cook.

The question nagged at her every evening. Should she try something new? Stick to what she knew the boys would eat? Cater to their individual preferences? Chicken? Beef? Vegetables? She didn't even *like* cooking. Most days, it felt like nothing more than a tedious, never-ending chore.

Then it hit her. *Pasta!* She chuckled to herself. Mondays were for pasta—quick, easy, and guaranteed to keep complaints to a minimum.

"Guys!" she called up the stairs. "We're having spaghetti tonight!"

Muted replies drifted down: *"OK!"* and *"Sounds good!"*

Julie opened a bottle of wine and poured herself a generous glass. She pulled her grade book and a stack of papers from her bag. *Might as well get some work done before dinner,* she thought.

The rest of the afternoon passed with her curled up on the couch, half-watching TV as she sifted through assignments. The piles of papers reminded her of everything she still needed to do for the field trip—or at least, it *felt* like she did. She wasn't even sure anymore. It was just a lot.

A lot of kids. A lot of planning. A lot of added stress.

But it was going to happen.

This week, she was determined to finish sorting through all the student paperwork and chaperone details. She still needed to double-check the bus reservations and reach out to the Village to confirm there weren't any last-minute concerns.

After a dull and uninspiring text exchange with Mike, Julie finished her second glass of wine, closed her grade book, and stacked the papers into a neat pile.

Time to call it a night, she told herself.

| 21 |

It was around 9:00 p.m., and Julie could see the glow of light spilling from beneath the doors of both boys' rooms.

"I'm going to bed!" she called out loud enough for them to hear. "Make sure you don't stay up too late," she added.

"OK, Mom! Love you!" they chimed from behind their doors.

Julie stepped into her bedroom, her gaze falling on the queen-sized bed. She sighed, already envisioning herself nestled under the covers—warm, safe, and at ease. She moved through her nightly routine: brushing her teeth, removing her makeup, and indulging in a short, hot shower.

She turned on the water, and the sound of it striking the shower walls was instantly soothing. This was her quiet space. Her escape.

Stepping into the warm cascade, she let the heat envelop her, melting away the chill clinging to her skin. She tilted her head beneath the stream, allowing it to surround her, muffling the outside world. The crisp scent of tea tree shampoo and her favorite shaving cream filled the air, heightening her sense of relaxation. She inhaled deeply, savoring the moment, wishing she could stay here forever.

But that thought passed as quickly as it came. With a sigh, she stepped out, dried off, and prepared for bed. At her dresser, she pulled out a pair of worn, comfy pajama shorts and an oversized tank top.

Sliding under the covers, she shivered at the cool burn of the sheets against her freshly shaved skin. So soft. So soothing.

She had once thought she liked sharing a bed with Mike. But now, she loved having it all to herself—stretching out without restriction, taking up as much space as she pleased. She spread her arms and legs wide, starfishing across the mattress.

"Ahhh," she whispered, a satisfied smile forming. "That feels so good."

Julie propped herself up and reached for the remote on her bedside table. *A little news before bed,* she thought. With the press of a button, the TV flickered to life, casting a bright flash of white across the dimly lit room.

Turn the volume down, she reminded herself, lowering it before setting the remote back in its place.

As she shifted under the covers, her eyes drifted toward the half-open drawer of her nightstand. Something about it snagged her attention. Then, like a spark igniting a memory, it hit her—this was where she had stashed her prizes from Barbara's party.

A quiet thrill ran through her. She had nearly forgotten about them.

She had never used a sex toy before, but now, the curiosity tugged at her, insistent and undeniable. Lying there, staring at the drawer, she couldn't help but wonder... *what would it be like?*

Julie slipped out of bed and knelt in front of the nightstand. With careful hands, she eased the drawer open, the soft glow of the TV casting light over its contents. The gift bag remained safely tucked inside, untouched since that night.

She reached in, pulled the bag out, and set it upright on the carpet. Her fingers brushed against two boxes inside.

The first box was nearly as wide as the bag itself, making it difficult to remove. As Julie tugged it free, the glossy pink surface gleamed under the soft glow of the TV. Across the top, bold capital letters declared: *OMG!* Below, a simple outline hinted at the device inside, its shape both mysterious and intriguing. She studied it for a moment before setting it aside and reaching for the second box.

This one was smaller, wrapped tightly in clear plastic. Printed on one side were the words: *Mighty Might.* On the other: *Awesome Night.*

Hmm... this looks a little less intimidating, she mused.

Setting the larger box back into the bag, she slid the drawer shut. Then, with a steadying breath, she peeled away the plastic wrap and separated the two halves of the box.

A surprising resistance met her effort—it was as if a vacuum sealed them together, fighting her as she pulled. The tension built until, with a sudden whoosh of air and a swift slide, the box popped open.

Instantly, the familiar scent of plastic and packaging filled the air. A small paper booklet slipped from the box, fluttering to the floor. Across the front, in simple lettering, it read: *Instructions.*

Inside the box, a molded insert cradled a sleek silver tube, short and rounded at both ends. No more than two inches long, its chrome finish gleamed in the dim light. The only distinguishing feature was a tiny red dot near one end, barely visible in the TV's glow.

Julie carefully lifted the bullet-shaped device from its casing, turning it over in her palm. Not too heavy, not too light—it felt exactly as she had imagined.

She placed the opened box back into the bag on the floor, nudging it just beneath the bed. Then, grabbing the instruction leaflet, she slipped under the blankets once more, the cool sheets embracing her warm skin.

Let's see how this works, she thought, propping herself up against the pillows as she unfolded the booklet.

There weren't any real written instructions—just a simple diagram of the toy with arrows and labels.

One end was circled and marked *Front.* Behind that, the tiny red dot was labeled *On/Off – Long press. Cycle – Short press.* Off to the side, a small box read: *3 Settings. Tap to cycle through.*

Julie held the toy in one hand and hesitantly tapped the red dot.

"BuzzzzzzHummmmm!"

The toy jerked to life, sending a soft but insistent vibration through her palm. A tingling sensation traveled up her arm.

Holy crap! She jumped, startled. The power was much stronger than she had expected.

She tapped the button again.

"BuzzzzHummmmBuzzzzHummmBuzzzzHummm!"

This time, the toy pulsed rhythmically. Each throb sent a faint, synchronized thump up her arm.

Curious, Julie pressed the button once more.

"BuzBuzBuzBuzBuz Buz!"

The toy vibrated in rapid-fire bursts, short and sharp.

Holy crap, she thought. *This is crazy.*

With another tap, she cycled it back to the gentle, steady hum of the first mode. Finally, she pressed and held the button. The vibrations stopped, and a small red light blinked three times.

Oh? What's that? She studied the diagram again and spotted another small box with the text: *Battery Charge: 3 – Fully, 2 – Partial, 1 – Recharge.*

Oh, so it's fully charged. She smiled to herself.

It was surprisingly simple to use. Yet as she sat there, holding it in her hand, she couldn't help but wonder—*how would it feel against her skin?*

She pulled the covers up over her shoulders, stretched her legs out, and bent them slightly at the hips, causing the blankets to lift just above her body. Taking a steady breath, she pressed the small raised dot and waited.

"Buzzz!"

The toy hummed softly in her hand. Julie traced it slowly down the center of her body, following her midline as she closed her eyes, letting the vibrations seep through her skin. A deep breath escaped her lips as she sank further into the mattress, tension melting away.

She could feel her body growing heavier, the weight of her sinking into her tailbone, pressing deeper into the bed. Her mind swirled with anticipation.

Slowly, deliberately, her hand crept down her body, tracing the curve of her waist until she reached the band of her shorts. She lifted the fabric just enough and slipped the toy beneath.

A sudden jolt coursed through her as the vibrations teased her skin, making her stomach clench in response.

Pressure began building deep within her chest, pulsing in sync with the rhythmic hum. As her fingers brushed over the soft curls between her legs, she could already feel the deep tremors resonating through her body—direct, insistent, reaching the most sensitive parts of her body with an undeniable intensity.

The vibrations deepened as she inched closer. Cradling the silver bullet in her palm, she let her hand glide lower, guiding the sensation where her body ached for it most.

A sharp gasp escaped her lips as the full force of the tiny motor met her, like an arrow finding its mark, sending an electric pulse through her body. The sensation intensified as the toy passed over, each movement amplifying the pleasure.

Julie instinctively pulled back, letting the toy glide along her sensitive skin before returning to target. With every slow pass, heat surged through her, her body growing wetter, hotter—responding to each rhythmic pulse.

She drew in a deep breath, then released it slowly, steadying herself.

With each glide of the toy, the tension within her coiled tighter, the pressure building higher and higher. Each pass became shorter, more deliberate, her touch growing firmer with every movement.

The toy slid over her skin, each pass leaving a trail of sensation in its wake. The cool air kissed her wetness, heightening the warmth building deep within. Up and down, her hand guided the toy with slow, deliberate strokes. The rhythmic vibrations, sending waves of pleasure coursing through her.

Her breaths came faster now, shallower with every stroke.

Her legs and butt clenched involuntarily as warmth spread through her, a tingling heat rushing over every inch of her skin. The pressure inside her swelled with every passing second, the relentless vibrations driving her higher, pushing her closer. She could almost see the release hovering just beyond reach.

She held her breath—then, in an instant, pleasure detonated inside her, a violent explosion radiating from her core, surging outward like a pulse of raw energy unleashed into the universe.

"Ahhhhhhh!!" A sharp cry escaped her lips as her body trembled, shaking as wave after wave overtook her. The toy's relentless hum carrying the sensation, sending aftershocks through her—muscles spasming beyond her control.

"Ahhhhh!" She bit her lip, trying to stifle the sounds spilling from her lips.

"Holy Fuck!" she gasped, the words barely contained. Desperate for relief, she tore the toy away from her body, the vibrations suddenly unbearable against her oversensitive skin.

Julie struggled to catch her breath, her chest rising and falling in shallow, uneven pants. Slowly, her muscles began to unwind, the lingering tremors fading into warmth. Beneath the blankets, the quiet hum of the *Mighty Might* still vibrated softly, muffled by the comforter and the sound of her own breathing.

She reached down, slipping the toy from beneath the covers, and pressed the little red button. At once, the vibrations ceased, leaving the room steeped in silence.

Julie lay still, her skin flushed and hot, her pulse gradually settling. Exhaustion seeped into her limbs as she set the toy on the bedside table. All she could do now was breathe—staring up at the ceiling, thinking...

Thoughts swirled in her mind, refusing to settle.

She exhaled slowly, her body sinking deeper into the soft mattress, the familiar weight of it supporting her. Focusing on each breath, she let the calmness wash over her, pulling her gently toward sleep.

| 22 |

The next morning, Julie woke up feeling different—eager, energized. The night before had been an awakening.

I deserve to be happy.

The thought echoed in her mind as she pulled on her clothes.

And I'm not.

I deserve to feel good. To feel loved, wanted... respected.

She glanced around her bedroom.

It felt big. Empty.

Her eyes landed on the tiny vibrator still resting on her bedside table. Quickly, she picked it up and tucked it into the top drawer. Everything was starting to make sense now.

This was what Barbara had been talking about. *This* was the empowerment she was so passionate about. .

How had she not seen how much of herself she had been giving up.

Emotions stirred inside her—years of neglect, of unmet needs—but now wasn't the time to unpack them.

She took a deep breath, finished getting dressed, and made her way downstairs.

The twins had already made breakfast and were nearly ready to go. Julie watched as they gathered their things, moving through their routine with effortless independence. If there was one thing to be proud of in her life, it was them.

But they weren't boys anymore.

Every day, she saw it more clearly—the way they had outgrown the softness of childhood, their faces now lean and defined. They were young men now, strong and sure of themselves.

And she was so proud of the people they were becoming.

Where has the time gone? she wondered as she watched them.

Julie snapped back to the present. It was time to leave, and she still hadn't finished getting herself ready.

"Crap!" she blurted. "Look at the time!"

"We're all set," Tommy called back.

"Ready when you are!" Chad added.

Julie groaned. "Ugh! Alright, let's just go. I'll grab something at work."

Everyone grabbed their bags and headed for the car.

"I *cannot* wait for you two to get your licenses," Julie laughed, shaking her head. Another reminder of how much older they were getting.

With the boys dropped off, Julie made the short drive from the high school to Franklin. Stepping out of her car, the sharp morning air stole her breath as she hurried from the parking lot to the front office.

"Good morning!" Mrs. Reed greeted with a smile. "Crazy morning?"

"If this morning is any indicator, it's going to be an even crazier *day!*" Julie laughed.

Her mind was already racing. There was so much to do, so much to sort out. But first—coffee.

Navigating the crowded hallway, Julie made her way to the cafeteria. There was just enough time to grab a cup before heading to Room 10. As she stepped through the classroom door, the bell rang right on cue.

She sank into her desk chair, already hearing the familiar thunder of students' feet pounding down the hall toward their homerooms.

"Tuesday. 8:00 a.m. Let's go," she muttered, psyching herself up for the day.

The morning routine moved like clockwork. Students filtered in and out of homeroom, leaving just enough time to take attendance, go over the lunch menu and morning announcements, and answer a few last-minute questions.

The rest of the day also hurried by faster than Julie had expected. Before she knew it, the final period had arrived.

Tuesdays meant prep during the last block of the day—a rare moment of quiet after the chaos of teaching. The stillness of the empty room settled over her, stark and noticeable after hours of nonstop movement.

She sat at her desk, feeling small in the silence. Her mind kept circling back—Friday night, the weekend, last night. So much had happened.

She had never felt more certain about her emotions—yet never more confused.

She still couldn't put a name to what she was feeling.

Her eyes drifted to the manila envelope in front of her, the task she *should* be focusing on. But her mind wouldn't let her. It kept tugging her in different directions.

Was she mad? Frustrated? Sad? Unhappy?

"Ughhh!" she groaned, rubbing her temples. "Come on now, Julie, you have work to do," she muttered under her breath.

Shaking her head, she rolled her shoulders, as if physically trying to shake off the tangled emotions. *Focus.*

She took a deep breath and poured the contents of the envelope onto her desk. Quickly, she thumbed through the stack, counting the permission slips held together with the green paperclip.

Green for "Good to Go."

Each one was complete, signed, and accompanied by any necessary medical paperwork.

"One hundred and twenty-four," she murmured, double-checking the number.

So far, she had 122 sixth-grade students, plus two additional slips for Alyssa and Lisa.

"So, 124 divided by 10 is..."

Julie hesitated, then groaned.

"Hum? And this is why I don't teach math!" she laughed to herself. *"Uh, 12. No! 13!"*

It was thirteen.

She had ten confirmed chaperones, which meant she still needed three more—or just two if she counted herself. Melanie and Cole had already offered to help, so that left only one more to find.

I better make sure Mr. Dryer is okay with this, she thought, opening her laptop to send him an email.

TO: Mr. Dryer
SUBJECT: Field Trip Chaperones

Dear Mr. Dryer,
As you know, the sixth grade is scheduled to visit Patriot Village next week. They recently contacted me with an updated chaperone policy requiring a 1:10 chaperone-to-student ratio.

I am currently short three chaperones. Mrs. Reed is working to recruit more via our Facebook page and the news blast. Additionally, Mr. Anderson and Miss Crane have offered to step in if needed, though they would both require substitutes for the entire day.

Please let me know if this is an option we can pursue.
Thanks in advance,
J. Tosh

And... send.

Julie exhaled, satisfied. At least now she had a plan, and she still felt confident she could secure a few more volunteers before the trip.

She sifted through the remaining paperwork—the day's itinerary, the bus reservations. One by one, she clipped each document with a green paperclip. *Good to go.*

Relief settled over her. For the first time, she felt like she truly had a handle on this trip. With everything laid out in front of her, she felt capable. Confident. In control.

I wish I felt like this more often.

The bell was about to ring again, signaling the return to homeroom for dismissal. Soon, the students would flood in, grab their coats, shove their belongings into their backpacks, and file out for the day.

Julie had no obligation to stay late, but the thought of lugging a stack of papers home wasn't appealing. It would be easier to get the grading done here.

The bell rang, and just like in the morning, the students swelled in—then rushed out.

Julie sat at her desk, savoring a second wave of quiet. She flipped through one stack of essays, then another. She had always loved reading what her students wrote, always surprised by the insights they shared.

Each paper offered a glimpse into who they were, their thoughts and experiences laid bare on the page.

Writing can reveal a lot, she mused.

Just then, a knock sounded at her open door.

"Hey, Jules! Sorry, didn't mean to startle you—you looked completely lost in your reading," Cole said with a grin, his laugh easy and warm. "I was just heading out, but I wanted to check in and just say, I hope you have a great rest of your day!"

He leaned against the doorframe, casually relaxed. Unlike the other male teachers, who always seemed to carry briefcases, Cole had a backpack slung over one shoulder and a gray hoodie tucked under his arm.

"And that's exactly why I don't teach English." He gestured toward the mountain of papers on Julie's desk, flashing another smile.

Julie smiled back but found herself momentarily lost, staring at him. The late afternoon sunlight filtered through the window, catching the ends of his brown hair, making them glow a deep amber. His eyes were bright, and his smile always reached all the way up his cheeks.

Realizing she had paused too long, she gave a small shake of her head. "Yeah!" she said, laughing lightly, trying to cover for herself. "It's the worst part, really! But once you get into it, it goes by pretty fast."

"Oh, I didn't mean to break your concentration! I saw the door open, and…"

"That's fine! I needed a break anyway." Julie waved off his concern, laughing a little more, trying to reassure him. "So, you're heading out?"

"Yeah," he said, adjusting his backpack. "I'm gonna try to get some shopping done before everyone else gets out of work. It's so much easier now than later—and *definitely* easier than the weekend."

He wasn't wrong. That was one of the perks of teaching—the early hours. Julie could be out by 2:30 p.m., run errands, finish shopping, and still be home before most people had even left work.

"Well, get going then!" she teased, waving him away.

"Alright! See you in the morning, Jules." Cole smiled—and then winked before turning down the hall.

Julie watched him go, a quiet thought settling in her mind.

I am so lucky to work with him.

Somehow, he always made her day better. His presence was calming, his friendship so easy, so genuine.

If she ever left Franklin, he was the one person she knew she would miss the most.

| 23 |

The rest of the day passed in a blur as Julie moved through her usual routine.

Dinner was done, the kitchen cleaned, and now she sat curled up on the couch, a glass of wine in hand, half-watching the news.

She tried to focus, but her mind kept drifting back to the way she had felt that morning—empowered, energized, ready to take on the world. Now, as the evening settled in, that ambition felt distant, swallowed up by the quiet comfort of routine.

With a sigh, she reached for her glass and took another sip. A second pour helped her relax a little more.

Ding!

The notification cut through the quiet hum of the evening news.

Julie reached for her phone.

7:30 on the dot.

Mike's text—right on schedule.

MIKE: Hey, just wanted to touch base and see how your day was. Busy here, but good!

Julie smiled faintly as she typed her reply.

JULIE: Hey. It's been a pretty good day too. I finally feel like I have the field trip under control. Can't wait for you to be back home. Miss you already!

His reply came quickly.

MIKE: That's good. Same. Hope you have a good day tomorrow too. Love ya!

Julie stared at the screen.
That was it?
She had been trying to share a piece of her day, her accomplishments—and all he had to say was, *"That's good."*
She shook her head. She spent more time talking to Cole about her day than she did with her own husband.
And they had actually talked.
Julie took a deep breath. Maybe she was overreacting. Maybe he was just tired. Or perhaps he was preoccupied with something else, and she was distracting him.

JULIE: Love you too.

Julie set her phone down and sank into the couch cushions. She looked around the empty room and sighed again.
She felt... off. Conflicted.
She didn't know exactly what she was feeling, but she knew she didn't like it.

Reaching for her glass, she tipped it back, finishing the last of her wine in one gulp. The warmth of the alcohol spread through her, softening her edges.

That's enough work for today, she thought, pushing herself off the couch.

She moved through the kitchen, turning off the lights as she passed, then climbed the stairs to her room.

A soft glow shone beneath the boys' doors. Chad's TV murmured quietly, and the faint sound of Tommy flipping pages told her he was still studying.

"Good night, boys!" she called. "I'm going to get ready for bed!"

"Good night, Mom!" they answered in turn.

Julie stepped into her bedroom and flicked on the light. She pulled open her dresser drawer, grabbing a sports bra and a pair of panties for the next day, then placed them on the chair next to her closet.

She reached for her black jeans and tossed them over the chair as well.

From the closet, she chose a sweater that paired well with the pants and added it to the pile.

That will do.

She opened her top drawer and pulled out an old, extra-large T-shirt—the one she loved to sleep in.

The fabric had faded over the years to an off-white color, and the word *BOSTON* stretched across the front in worn maroon letters.

She had bought it years ago on a family trip to walk the Freedom Trail. It had originally been for Mike, but he refused to wear it. Said it wasn't his style.

So, it became hers.

But only when he wasn't home.

If Mike saw her wearing it, he'd get irritated, telling her to *"take it off"*—*"That's mine"*—not because he wanted it, but because it gave him an excuse to get her naked.

With him away, though, she could wear whatever she wanted.

She could be comfortable in her own home.

Lost in thought, Julie undressed and stepped into the shower. The warmth of the water mixed with the lingering buzz from the wine, making her movements slow and deliberate.

As she lathered up, her eyes drifted over her body, and she sighed.

She hated what she saw.

Two babies, years of exhaustion, and time itself had left their marks.

Others told her she looked great, but she couldn't see it.

All she saw were the extra weight, the less-perky breasts, the stretch marks, the wrinkles.

Ugh. I should probably do a full shave.

Julie usually shaved every few days—unless a specific outfit called for it. But it was winter, and no outfit required it.

At least, not until Mike came home.

For now, a quick maintenance shave would do.

Once she was done, Julie sighed and plunged her head under the running water. The steady stream drowned out her swirling thoughts, granting her a fleeting moment of peace.

Stepping out, she dried off and slipped into her oversized T-shirt. The fabric was soft, worn in all the right places—it really was her favorite.

Padding across the carpeted floor, she crawled under the covers.

The cool sheets against her bare legs sent a shiver through her, both relaxing and stimulating. She pulled the blankets up over her shoulders, savoring the contrast.

Reaching for the remote on her nightstand, she clicked through channels until she landed on a mindless sitcom. The soft glow from the screen made the room feel a little less empty.

9:30 p.m.

Where did the day go?

Her mind was still too restless for sleep. She exhaled, staring up at the ceiling, then over at her nightstand.

Slowly, Julie slid out from under the blankets and knelt beside the bed.

She opened the top drawer, her fingers brushing against the small vibrator she had used the night before.

Should I use it again? she wondered, warmth already blooming beneath her skin.

Or...

She hesitated.

Then, reaching under the bed, she pulled out the hidden bag.

First, the smaller box from the night before.

Then, the larger one.

The powder-pink box read **OMG** in bold white letters. A picture of the device was printed on the front, its sleek, ergonomic shape intriguing her—a cone-like opening at the top catching her eye.

Barbara had raved about it at the party. *"It's NOT a vibrator,"* she'd said. *"It's something completely different."*

Julie scanned the box, her eyes catching words like *"Waterproof.", "Air-Wave Technology."*, and *"Virtually Silent."*—prominently displayed.

She peeled the plastic wrapping off the box, tossing it into the bag by her knees. With a soft magnetic release, the lid flipped open. Inside, the device sat cradled in molded packaging. Julie picked it up, marveling at how light and comfortable it felt in her hand.

The back featured three buttons labeled (+), (-), and (P). The front had that cone-shaped opening, which only piqued her curiosity more.

Reaching deeper into the box, she found the charging cable and a small instruction booklet.

Flipping through the pages, she landed on a diagram of the toy, complete with labels and more details. It was easy to follow. The (+) and (-) were labeled as *"Intensity,"* and the (P) as *"Power On/Off."* Arrows pointed to the *"Magnetic Charging Port"* and the *"Stimulation Head."*

Julie continued through the booklet, her eyes landing on a section marked *"USE."*

Ah, here we go!

The booklet read:

"Press and hold (P) for 1 sec to turn on your OMG. The stimulation head will create a light puff sensation, and you will feel the OMG turn on. Gently splay your labia to expose your clitoris. Place the stimulation attachment tightly on your clitoris and apply light pressure. Use the (+) and (-) buttons to increase or decrease the Air-Wave experience. Enjoy! Press and hold (P) for 1 sec to turn off your OMG."

Julie pressed and held the power button. A faint rumble came from the toy, and the button lit up a bright blue. Aside from a gentle hum from the base, there was hardly any noise. She placed the cone end over her knuckle and felt rhythmic puffs of air against her skin.

Oh, wow! she thought. *This is different.*

Julie pressed the power button again, and the toy gently powered off. She quickly tossed the box back into the bag and slid it under the bed.

With a swift motion, she jumped into bed, pulling the covers up over herself.

The blankets settled under her chin, and she closed her eyes, letting out a deep breath. Slowly, she pulled her knees up, tugging her T-shirt over her hips. The cool sheets slid over her skin, sending a shiver through her. Her freshly shaved legs felt soft, smooth, and silky.

Slowly, she slid her hand down her right leg, focusing on the sensation of her own touch. As her hand moved closer to the inside of her thigh, her bottom sank deeper into the mattress. Her breathing deepened. She could feel her chest rising and falling beneath the weight of the covers.

Her hand moved softly between the crease of her leg and the edge of her trimmed pubic hair. With each movement, her breath grew deeper, anticipation building.

Her middle finger deliberately glided between her skin, while her ring and index fingers traced the outer edges of her swollen flesh. With each movement, she felt her body growing wetter. She slid her hand lower, then brought her fingers back up, gently stroking her sensitive lips. The pressure sent waves of pleasure rippling through her abdomen.

Julie let her hand drift lower, gently tracing over her skin, a shiver running through her as the cool air met her heightened sensitivity beneath the sheets. She felt herself growing more aroused, her body temperature rising. She pinched her flesh together, folding them inward, before slowly pulling them apart once more.

Each exhale sharpened her focus on her own touch, amplifying the sensations it created. With every movement, she grew wetter, her desire building.

Her eyes still closed, she reached for her new toy, eager to explore. She found the power button with her thumb and pressed it, feeling the slight vibration hum through her hand. The soft pulse of the vibration gently cycled in her palm.

She reached further down, guiding the pulsating cone directly over her most sensitive point. She pressed down, and the steady rhythm wrapping around her perfectly, with a gentle yet firm, steady pressure.

The toy created an unusual sensation—like a soft pocket of air gently tapping in a slow, continuous rhythm.

Julie lay in bed, breathing in sync with the rhythm of the pulses, moving the cone in small, slow circles as the magic puffs kept time. With her left hand, she continued to explore herself, the touch and the toy working in perfect harmony.

Julie sank deeper into a focused state of pleasure. Her mind emptied of everything that had once weighed so heavily on her. She was lost in the rhythm. Lost in the moment. She slid her finger up the toy and pressed the button to increase the intensity.

Click.

The toy hummed stronger, and Julie immediately felt the change. The pressure became more intense, more direct. She focused on the sensation, surrendering to the feeling—the rhythm, the circles, the pressure. The rhythm, the circles, the pressure.

She could feel herself building, her breath shallow and quickening.

Click.

She increased the intensity again. This time, the gentle pulsation transformed into a rhythmic thumping directly on her clit. Her breathing quickened, growing more shallow. She could feel her abdomen tightening as the pressure built deeper within her.

Her eyes squeezed shut, still focused on the pinpoint pleasure. Her muscles began to contract, her body responding involuntarily. She let herself sink deeper into the sensation, building and building.

She surrendered as the pleasure overwhelmed her, her mind free to relax. It spun like a prize wheel. Without warning, an image of Cole flashed in her mind—standing in her classroom doorway. His smile. His silly backpack slung over his shoulder. His hair. His eyes. His smile again.

The urge became too strong to resist, and Julie felt her body reach its peak, exploding in ecstasy.

"Aghhhhhhughhh!!" Julie gasped as her muscles contracted, her body trembling. The toy, still firmly in place, continued to pulse against her, each vibration intensifying the waves of her climax. She couldn't fight her body, still tense, pulling her in every direction.

"Aghhhh!" she cried out. "Too much! Too much!" she panted, pulling the toy away from her shaking body, her nerves tingling and hypersensitive to the slightest movement.

"Holy fuck!" she gasped.

Julie forced herself to reach for the power button, pressing it down and waiting for the toy to fall silent.

"Oh my God!" she laughed, still struggling to catch her breath.

Unable to move, Julie stared up at the ceiling, trying to process the overwhelming sensations.

Oh my God, she thought. *That was incredible. Abso-fucking-lutely incredible!*

What the hell?

Cole?

Julie couldn't believe it. In the middle of her orgasm, she found herself thinking about Cole. *Mr. Anderson. Cole!*

She wondered what this meant. Where was her mind? But why not? He was an amazing man—handsome, thoughtful, kind, warm, friendly, funny—just... *Cole.*

Her thoughts swirled as her body sank deeper into sleep.

| 24 |

The next morning, Julie woke up to the sound of her alarm. Her brain was still processing all the thoughts from the night before. Her mind kept jumping to those events as she got ready for school, made breakfast, and ensured the boys were set for the day.

Looking at the clock on the kitchen stove, Julie called to the boys sitting at the kitchen table, "Leaving in five minutes! So let's wrap this up!"

For the second morning in a row, Julie felt a newfound energy and focus. There was a spring in her step and a sharp sense of confidence. She thoughtfully planned her day in her head as she packed her school bag and ensured the boys were following her lead.

Five minutes were up. "Alright, let's go, guys!"

Julie dropped the boys off at school and made her way to the parking lot at Franklin. All she could think about was hoping she wouldn't run into Cole on her way into the building or in the office. Just the thought of seeing him made her feel hot and blush with a mix of excitement and embarrassment.

Come on Julie, she thought to herself.

Shake this off! You're a grown woman, and this is no big deal.

She tried to convince herself.

But deep down, she knew it wasn't really that simple. The more her mind processed in the background, the more she realized how special and amazing Cole truly was. He was... Cole.

"Ugh!" she let out an exasperated sigh. Julie took a deep breath and exhaled slowly. *Let's do this, Mrs. Tosh*, she cheered herself on.

Julie hurried across the parking lot in the crisp morning air before diving into the warm building. The sounds around her, the scent of the old building, and the familiar surroundings pulled her back into the present moment. She had a lot to do today and couldn't afford any distractions.

Julie made a quick stop in the office to check her mail and say hello to Mrs. Reed. The secretary was buried in papers and announcements for the morning but caught sight of Julie out of the corner of her eye.

"Julie!" Mrs. Reed called out to get her attention. "I wanted to let you know I spoke with Mr. Dryer, and he said you're all set if you need extra teachers for the field trip. Just let me know for sure by Friday so I can have the substitutes scheduled. And Paul said, 'If you need any more, let me know.' We can spare a few aides if needed."

This was wonderful news. Julie had worried Mr. Dryer might not approve adding extra teachers to the trip. But what could she do? These days, most parents work full-time and can't take time off like they used to. Among all the stress and anxiety Julie carried, this was one weight she was relieved to shed.

"Thanks, Beth! I really appreciate it. I'll definitely let you know!" Julie said with a wide smile. She turned to leave with a sense of excitement and accomplishment. Each day, she felt more confident and in control.

Julie made her way down the halls toward the teachers' lounge for a quick cup of coffee before heading to her classroom. On her way, she noticed Barbara walking out of the lounge, laughing as she always did. Her laugh was so distinct—booming yet playful, exciting yet friendly. It defined who Barbara was as a teacher and a friend. Barbara noticed Julie approaching.

"Well, look at you!" Barbara called out loudly enough for the whole cafeteria to hear. "You've got a spring in your step, don't you?" she teased with her trademark smile and sass. "I told you!" she said, laughing.

Julie quickened her pace and grabbed Barbara's arm, pulling her to a quieter corner near the lounge door.

"Shhh!" Julie whispered frantically. "You're so loud!" she said, laughing.

"Yes, yes, you did! And yes, yes, you were right! Oh my God, Barb, that thing is AMAZING!" Julie's face turned bright red as a giddy smile spread across her lips. "I don't even have words to describe it. Just... amazing!"

"That's what everyone says!" Barbara replied with a grin. Pulling Julie closer, she whispered, "I'm so happy for you. This is why I do what I do! It's important, and it's fun!" Barbara patted Julie on the shoulder reassuringly. "I'm so glad you came to the party. You deserve this. If there's ever anything you need, just let me know. I'm here for you."

"Thanks," Julie replied with a grateful smile. "I can't think of anything right now, but I'll definitely let you know."

Barbara winked. "I know you will, dear." Then, more loudly, she added, "Go get your coffee, or we'll both be late!" She gave Julie a quick hug before walking away.

Julie watched Barbara leave the cafeteria, a small smile still on her face, the warmth of their conversation lingering. Yet, something about it unsettled her. Barbara had meant well, but Julie knew she'd never actually go to her if she needed anything—or had a question.

Not about that stuff anyway.

If I ever had a question... she thought.

Her mind searched for a name—someone she could turn to, someone she could confide in.

But there was no one.

The realization settled in—slow at first, then all at once—as she struggled to come up with even one name.

Who could I talk to? she wondered. *About this? About anything?*

The thought sat heavy in her chest, pressing down like a weight she hadn't noticed before.

Her stomach sank as the reality hit her—she had no real friends.

For nearly half her life, the boys had been her entire world, filling every corner of it. But now, as they grew older and more independent, that space was shifting—widening, stretching into something empty.

And Mike? Talking to him wasn't an option.

He dismissed anything that wasn't about him—brushing off her feelings, her thoughts, her concerns, and any attempt at real connection. If she so much as hinted at pursuing something for herself—*beyond just being a wife and mom*—he always had the same tired excuse: "*Why do you need friends when you have the boys and me?*"

It always sounded so logical when he said it—so reasonable. And if she ever questioned it, he'd twist it around until she felt guilty for even wanting more.

Now, standing in the cafeteria, that loneliness wasn't just creeping in—it was settling deep into her heart.

Julie sighed and glanced at the clock. "Fuck!" she muttered. Nearly 8:00 a.m.

She hurried out of the cafeteria, sped past Mr. Anderson's door without so much as a glance, and darted into her classroom.

Tossing her bag on the desk, she let out a deep breath, relieved she'd made it on time. Down the hall, she could hear the students' footsteps as they stampeded from the gymnasium. *Here we go*, she thought as another day began.

Homeroom passed quickly. Julie checked off the usual boxes—attendance, announcements, answering questions—before releasing the students to their first-period classes.

As she stood by the door, she heard a voice over her shoulder.

"Hey! Good morning, Mrs. Tosh!" called out Mr. Anderson from across the hall. He smiled and gave a slight wave, his eyes lighting up when he saw her turn.

Julie stepped into the hallway, meeting him halfway through the crowd of students.

"Just wanted to say hi!" Cole said. "I didn't see you this morning and wasn't sure if you made it in. You look like you've already had a full day. Everything okay?"

Julie gave him an exhausted smile. "Yeah, I'm good. I was just running late and didn't have time for coffee this morning, so I'm a little off. But good morning!" she added, smiling back. She couldn't help but notice his brown eyes, warm and inviting, as if he genuinely cared.

"Good," he said. "I talked to Beth in the office, and she said you got the okay for extra teachers on the field trip. If you still need me, let me know. I've never been to the Village, and it sounds fun."

"Absolutely!" Julie said, a bit more excitedly than she intended. "I should have everything finalized by Friday, so I'll definitely let you know."

"Sounds good!" Cole said, raising a fist for a fist bump. Julie laughed and met it with her own.

As she turned back toward her classroom, Julie smiled to herself.

That wasn't so bad? she thought, stepping inside.

Time to start the day.

| 25 |

Julie's first class of the day consisted of students who faced significant challenges in English. It was her most demanding class to teach, as it included both students who struggled with state performance exams and those for whom English was not a native language.

All of the students met a required baseline, but each needed individualized attention and tailored teaching methods. With only fifteen students in the class, Julie often felt like she had taught fifteen different lessons by the end of the period.

It was also the only class where she had an aide to assist her.

Mrs. Martinez primarily worked with Hispanic students, accompanying them from class to class and occasionally serving as a translator.

Julie knew little about Mrs. Martinez beyond her first name, Maria. Their class was always so busy that they rarely had time for casual conversation. However, this morning's lesson was going unusually smoothly.

The class had spent most of the year mastering basic grammar and sentence structure, with a strong focus on diagramming sentences. Today, they were working on a worksheet to prepare for tomorrow's quiz. With the students absorbed in their work, Julie finally had a moment to discuss her plans for Monday with Mrs. Martinez.

Since Julie would be away on the field trip, Mrs. Martinez had been assigned to cover her classes for the day. To keep the students who weren't attending engaged, Julie had suggested showing a film about colonial New England, giving them some historical context for their peers' experience at the Old Patriot Village museum.

They had just begun brainstorming possible films when a knock sounded at the door. Slowly, it creaked open, revealing Mr. Anderson's head peeking inside.

Cole's eyes widened when he spotted Julie sitting at her desk with Maria. "Hey, I don't mean to bother you," he said, stepping cautiously into the room so as not to disturb the class, "but I just finished my prep period and went across the street to Dunkin' for a real cup of coffee. I figured you could use one too."

He approached Julie's desk with a warm smile. "I wasn't sure how you take yours, so I grabbed a handful of sugar and creamers," he added, offering a lopsided grin.

Cole pulled a cup of coffee from the holder and set it beside Julie's papers, along with a small pile of sugar packets and creamers.

"And I didn't forget about you, Maria," he said with a laugh, placing another cup near her. "Just how you like it—Extra Extra!"

Maria grinned and raised her cup. "This is why you're my favorite teacher!" she teased. Then, more sincerely, she added, "Thank you, Mr. Anderson. You didn't have to do this."

"Thanks, Cole! You really didn't have to," Julie said, touched. "I'll pay you back later," she insisted.

"Don't even think about it. It's no big deal," Cole said with a shrug.

"Anyway, gotta go! The bell's about to ring." He flashed one last smile before heading out the door.

Julie glanced at Maria and smiled. Maria smiled back knowingly.

"If I were twenty-five years younger," Maria said with a wink, "that one would be mine! They don't make them like that anymore. He's so good with the kids, always in a great mood. And, of course, he knows how I like my coffee!"

"Yeah, he's something," Julie replied with a smirk, her thoughts briefly drifting to the night before.

"Okay, kids! Let's start wrapping up," Julie called out. "The bell's about to ring. Finish your worksheets for homework, and don't forget—quiz tomorrow! If you have any questions, ask before the quiz starts. Got it?"

She scanned the room for any puzzled faces. "Enjoy the rest of your day! See you tomorrow."

After a quick chat with Maria to finalize their plan to research movies during tomorrow's quiz, the bell rang, signaling the end of the period.

The rest of Julie's morning flew by. At times, it felt like she spent more energy keeping students entertained than actually teaching, but that was just part of the job. She had always believed school should be as fun as it was educational—after all, who would want to sit through a miserable class every day?

Still, making sixth-grade English exciting wasn't always easy. Shakespeare, grammar, spelling, vocabulary—even she found it dull at times.

She couldn't help feeling a little jealous when students came in from Mr. Anderson's class, raving about making silly putty, inflating balloons with vinegar and baking soda, or cooking hot dogs with the sun. But she loved what she did and found joy in those moments when students were genuinely excited to learn.

Julie gathered her papers into a neat pile and headed to the cafeteria for lunch duty. As she walked down the hall, her thoughts raced—she couldn't shake the events of last night, her conversation with Barbara, or the growing anticipation for the field trip. It was all too much.

"Ugh," she groaned aloud, frustrated by her swirling thoughts. Taking a deep breath, she exhaled slowly, trying to steady her mind.

Lunch duty, as usual, ran itself—a relief given Julie's distracted state. She paced rhythmically between the rows of tables, the white noise of chatter and clattering kitchen equipment lulling her into a trance-like drift. Occasionally, she paused to sidestep an obstacle or change direction, but her mind was elsewhere.

Ring! The bell jolted Julie back to reality. She shook her head, trying to regain focus. "Wow, that went by fast," she muttered.

As students filed out of the cafeteria, she decided to slip into the teachers' lounge for a brief respite.

As Julie stepped inside, she heard Melanie's familiar voice.

"Hey, Julie!" Melanie called from a worn-out chair along the wall, sealing a plastic container—presumably from her lunch. She flashed a curious smile. "Do you have plans for Saturday night? CJ and I are going out for drinks and thought it might be fun to invite you and your husband along."

"Huh?" Julie replied, caught off guard. "Saturday?"

"Yeah," Melanie said. "Nothing crazy—just a few drinks and some company. Thought it'd be nice since we had so much fun the other night."

Julie hesitated. "Um, yeah. Just... yeah. Mike's out of town until Wednesday, I think, so..."

Melanie perked up. "Oh, I didn't realize he wasn't around... See? That's why we need to hang out more!" she teased.

"But seriously, if you want to come without him, you're more than welcome. There might even be a few other people joining us. Don't be shy. Seven o'clock at The Tap House. You know where that is?"

Julie nodded. "I've never been, but I know where it is. I'll let you know," she said, still processing the invitation.

"Great!" Melanie said, gathering her things. "It'll be fun!"

Julie sat down, still puzzled by the exchange.

Melanie had just invited her out.

Did Barbara put her up to this?

She'd never, ever been invited out before. Then Barbara's party. Now this.

Sighing deeply, she thought, *I've got to talk to Barbara.*

| 26 |

Julie made it through the last two periods of the day without overthinking—without letting herself spiral into questions about why Miss Crane had invited her out.

But the thought still lingered at the edges of her mind.

She had never been invited out by a coworker before—aside from Barbara's party. And now, here she was, being asked out again.

Was she reading too much into it? Maybe Melanie really did just want to hang out.

And then again... would Barbara really try to set her up?

Julie wasn't sure whether the thought made her anxious—or intrigued.

She shuffled the papers on her desk into neat piles, organizing the remnants of the day. Sliding her grade book, laptop, and a stack of assignments into her bag, she readied herself to head home.

As she turned to leave, her eyes landed on the empty coffee cup still sitting on her desk.

She picked it up, turning it absently in her hands.

That was really thoughtful of Cole today.

A small smile touched her lips. *I'll have to do something for him,* she thought.

The room was too quiet.

The empty stillness settled over her, making the space feel larger than it was. The soft hum of the heating vents was the only sound filling the chilly silence.

Julie set the cup back down on her desk. Then, without another glance, she headed for the door.

Her steps were soft, almost hesitant, as she made her way down the hallway.

Instead of turning right toward the main corridor and heading out the front door, she kept walking straight—toward the other wing of the building.

Toward Barbara's room.

The right wing mirrored the left, designed for efficiency with a near-identical layout. Sixth-grade classrooms occupied the first floor, while seventh and eighth grades were housed above. The cafeteria and gym were the only shared spaces, keeping movement structured and minimizing unnecessary crossover.

The design simplified logistics, especially in the early months of the school year when sixth graders needed extra supervision in the hallways.

Barbara's classroom, Room 1, sat at the far end of the hall. Julie quickened her pace, hoping to catch her before she left for the day.

As she neared the door, she heard the faint sounds of movement from inside—papers shuffling, the soft rustling of fabric.

Good—she's still here.

Julie stepped inside to find Barbara slipping on her coat, struggling to pull the shoulders up over her blazer while simultaneously pushing in her chair.

"Why, hello, Julie!" Barbara greeted, fumbling with her sleeves. "Don't see you down this way much." She gave her a knowing look with her eyebrows raised. "Something I can help you with?"

Julie paused for a moment, trying to figure out exactly what she wanted to say. "Yeah, if you have a second, I have a couple of questions. If that's okay?"

"Absolutely! I was just on my way out, but I really have nowhere to be at the moment. Have a seat!"

Barbara motioned Julie to pull a chair up next to her desk. They both sat down.

Julie crossed her legs and folded her arms across her lap.

Barbara leaned back in her chair with an inquisitive grin. "What can I help you with? Do you have a question about the field trip? From what I hear, that's pretty much all set. Mrs. Reed says you have all the chaperones you need, and the paperwork is just about delivered."

"Yes. Um. Yes, that's true," Julie remarked, still trying to figure out why she was there—what she wanted to say.

"That's not it. It's not the field trip. It's… it's…" She exhaled sharply, raising her shoulders as she scrunched her face. "How do I put this?"

Julie took a deep breath. "Did you ask Melanie to invite me out for drinks?"

Barbara leaned back in her chair, her expression shifting. "Did I ask Miss Crane to invite you out?" She raised an eyebrow. "Absolutely not. Why would you think that?"

Julie sat still, searching for an answer. *Why do I think that?*

"I don't know!" she blurted out. "It's just... I've never been invited to hang out with anyone from work before. Like, ever. And I only just really met Melanie at your party. And now she wants to hang out? I didn't know if, for some reason, you thought she should. I just know you've worked with her and been friends with her longer than me, and I don't know... it just seems like something..."

"Something I'd do?" Barbara asked, amusement coloring her voice. "You think I have the time or energy to coordinate evenings out with fellow faculty?" She shook her head.

"Mel is a great teacher, a wonderful woman, and a pleasant acquaintance, but faculty playdates aren't something I get involved in." Barbara looked at Julie sternly, though her expression held a trace of warmth. "Tell me, Julie, what do you really think? How do you really feel?"

"I don't know!" Julie sighed. "Ever since your party, I've been feeling... off? No—just different. I don't know how to describe it. I don't know exactly how or what. But definitely not myself."

"Oh no, Julie," Barbara said with a light laugh, shaking her head. "I think you've got it all wrong! I think you've actually been feeling *more* like yourself. And now, you're just scared because you don't know who *you* really are."

"Let me tell you something," she continued. "Honestly, I wasn't even sure you were going to come to my party. And now, let me be brutally honest here, hun—you do *not* make yourself *invitable*. You're so closed off, so reserved, so withdrawn. It surrounds you. And if people can't see it, they can definitely *feel* it." She paused.

"Don't get me wrong—you are a lovely person. But you are extremely difficult to approach."

Julie sat there, unsure of what to say.

"But seriously, Julie, you must have friends—some kind of social life? You can't be a complete stranger to going out. After all, you have a husband, right?"

Barbara tilted her head. "If you ask me, I think Mel met you for the first time at my party, thought you seemed fun, and simply wanted to get to know you better. So she asked if you wanted to go out and do something fun. Is that so hard to imagine?"

Julie looked at Barbara, then dropped her gaze to the floor. "Truth is, I don't. And yes... it kind of is."

Barbara's caring smile faded into a concerned frown as realization set in. "What do you mean?" she asked. "You don't go out? You don't have friends? Hobbies? Anything?"

She was as shocked as Julie was embarrassed to admit the truth out loud.

"No," Julie said, looking back up at Barbara. She shrugged, inhaled deeply, then exhaled with another instinctive sigh.

"My poor thing! Tell me something—how long have you been married?" Barbara asked, concern creeping into her voice.

"This year, it'll be fifteen years," Julie said, clearing her throat. "That one's easy—it's one year more than the twins' age."

"Twins?" Barbara repeated, eyes widening. "I didn't know the boys were *twins!* And they're fourteen now? How exciting. You must feel pretty blessed." She shook her head with a smile. "See? This is what I mean. Who else knows you have twin boys?"

"Hmm? Mr. Dryer, I guess?" Julie said, thinking. "I'm sure I mentioned them during my interview. And Mr. Anderson knows." She struggled to think of another faculty member she had told. "I'm sure I've mentioned them to Mrs. Martinez too!" she added confidently.

Barbara raised an eyebrow. "So, out of the entire faculty, only four people know that Julie Tosh has twin boys? That's *it*? Oh, honey, that's not good."

Barbara shook her head. "You can't believe you've been invited into Mel's life because you don't invite people into yours. Why do you think that is?"

Julie sat in her chair, thinking. Her mind was blank.

Why? she wondered. *Why would I? Why would I want more people in my life? What good would that do me? What would be the purpose?*

"I don't know!" Julie snapped, frustration creeping into her voice. "Maybe because more people in my life would mean more people to take care of? More people to worry about? More people pulling me away from the boys and Mike? More people I'd have to share my time with?"

"Oh, honey," Barbara said, shaking her head. "Friends don't take time away—they add to it. Or at least, that's what they're supposed to do, if you ask me." She gave Julie a thoughtful look. "Don't you and your husband go out at all? Fifteen years isn't long enough to stop dating and doing things together. Harold and I have been married nearly thirty-five years, and we still find time for all sorts of things!"

"Not really." Julie shifted uncomfortably in her chair, leaning closer to Barbara. "Honestly, I can't remember the last time we went out—besides carpooling the boys to practice or something."

"He isn't the going-out type. At least, I don't *think* he is. I really don't know anymore. He works so much, always on the road, so we never really get the chance. And whenever he *is* home, he'd rather sit on the couch and watch TV or nap than do anything else."

Julie sighed. "So, no, we don't go out. Not really."

"*Anything?*" Barbara exclaimed, throwing her hands in the air. "Oh, honey, my heart is *breaking* for you! *Please* tell me you at least still wrestle in the sheets! *Please!*"

Julie took a deep breath and rolled her eyes. "That's the only thing he wants to do—but I wouldn't call it *wrestling*," she said with a half-hearted laugh.

"Oh?" Barbara's brows lifted. "No? Why not?" She leaned in, pushing Julie for an answer.

"Oh, it's just that… I don't know. He's… hmm… how do I say this? *Not very good?*" Julie sank her head, raising her shoulders. "He's…"

"*Not* the best you've ever had?" Barbara interrupted before Julie could finish.

Julie took a deep breath, steadying herself. "No, actually… he is," she admitted. "He's the only guy I've ever been with."

Barbara's eyes widened in disbelief. "*Seriously?*" she asked. "Then what makes you think he isn't that good in bed?"

Julie hesitated, then shrugged. "Well... he's painfully overweight and out of shape, actually has a tiny—you know what—and he's done in no more than thirty seconds. I'm *clearly* no expert, but that doesn't sound good to me."

She felt her cheeks flush as the words left her mouth. *How did the conversation even get here?*

"Wait—back up. *Back. UP!*" Barbara exclaimed. "You've got me in too deep now! How did you two even end up together? And never anyone else? *Ever?* Come on, I need to know."

Julie took a deep breath, exhaling slowly. "It's really not that exciting of a story," she admitted with another sigh.

Barbara tilted her head, waiting.

Julie hesitated before continuing. "We started dating a few months before the start of our senior year of high school. I remember thinking how different he was from the other boys—funny, goofy, silly. He made me laugh, made me smile, made me feel comfortable in a way no one else really ever had. He was sweet and kind. He made me feel safe... like... I could let my guard down. Like, I didn't have to worry about... things." She exhaled softly.

"But even then, if I'm being honest, I wasn't really *into* him. Not really. Not like that. But he was nice." She shrugged. "So when he asked me out..."

She cleared her throat, the memory still oddly vivid. "... I actually flipped a coin."

Barbara's lips quirked in curiosity. "A coin?"

Julie nodded. "Heads—yes. Tails—no. And I flipped heads. So, I figured, *why not?* What's the worst that could happen, right?"

Barbara let out a curious hum. "And...?"

"Well, the first few months were okay," Julie admitted. "Pretty normal, I guess. He was nice. We'd go out—movies, stuff like that. When school started again and people found out we were dating, they thought it was great. Everyone kept telling me how lucky I was, how he was such an amazing guy—'one of the good ones,' you know."

She gave a small, humorless laugh. "So, I figured things were going pretty well, too."

She paused, shifting slightly in her seat. "Believe it or not, he used to bring me flowers every Friday at school. At first, I thought it was sweet. But then..."

She trailed off, shaking her head. "He loved the attention way more than I did—so much that he insisted I carry them around all day just to make sure everyone noticed."

Julie's fingers fidgeted absentmindedly. "I hated it. They were awkward to carry around, and I felt so embarrassed. But if I tried to put them in my locker..." She exhaled sharply. "He'd get so mad. *'I didn't give you those to hide in your locker!'* he'd say."

She shook her head. "So, I just... went along with it. I didn't want to make a big deal out of it. I mean, he was trying to be nice. So..."

Barbara's expression shifted, curiosity giving way to quiet concern.

"I see," she said gently. "You think that sounds, *nice?*"

Her words weren't a question but an invitation—urging Julie to continue.

"Maybe two or three months in, all he started talking about was wanting to have sex," Julie admitted, her voice tinged with an old, familiar exhaustion.

"He'd go on about how all the other guys with girlfriends were doing it, and how his friends on the football team made fun of him because we hadn't yet. He said *I* was the reason he was being made fun of. And *I* was the reason he was getting laughed at."

She let out a humorless breath. "I told him I just wasn't ready. Not yet, anyway."

Julie hesitated, glancing down for a moment before continuing.

"It's not like I wasn't curious. We had made out and done... other things. But I just wasn't into him like *that*. Not really.

"I mean, it's not like I was necessarily waiting for marriage or anything. It's just that... I don't know. I guess I just felt that maybe there was someone better out there. Someone who just... felt *right*."

She swallowed hard. "But deep down, I didn't really believe I'd ever find that. We lived in such a small town, and he was the only guy who had ever shown any real interest in me."

Julie took a deep breath, her voice growing hollow, tightening with emotion.

"Everyone at school loved how he paraded me around like I was his perfect girlfriend. They thought we—*he*—was so special. But I hated it because I knew the truth. They didn't see it... but I did. Every day."

She let out a bitter laugh. "We were even voted *Class Sweethearts* in the yearbook."

Her hands clenched into fists in her lap.

"He told me that now we *really* had to have sex—because now everyone expected it. And because now, I *owed* him. Owed him because the jokes had gotten worse. Because it was all my fault. Owed him for all the dates, all the movies, all the dinners...all of it"

Julie's voice cracked.

"He told me that if I didn't, he was going to break up with me—and make sure everyone knew why. And he *promised* he'd make the rest of my year unbearable."

Julie's tone fell dark and hollow. She had never shared these feelings or stories with anyone before, and hearing them out loud made the truth feel even more awful. Even more *alarming*. Even more *disgusting*.

"I guess at that point, I was just exhausted from saying no. He knew how embarrassed I'd be if he broke up with me. So, he just kept pushing and pushing—pressuring me, threatening me—until I gave in."

Her chest ached as she forced herself to keep going.

"I don't really remember much about that first time—it hardly even feels like a real memory now. But what I *do* remember is that it was fast. And I mean *fast*. And it never got better after that. Nothing did."

Julie shook her head and sighed, rubbing a hand over her face.

"I remember every time he wanted to, I felt... forced. You know? Not *physically*—exactly. But I knew that if I said no, he'd probably follow through on his threats to break up with me. Or worse... he'd find a way to make me pay for *disrespecting* him or causing him any embarrassment."

Julie glanced away, as if trying to distance herself from the memories. But they were still there—buried, but there.

"By then, it already felt like I'd gone too far. And I didn't feel like I had anyone to turn to for help. He became so jealous and possessive. He wouldn't let me go to parties—said they were full of bad influences—and he insisted I spend all my free time with him."

Julie continued, "After that, it seemed like all he wanted from me was sex. And if I ever said no, he'd get so angry. In the end, it just became easier to give in, you know?"

"I mean, it was so bad and over so fast, it almost didn't even matter." She let out a weak, forced laugh.

She exhaled heavily, as if the weight of her own words had pressed deep into her.

Julie wiped her eyes, staring down at the scuffed tiles of Barbara's classroom floor. The silence between them felt heavy, thick with unspoken truths.

Across the desk, Barbara shifted, the soft creak of her chair breaking the stillness. She leaned forward, resting her elbows on the surface.

Her voice was low, calm—but unshakably firm.

"Conceding is *not* Consenting."

She folded her hands and let the words settle, the weight of them stretching across the space between them.

Julie's breath hitched, but she stayed quiet.

Barbara exhaled softly before continuing. "I've known so many women who've been in your shoes—coerced, controlled, trapped in situations where they felt they had no choice. Men can force you with fists, and they can force you with feelings."

She hesitated, her voice dropping just above a whisper.

"The first are *monsters.*" She paused. "The second... *worse.*"

Julie glanced up at Barbara, her words sinking in. The classroom felt smaller now, quieter. Barbara's gaze was steady, her presence a lifeline Julie hadn't known she needed. The words hung in the air, heavy but brimming with understanding.

"I think, deep down, I knew I wanted out," Julie admitted, her voice a little more at ease. "But I was so scared. And alone. I didn't have anyone I could turn to or talk to."

She forced a light laugh.

"He kept buying me flowers, putting on this show like we were the perfect couple. And I just played along because he promised not to make my life difficult... as long as I did what he wanted."

Julie took another deep breath.

"Why did you stay with him? Even after school?" Barbara asked, her voice laced with quiet concern.

Julie let out a small, hollow chuckle, lifting her gaze from the floor to meet Barbara's.

"Honestly? I couldn't wait for graduation," she admitted, her voice cracking slightly as her eyes shimmered with unshed tears.

She swallowed hard before continuing. "I knew once high school was over, I could go off to college—I wouldn't feel so boxed in anymore. If that makes any sense."

She exhaled, shaking her head. "I thought college would be my escape."

Barbara listened intently, waiting.

"But the only school I could afford was close to home," Julie continued, her voice softer now. "And it was a small town. I never really felt like I could get away from him."

She hesitated, then offered a small, wistful smile through her tears.

"I tried, though," she said. "In my freshman anthropology class, I met this guy. I had the biggest crush on him."

Her smile grew, tinged with something bittersweet.

"He felt so out of my league—so smart, so handsome. And he was *so* nice to me."

She blinked rapidly, letting out a quiet laugh. "I definitely wasn't used to that."

Julie wiped her face with both hands as Barbara handed her a tissue.

"I don't know," Julie admitted, her voice barely above a whisper. "I guess I figured Mike was the type of relationship I deserved."

She let out a shaky breath. "It had all just become... normal to me."

Barbara shook her head. "That's not your fault, dear. It's not. Don't ever think it is." She sighed, quiet understanding softening her expression. "You see, that kind of pain is like cold water—shocking at first. But eventually, your brain just gets used to it. And you forget it's even there."

Her words carried a weight that felt deeper than just support.

Letting the sentiment settle, Barbara remained quiet, giving Julie the space to speak when she was ready.

"Before I could really do anything about it, I found out I was pregnant." Julie swallowed hard. "I had to drop out of college after my first semester. Mike got a job at the warehouse, and after the twins were born… they became my whole life."

Her lips pressed together for a moment before she continued.

"Mike worked hard so I could stay home with them. And I guess… I felt like I *owed* him for that."

She rubbed her hands together, as if trying to warm them.

"When they got older, going back to school was *my* idea. Mike was against it—at first." She shook her head. "He worried that if I was working, I wouldn't be able to take good care of the kids."

Her voice dipped slightly with frustration. "But I convinced him the hours worked out perfectly while they were in school."

Julie exhaled a slow breath, glancing away. "So here I am," she said, forcing a half-hearted smile. "A second-year middle school teacher. Over thirty."

She shook her head again, suddenly overwhelmed by everything she had just laid out.

"I'm sorry!" she blurted, snapping herself back to reality. She sniffled, wiping at her eyes. "I don't know why I'm telling you all this. This is *too much!*"

Her breath hitched, her emotions teetering on the edge.

But Barbara didn't flinch. She just waited.

Because this wasn't too much.

This was Julie—*finally* letting it out.

Barbara sat back in her chair, shaking her head, a mix of disbelief and understanding in her eyes.

"Don't be sorry, love," she said gently. "You're telling me because I asked. And, honestly? I'm convinced no one else ever has."

She sighed, her voice softening as she leaned forward.

"Oh, honey. *Oh, honey.*" She reached for Julie's hand, giving it a squeeze. "You poor thing."

Barbara's eyes searched Julie's, full of something that felt like both sympathy and urgency.

"You're telling me you don't have time for friends because you're saving all your time for two boys who, sooner than you realize, will be spreading their own wings—and for a husband who's always on the road, never home, and pays you no genuine attention?" She shook her head.

"What, my dear, do you *do* with yourself?"

She paused just long enough to let the question settle.

"No friends? No hobbies? *Oh, honey!*" Barbara leaned in, her voice laced with a mix of encouragement and insistence. "Not only *should* you go out with Mel, but you *need* to. Understand?"

For the first time since sitting down at Barbara's desk, Julie *really* smiled.

"I hate to say it," she admitted with a small laugh, "but I think you might be right."

"Oh, dear, I am *so* glad you won that raffle," Barbara said with a warm smile. "If anyone deserves it, it's you."

She leaned in slightly, her expression bright with encouragement. "Now, come on—be honest. It's pretty amazing, isn't it?"

Her smile grew wider, her gentle nod coaxing Julie to relax, to let go of some of the weight she had been carrying.

Julie let out a tearful laugh. "They *both* are!"

Barbara chuckled along with her. "Oh, trust me, I could tell."

She glanced at the clock and sighed. "But look at the time. We've been going on and on. If I don't get home to make dinner, nobody's going to make it for me." She smirked. "But I'll give you this."

Barbara reached into her desk drawer, pulled out a small scrap of paper, and wrote on it before folding it in half.

"If you can't find the time to make new friends away from home, try this."

She handed Julie the folded note as she pushed herself away from her desk and stood.

"It was so nice talking with you. I will *definitely* keep you in my thoughts and send you all the positive energy I can," Barbara said with a warm smile.

Julie took the note and slipped it into her coat pocket as she got up to follow.

"Thanks for listening," Julie said. "I feel better." She forced a smile. "It's just…"

"Don't worry, sweetie. Whatever these ears hear never crosses these lips. That, I *promise* you," Barbara said as if reading Julie's mind. "God gave women such big hearts so we could help each other carry the pain. *God knows* there have been times when I needed another woman's ear like you wouldn't believe."

She paused slightly. "Only a woman feels what a woman feels."

Barbara moved around to the front of the desk and gestured Julie in for a hug. "Now, you go home and take care of that anxious brain of yours. *You got this!*"

Julie hugged Barbara back. "Thank you!" she said, smiling before turning for the door.

She wasn't sure what had just taken place. She had come to Barbara with questions, but somehow, she had even more now.

Julie tried to shake the thoughts out of her head as she made her way across the parking lot and into her car. The clock radio lit up as she turned the ignition. It was already almost 4:00 p.m.

"Ugh," she huffed.

I don't really want to make dinner tonight.
Looks like we're doing pizza.

| 27 |

Julie arrived home with a large pizza for her and the boys. It was hard to tell nowadays what size to get. She remembered when a medium was more than enough, with plenty of leftovers for lunch the next day. But now that the boys were older—and bigger—they could probably devour an entire large pizza on their own.

"I'm home!" Julie called up the stairs. "I have *PIZZA!*"

The boys immediately dropped what they were doing and thundered down like starving cannibals.

"Hey, Mom!" Tommy grinned. "Good call."

"Yeah!" Chad blurted out with a mouthful of pizza. "We figured you were gonna stop and get something since you weren't already home."

"Come on, guys! At least get a plate!" Julie scolded, watching them tear into the slices. She shook her head as she took off her coat and handed them each a plate from the rack near the sink.

"You know, you *can* make a snack on your own if I'm not here, right?" she reminded them.

Julie watched the boys as Barbara's words echoed in her mind. *They were getting ready to leave the nest.*

They still had time. But they were growing up fast.

She grabbed a slice and sat down at the kitchen counter.

They didn't need her as much as she needed them.

She watched them with a newfound appreciation. Her boys were really growing up. She had always known it, but she had never *really* taken the time to notice it.

"Do you guys want to join me at the table and tell me about your day?" she asked, hoping one of them would bite.

"Nah, it was stupid, really," Chad blurted out. "I had swimming in gym this morning and spent the entire day smelling like chlorine. That's pretty much it. Oh, and I got a Bronze Star award on *Medal of Glory,* the game I've been playing."

Julie tried to look genuinely interested. Video games and music—those were the only things the boys seemed to care about these days. And neither of them really interested her.

"Oh! Congratulations, I guess?" she said, searching for some kind of reassurance.

"Eh, it's no big deal. Just a thing." Chad shrugged. "Justin's getting on in half an hour, and we're launching a new campaign. So that should be fun."

He grabbed what looked like *half* the pizza.

"Hey, guys! Slow down! And save some for me, you know!" she called out, locking eyes with both of them. "I want to take some to work tomorrow, too."

Chad and Tommy each grabbed hefty slices, piled them onto their plates, and headed back upstairs.

"We'll bring the plates back down when we're done," Tommy said, nodding for approval. But Julie knew they'd probably forget.

"Sure, have fun!" she said, watching them disappear up the stairs into their rooms.

Julie looked around the kitchen and found a small pink Tupperware container. *I'll just grab these two slices for tomorrow,* she thought, loading them into the container and stashing it in the fridge. The best part about having boys? They never touched anything pink.

With that, she placed the remaining slices in a separate container. *And that's for you guys,* she mused to herself.

She tossed the empty pizza box into the recycling bin and wiped down the counter. At least pizza was easy to clean up after.

Reaching for her favorite wine glass, she pulled a new bottle of Chardonnay from the cupboard. *I deserve this,* she thought, pouring herself a generous glass.

Her eyes drifted toward the living room. The couch looked *so* inviting.

Grabbing her bag off the floor, Julie made her way to the sofa. It felt like sinking into a cloud as she fell into the deep, soft cushions. Letting out a deep breath, she closed her eyes for a moment.

What a day.

She turned on the TV. It was almost 6:00 p.m.—time to catch up on the news.

Julie wasn't a big news buff, but she liked to check the weather and stay somewhat aware of what was happening around her. Most of the general news felt like filler—forced stories just to eat up airtime. She could definitely do without the politics, but it provided a soothing backdrop as she sipped her wine and sorted through her papers from the day.

Before she knew it, it was already 7:30 p.m.

Right on time, her phone chimed with a new text message. She set down her glass and picked up her phone.

Mike.

Just as she suspected.

A small feeling of guilt settled in her chest. She had been so negative about him earlier with Barbara. *After all, here he was—checking in like clockwork after a busy day of work.*

MIKE: Hey! Hope you had a great day!

I'm not really sure what kind of day it was, she thought to herself.

JULIE: It's been a day, but so far, so good!

Wait, what's that even mean? Um...?

JULIE: Going good!
JULIE: Just finishing up some papers and having a glass of wine. You?

That was better.

MIKE: Glad to hear. You know, just another day.
MIKE: Bed soon, and then hitting the road in the morning.
MIKE: So, I should probably keep this short.

Julie wasn't sure how to respond or what to say.

JULIE: OK. Drive safe!

That was the best she could come up with on the spot.

MIKE: Love you!

JULIE: Love you too.

And the conversation was over. Julie looked at the phone in her hand, struggling with what to think. But her thoughts kept circling back to the same idea. *Here's the man I built a life with, and he only has time for a five-sentence text conversation.*

She wanted to tell him about her day. She wanted to tell him how she felt. She wanted more from him than a few short sentences.

Her frustration grew. There was a part of her that understood. She got it—he was tired. He was busy all day. *But so wasn't I.*

She had nobody to talk to because she had *nobody* to talk to. The boys weren't interested in her life outside of the house, and clearly, her husband wasn't interested in her day at all either. Yes, he texted her every night. But seriously, where were the phone calls? The *real* conversations?

"Ugh!" Her frustration swelled. How would he feel if the script were reversed and she only answered his questions with basic responses? If she put in minimal effort? How would he like it? He *fucking* wouldn't. He'd have a meltdown and a temper tantrum, like he always does when he doesn't get his way. *Ugh!*

Her frustration and resentment deepened.

What if Barbara was right? What if she wasn't who she *is*, but just who everyone else made her to be? Made her THIS mom. Made her THIS wife. How would she know? How could she tell?

Julie grabbed her glass of wine and finished it in one swallow.

Fuck! she thought. *FUCK!*

Ugh! The conversation with Barbara. Why had she said so much? Why had she revealed so many details of her life? So many personal details.

It felt so freeing. So therapeutic to share. Julie had held on to those feelings for so long. She'd harbored them inside, never given the chance to say them out loud. And once she started talking, she just couldn't stop. The truth was, there was still so much more she hadn't shared with Barbara.

For the last fifteen years, she'd used every coping mechanism in the book to justify her life. But saying it out loud forced her to hear it for herself. The truth was, if anyone else told Julie her story, she would never be able to excuse what she had been through—or accept it.

Could this be the real reason Mike never allowed Julie to have a social life? To never have friends? Was it because they would be able to see through his tactics, his plan, and his manipulation?

Julie walked into the kitchen and placed her glass on the counter. Her eyes drifted toward her coat, still hanging on the chair by the kitchen table. *The note.*

Julie hesitated for a moment before reaching into the pocket of her coat and pulling out the folded piece of paper.

Barbara had handed it to her so deliberately, as if it meant something.

She unfolded it and looked at what Barbara had written. In red pen, it read: **www.cucme.com.**

Julie frowned slightly. *What is this?*

She ran a finger over the ink, reading the name again.

A website?

| 28 |

Julie poured herself another glass of wine before settling back onto the couch. Her laptop was still open on the coffee table. She set the paper aside and pulled the computer closer, opening her web browser. She typed in the website address and hit enter.

The page loaded. Across the screen, she read:

"CUCME (See You See Me) – Global Online Community And More! Connect with people from around the world or next door! Connecting is easy with public directories, video rooms, and a live contact list. Download Today!"

So, it's a chatroom.

She glanced over the site more carefully. In the corner of the page, *"30 Day Free Trial!"* flashed. *This must be what Barbara meant. I could make friends from home,* Julie thought to herself, nodding. She studied the page a little longer.

Oh, what the hell, she muttered, hitting the *"Download Now"* button.

The screen flashed, and a window popped up over her web browser. It was labeled *"CUCME INSTALLATION."* Julie clicked the [Next] button. The computer whirred as the installation began. The progress bar quickly moved from left to right, and file names flashed across the screen.

"INSTALLATION COMPLETE." appeared, and Julie clicked the button labeled [Run Now].

The computer whirred again, and a new screen appeared. "CUCME SET UP." Julie scanned the page.

Okay. This doesn't look so bad.

She started filling out the information requested on the screen.

"COMMUNITY USER NAME?" Julie already knew what that would be. She used the same username for nearly everything: "*Jules555.*"

It was a silly username, but it always made her smile. Her dad had called her *Jules*, but he also had this odd habit of shouting, "*Triple Nickels!*" whenever a clock hit 5:55 or anything displayed three 5's in a row.

Her dad was a history buff, and she knew it had something to do with World War II. Beyond that, she wasn't entirely sure, but it was a fun memory she had of him.

So, whenever she had to create a username, she always went with "*Jules555.*"

"PASSWORD?" This was another easy one. Julie used the same password—or at least variations of it—for practically everything: "*Hero2124!*" It was the name of her first dog growing up, plus the last four digits of her social security number.

Julie clicked the [Next] button.

"SEX?" Female. *Next.*

"AGE?" Julie was relieved to see a [Skip] button next to that question.

"*STATUS?*" Julie selected *"Married"* from the drop-down menu.

"*LOCATION?*" She clicked the down arrow and scrolled through the listed countries, looking for *"United States of America."*

"*ZIP CODE?*" She clicked the [Skip] button again.

"*COMMENTS?*" *Skip.*

A new screen appeared: *"Profile Picture."*

That makes sense, Julie thought to herself. *After all, it's a chatroom.*

There were two options: *WEBCAM* and *FILE.* She clicked the [File] button, and a window showing computer folders opened on the screen.

She knew there were at least a few good selfies on her computer that she had downloaded from her phone. She browsed through the folders: *"Media."* Nope. *"Pictures."* Nope. *"Downloads."*

Ah, yes! Here they are, she smiled.

There were really only two decent ones to choose from.

"This one," she said aloud as she clicked on a selfie she'd taken sitting at the kitchen table a few months ago, when she'd thought her hair looked super cute and wanted to show Mike.

The screen closed, and another one took its place: *"INFORMATION VERIFICATION."*

The screen displayed all the information Julie had entered, along with her profile picture. She reviewed everything and clicked the button labeled [Complete].

The screen disappeared, and a new one filled the window. In the top left-hand corner, the screen was titled *"CUCME – Online."*

Across the top were a series of buttons with icons: [Global], featuring a picture of a globe, and [Local], with an image of a phone book.

Below that, a rectangular box displayed her profile picture and the personal stats she had just entered: *"Jules555, Female, Age Unknown, United States."*

To the right, another small rectangular box showed *"Current Room: General Chat."* Next to it, a larger box listed other available rooms: [Clean Chat, Friends and Family, Hearing Impaired, Meeting Zone, Adult Chat, Gay Chat].

Under the top section was a large directory with vertical columns labeled *"Name, Location, and Comments."* Julie clicked the header titled *"Name,"* and the list shuffled, reorganizing itself alphabetically.

This must be all the usernames of people in the room.

She scanned the screen more closely. Above the list of users, there was a small text box that read *"244 – Online."*

Wow! That's a lot of people!

Julie clicked on the header labeled *"Location."* Again, the list of users resorted, this time with *United States* at the top.

She continued scrolling through the usernames: *Aspin, BBQSauce, Bruno14, Catherine, George, Jenny616...* The list went on and on. She clicked on the *"Name"* header again, and everything resorted by username.

"MESSAGE!" blared from the computer speaker, startling Julie as she focused on the screen.

A message? Where?

She scanned the screen and noticed a small tab on the right-hand side: *"Messages."* She clicked it, and a new side window opened.

The window displayed a username: *Larry 1* and a short message.

Julie leaned in closer to the screen.

"Hey, how are y..." the message partially read.

She clicked on it, and a message window popped up.

On the left was an image of an older man, maybe in his 40s, smiling and sitting in an office chair. To the right of his picture was a box that read, *"Hey, how are you? I'm Larry from Wisconsin."*

"MESSAGE!" Julie jumped again at the sudden notification. She closed Larry's window and noticed another new message beneath his. This one was from the username *Ryan.*

Julie clicked on his message. Another window opened, this time displaying a picture of a younger, possibly college-aged guy smiling and sitting in what looked like a dorm room. His message simply said, *"Hi."*

"MESSAGE!"

"MESSAGE!"

"MESSAGE!"

The computer kept blaring new notifications. Julie frantically searched for the volume button to turn it down.

She now had five messages in her inbox: *Larry 1, Ryan, soulman123, Wolfman Jack,* and *NJ DAVE.*

She clicked on the messages one by one. Each was much like the last— a man sitting in a chair, saying some version of, *"Hello."*

Julie clicked the *"Messages"* tab again and closed the window.

She scrolled down the list of usernames. *Larry 1.* There he was. She clicked on his name, and the row became highlighted. In the upper right-hand corner, a new rectangular box appeared, titled *"USER PROFILE."*

There was Larry's complete profile.

"Larry 1," it read at the top. Below that was his profile picture. It looked like the man from the message, but now standing in front of a boat holding a fish. The box also included: *"Location: Wisconsin : Male 35-45 : Single."* and the comment, *"Republican For Life."*

Julie heard another notification: *"Message!"* but it was almost inaudible now, thanks to the low volume.

Curiously, she scrolled down the list of usernames, clicking on names and viewing their profiles.

Ryan, a picture of a young man drinking a beer, *Texas : Male 20-25 : Single.*

soulman123, a picture of a guitar, *Louisiana : Male 30-40 : Dating.*

She scrolled further.

Tracy, a picture of a blonde woman, *United States : 40-45.*

And continued scrolling.

Archer, a picture of another young man drinking a beer, *London : 20-25 : Single.*

Julie kept browsing the pool of users and usernames. Some were as plain and basic as hers, while others were creative and funny. Meanwhile, the computer kept sounding out notifications: *"Message! Message! Message!"* Julie definitely wasn't in the mood to talk to anyone, but she enjoyed navigating the room and viewing all the different profiles.

She continued to explore the chat room, becoming more and more familiar with its controls and how everything worked.

Julie glanced at the clock.

"Holy crap!" she said out loud.

How had it gotten so late? It was already after 10:30 p.m. She powered down her laptop and headed upstairs.

She quickly freshened up, showered, and then lay down for the night.

| 29 |

The following morning went as smoothly as Julie could have hoped. She was exhausted from the night before, still unable to believe she had stayed up so late scrolling through a computer chatroom. But after going upstairs, taking a shower, and lying down, she couldn't stop thinking about her conversation with Barbara the afternoon before.

Lying in bed, she couldn't help but wonder: If she hadn't gotten pregnant, would she ever have ended up marrying Mike? She thought about how close she had been to breaking free from him in college, how much she loved her boys, and how she couldn't imagine her life without them. But she also reflected on how hard it was to love their father. While she didn't want to admit it, she truly hated how he had treated her—not only when they were younger, but even more so now.

He had pressured her into decisions she never wanted to make. What saddened her even more was realizing that what she had told Barbara wasn't even the complete truth. There was so much more—so many other moments when he had imposed his control, made her feel worthless and small, and made her utterly dependent on him.

In private, he treated her terribly, but in public, he put on a show, pretending to be her white knight.

Julie never liked dwelling on the past. *It is what it is*, she always told herself. *You can't change it.* But remembering still left her feeling depressed, frustrated, and angry. She wondered what had happened to the nice guy she had met in college. What would her life have been like if she hadn't gotten pregnant and decided to stay with Mike?

Her thoughts raced until the early morning, when sheer mental exhaustion finally pulled her into sleep. Now she was paying the price for her overactive mind. However, she was fortunate enough to arrive at school early enough to fill her mug with enough coffee to last her through the first half of the day.

Sitting at her desk before homeroom, Julie couldn't help but notice the coffee cup Mr. Anderson had brought her yesterday during class.

Cole, she smiled to herself.

She still hadn't stopped thinking about him since the other night. Mrs. Martinez was right—they didn't make them like him anymore. *What was she doing? What was she thinking?* She sighed, exhausted, taking a sip of her coffee.

The bell rang, and Julie heard the stampede of sneakers down the hall. She took a deep breath, bracing herself to get on with the day.

For the first two periods, Julie struggled to stay motivated and energetic. The classes dragged on as she talked about metaphors and similes with sixth graders who didn't seem to care.

She had them go around the room, coming up with examples of both and discussing how they could use them in their own writing.

Julie ended the classes early, assigning a worksheet that the students needed to finish for homework. At the end of both classes, she sat at her desk with her head in her hands, trying to sort through her feelings and the situation that wouldn't leave her mind.

When the bell rang to end the second period, Julie felt a brief sense of relief—she now had 45 minutes to herself. But that relief was quickly cut short, as she knew she still had to finalize everything for the field trip. And unless she wanted to be up late again, she had to do it now.

She pulled her green folder out of her bag and opened it on her desk. Inside, she had all the completed permission slips, grouped together, that she now needed to reorganize into piles of ten. She pulled all the paperclips off and stacked the pile of papers neatly on her desk.

"One, two, three, four, five…" she counted softly to herself as she made new piles across the desk.

There were 160 sixth-grade students, but as of Monday, only 124 were cleared to go. This made for 13 piles, meaning Julie would need at least 13 chaperones.

She turned to her computer and pulled up the spreadsheet with the most up-to-date volunteer list, which she had received from Mrs. Reed earlier that morning. Fourteen names were listed as approved and available to chaperone for Monday's trip.

Julie let out a deep breath. "We'll be good!" she murmured again to herself.

She quickly put together a short email for all the volunteers, reminding them of the field trip and confirming that they had indicated they could help for the day.

She asked if anyone would *not* be able to make it, to please let her know or call the office ASAP so she could make alternative plans.

With a keystroke, the email was sent. She unlocked the bottom drawer of her desk, where she had been collecting all the field trip money.

She pulled out the deposit pouch and carefully counted the money one last time.

I think we're all set! she smiled as she placed the money back into the pouch.

Julie couldn't forget that she had to bring the money down to Mrs. Reed today and have her pay the balance due with the school credit card. Julie thought about doing it right then, but she really didn't want to. She was enjoying her quiet solitude, at least for the moment.

Julie sat back in her chair. This was it. Everything was done and ready for next Monday. She was so excited for the trip. It was her first "Big Project." She felt like she had done a great job with little to no guidance or help. Everything seemed to be falling into place. She felt relieved—and an incredible sense of pride.

Next year, I'll give myself an extra week, though.

She felt like she had waited a little too late to finalize everything, and a little more buffer room would make things a lot less stressful.

She closed the bottom drawer and locked it. Then, she piled all the grouped permission slips, neatly placed them in her green folder, and slid them into her desk drawer.

Julie turned to the computer on her desk and pulled it closer to her. She closed her email and calendar, then sat there, looking at the bare desktop. Her eyes scanned over the icons.

At the bottom of the last row, she noticed a new one—the one she had installed last night.

She hovered her mouse pointer over the icon and paused.

Should I? she wondered. *Why not?*

She glanced up at the clock.

I have some time, she convinced herself, and double-clicked on the tempting icon.

A new window opened, taking over the entire screen, just like it did the night before.

By now, she had become more familiar with navigating the program.

The "Messages" tab was blinking on the right-hand side of the screen, and the list of usernames was just as full as it had been the night before. Countless identities of people looking to connect with others. She clicked on the blinking tab—it was too distracting to ignore.

There were even more messages than when she closed it last night. She clicked on them one by one, reading more versions of "hello" than she had ever heard in real life.

The message section worked pretty much like her email inbox. She had figured out how to delete messages the night before, as well as how to save the ones that piqued her interest. She'd also learned how to add people to her friends list, so she could see if they were online when she was.

What would I even talk to these people about? she thought. *I'm not comfortable in a room full of real strangers. How could I be comfortable in a room full of online ones?*

Continuing through the new messages, she decided there wasn't anyone remotely interesting enough to engage with. She wasn't into music. She wasn't into sports. She didn't want to talk about fishing, or cars, or whatever these guys were talking about.

Delete.

Delete.

Delete.

She removed all the messages from her inbox.

"Message!"

As soon as she had deleted the last one, a new one popped up. The username was *JustinTime*. She thought that was kind of cute. Julie had become fairly comfortable with all the program's controls last night and had also learned that if she right-clicked on the message, she could open the sender's profile without having to find them in the directory screen.

JustinTime, it read. *Male: 65-70: Florida: Widowed: Nascar/Dogs/Grandkids – In that order.*

Julie laughed. His profile picture looked like it had been taken with his webcam. It showed an older man who looked a lot like Santa, minus the beard, sitting at a computer. His face was round with gray hair and large cheeks. She opened the message.

The picture in his message looked a lot like the profile photo, except this time he was wearing what appeared to be a Hawaiian shirt. The attached message read, *"Good morning! Justin here. I just wanted to say 'Hi' from sunny Florida. Hope you're having a great day?"*

Julie smiled. "What a sweet old man," she sighed.

She clicked on the [Reply] button.

A new window popped up on the screen. On the left-hand side was her face, recorded by her laptop's webcam. On the right was a text box for her to write a reply.

Under her video was written *"Take Picture."* with a [Now] button, and another one that said [In 5 Seconds].

At the bottom, there were two more buttons—[Cancel] and [Send].

Julie moved back and forth, watching herself move in the video window. It was strange to see. She had never used a webcam before. She backed up a bit, smiled, and clicked on the [Now] button.

The video window flashed, and a still image took the place of the moving video. She clicked on the [In 5 Seconds] button, and, as she expected, a countdown timer appeared as she moved again in the video.

The timer counted down, and when it reached 0, the video window flashed and took a still picture again.

Julie backed up and smiled one more time before clicking on [Now].

The image was replaced again with her current one.

She typed into the text box, *"Hi. Good morning. I'm Julie. I am having a great day so far. Jealous you are in Florida. It's cold here in Massachusetts."* Julie hit send and waited.

A new message popped up from *JustinTime*. There was another image of him smiling, along with a typed message: *"Good to meet you."* He wrote, *"It's sunny but still cold here today. It won't be warm until the early afternoon. So, just enjoying the sunshine and breakfast. Thought I would pop on here and see what everyone else was up to!"*

Julie replied, posing for another picture and typing, *"Must be nice to relax in the morning like that. I am at work right now."* She paused, thinking about what to write next. *"Can't talk too long because I have to get back to work soon."*

Send.

Justin and Julie continued to message back and forth with a relaxed rhythm. He explained how he was from Ohio, used to work as a civil engineer, and was now retired in Florida.

He spoke about his late wife and their kids, his two dogs, and how he used the chat room to meet new people and pass the time during the day. He also explained that his name was really *JustinTime*—spelled *"Thyme."* And how it has always been a funny conversation starter.

Julie confessed that this was her first time actually using the chat room. She shared that she was a school teacher in Massachusetts. She talked briefly about Mike and the boys, and about the dog she had when she was younger.

Julie felt awkward talking to a complete stranger, yet, at the same time, unexpectedly at ease. He was miles away—distant enough to feel safe, free from judgment or expectation.

In a way, it was liberating. She didn't have to worry about being liked or saying the right thing. It felt almost anonymous, almost unreal… like a conversation that existed in some in-between place, immune to consequence.

The bell rang, and Julie jumped in her chair. *"Lunch!"* she blurted out. *"Fuck!"*

She quickly wrote back to Justin. *"Sorry, I have to work."*
Send.

She closed all her windows, shut down the laptop, and dropped the screen as she hurried toward the door.

"Aghh! Fuckkk!" she yelled out again, looking back at her desk.

Still sitting on her desk was the deposit pouch full of money. She quickly grabbed it and dashed out the door. Julie walked down the hallway with a heavy step. She had to get the money to Mrs. Reed if she wanted the trip balance paid today.

Looking down the hallway, Julie spotted the back of Mr. Anderson. He clearly stood taller than all the students.

"*Cole!*" Julie yelled out, still marching down the hall.

Mr. Anderson stopped and turned around.

"Hey, Jules! What's up?" he asked calmly, his eyebrows raised. Julie caught up, breathing deeply.

"Huge favor! Please?" she asked, still trying to catch her breath.

"I have to drop this pouch off with Beth so she can pay for the trip before the end of the day. Is there any way you can watch the cafeteria for me? Just for a couple minutes while I run to the office? Please?" she added in a desperate tone.

"Sure!" Cole said, his face squinting as he smiled. "No problem."

"You are a lifesaver!" Julie cried. "I'll be RIGHT back! I *SO* owe you!"

Cole watched as Julie continued her hurried pace down the hall and turned right.

In the office, Julie confirmed with Mrs. Reed that she was able to get the payment processed today. She also let her know she had messaged all the volunteers about Monday, in case any of them needed to reach her.

Julie rushed back to the cafeteria to relieve Mr. Anderson.

She walked through the cafeteria doors, scanning the room for where he might be.

Oh! There he is!

She noticed him standing in the middle of the cafeteria. His back was to the door, so he didn't see her come in. Julie paused for a moment, watching him.

She could feel herself start to smile despite her exhaustion as she watched him interact with the kids. She looked at their faces—they were all smiles too.

He is so good, she thought to herself, just taking it all in.

"*Ugh!*" she let out a sigh as she continued walking in his direction.

"Thanks again!" she called out behind him, loud enough to get his attention.

Cole turned around, still wearing a calm smile.

"No big deal!" he replied. "That was what? Five minutes? Tops!" he added. "Listen, you look exhausted. I know you've been working really hard on the field trip, and it can be a lot of stress. Do you want to take a full lunch and just relax until the next period? I can cover for you. It's not a problem."

Julie didn't know what to say. She was exhausted, and the extra stress was more than she had anticipated. She would love to spend the lunch period at her desk with her eyes closed.

"Oh my God, *NO!*" she yelled at him. "You've already been too nice to me this week. I don't even know how I'm going to pay you back," she laughed. "I really appreciate you helping me out. I really do. But that's just too much. I can't ask you to do that."

"You're not asking me. I'm offering!" Cole said, a little insistence in his voice.

"That's too much! You work hard too, you know," Julie replied. "You go enjoy your lunch. You're going to need your energy for the next time I need you to bail me out!"

They both laughed and smiled.

"OK," said Cole, raising his fist for their signature knuckle punch, and giving her a wink.

Julie knew all she had to do was get through the rest of the day, and then she could go home and take a much-needed nap.

| 30 |

The day seemed to never end for Julie. The clock might as well have been standing still. Fortunately, the last period of the day was shared with Mrs. Martinez, and the students were taking a quiz. All Julie had to do was get the students situated and let the rest of the day take care of itself.

Julie could tell the students were also feeling the weight of the day. They all seemed to be dragging. She waited for the class to settle down.

"Alright, everyone. Does anyone have any questions on the worksheet from yesterday before we take the quiz?" Julie asked.

The students looked around the room at one another.

"Nothing? You all understand it?" Julie asked again. "You're all ready?"

Some of the students nodded their heads. Some just stared at Julie.

"Well, I guess we're going to find out!" she said jokingly.

Julie gathered the quizzes off her desk and began passing them out.

All of Julie's students knew how Mrs. Tosh expected them to do it. The students at the head of the row received a stack of papers, took the first one on top, and handed the rest of the pile to the student seated behind them. The quiz was two pages long, and Julie expected it would take the class all period to complete it.

"Make sure you read carefully and take your time!" Julie reminded them all. "If you have any questions, remember to raise your hand, and Mrs. Martinez or I will come to your desk to help you. You may begin," she added.

The students all looked down at the quiz and began working on correctly identifying the comparative and superlative forms of adjectives.

Julie sat down at her desk next to Mrs. Martinez. "So, have you thought of any other movie ideas?" she asked.

Julie and Mrs. Martinez listed as many movies as they could that would be age-appropriate. Some included *Johnny Tremain, The Last of the Mohicans, The Patriot,* and *This Is America, Charlie Brown.* All of the movies were available in the library, so any of them would do.

Mrs. Martinez agreed that on Monday, she would grab them all and let the kids choose which ones they wanted to watch. This way, the students would be less likely to complain, and Maria wouldn't have to sit through five periods of the same movie.

The last period was the only class that seemed to fly by. Before she knew it, the class was over—and so was the day.

Maybe it was the hecticness of the afternoon or all the caffeine finally kicking in, but Julie didn't feel as tired as she had earlier. With her classroom empty, she shuffled the papers on her desk and put them in her bag along with her laptop. She really needed to get home and just relax.

I don't think I'll have time for a nap, she thought.
I just need to put my feet up and close my eyes for a bit.

Full of anticipation, she drove home, eager to enjoy a moment or two of rest before the dinner routine took over.

| 31 |

The drive home was quiet, peaceful, and relaxing. The sun was bright in the sky, and Julie could feel the coming of spring in everything around her. She could tell the boys were home by the collection of shoes, coats, and backpacks on the hallway floor. But that didn't concern her at the moment. Right now, all she wanted to do was lie down on the couch and relax.

She threw her bag on the counter, placed her coat on the chair, and headed for the living room.

Her body sank into the soft couch cushions.

"Ahhhh!" Julie let out a sigh of relief. She lay her head back on the pillow resting near the armrest. She could feel the soft firmness of the cushions supporting her as she melted deeper into their comfort. She kicked off her shoes and closed her eyes.

Julie inhaled deeply, clearing her mind, then exhaled completely. With each breath, she could feel her body becoming more and more relaxed. The tension and exhaustion she had carried all day began to melt away.

As she closed her eyes, she felt herself sink deeper into the couch. In her mind, she replayed the events of the day. She thought about how the morning had dragged on. She thought about talking to Justin in Florida.

He was such a nice old man. Julie felt a twinge of sadness when he talked about his late wife, but she could tell he loved and missed her deeply.

Julie wondered how she would be missed if she were suddenly gone. The boys would absolutely miss her. They would be devastated, she thought. Mike? She really wasn't sure how he would react. He would definitely miss everything she did for him. But would he truly, deeply miss *her*? She didn't have an answer. Barbara would miss her. That, she was sure of. And Cole.

Ahh! Cole, she thought again. *I would definitely miss him if he were suddenly gone. I would miss him so much.*

In her mind, his face came into focus—those caring brown eyes, his chiseled cheeks and chin, that smile. Oh, that smile. It made everything feel OK. He was always so happy, so calm, so... Cole.

She pictured him standing in her classroom doorway, sunlight catching on his broad shoulders. He always dressed so well—those neatly pressed chinos and tailored shirts. His frame was so put-together—strong and steady, yet effortlessly warm. And that smile. That wonderful, reassuring smile.

I bet he's a good kisser, she thought to herself.

Her imagination carried her, and she let it.

She pictured his arms around her—a real embrace, not the casual fist bump they always shared. She could almost feel his chest against her cheek—strong and solid, yet somehow gentle and comforting. His arms seemed so warm, so safe.

Julie found herself breathing deeper, giving in to the thought. Suddenly, it felt real: his hands resting firmly on her back, pulling her closer, his heartbeat thudding in time with hers. She imagined the faint scratch of his stubble against her cheek, the clean scent of his cologne. Her own hands drifted around his waist as if to pull him closer still.

As she pictured him leaning down, brushing his lips along her neck, a shiver ran through her entire body. She imagined her breath catching, her eyes fluttering closed. Her mind wandered further, feeling the warmth of his mouth, the gentle pressure of his hands on her waist. Her breath grew heavier as she let herself sink into the fantasy.

"MOM! MOOOOM!"

Julie's eyes flew open. "What? What?" Her pulse raced as she tried to remember where she was. "Fuck," she muttered under her breath, glancing around the living room.

The once bright room was now dim, cloaked in twilight. "What time is it?" she called out, her voice still groggy.

"It's 6:45, Mom!" came Tommy's voice from the other room. "You fell asleep on the couch. I didn't want to wake you, but I didn't know what to make for dinner."

Dinner! "Fuck!" she said again, scrambling to sit upright.

"I'm so sorry. You're right, I fell asleep. I can—how about…" She ran a hand through her hair, trying to regain focus. "I can make chicken nuggets. Do you guys want chicken tenders and potatoes?"

"Sure," Tommy replied. "That's fine. I can grab them from the freezer if you want."

"Yeah, that'd be great," she said, grateful for his help.

With Tommy out of the room, she let herself catch her breath. Her thoughts drifted back to her daydream.

Holy crap, she thought. *What the hell was that?*

Shaking her head, she pulled herself together and made her way to the kitchen.

"OK," she muttered to herself. "Dinner. Just focus on dinner."

| 32 |

It didn't take long for Julie to whip up something for the boys and herself to eat. She always kept some frozen foods in the basement freezer just in case they were running late or she didn't want to cook a full meal.

She sat at the kitchen counter, staring at her plate of breadcrumbs and barbecue sauce.

This would never fly if Mike were home. He refused to eat chicken nuggets or microwavable pizzas. He insisted on eating real chicken or beef when he was home.

"*Fuck!*" Julie gasped, her voice sharp in the quiet kitchen. She whipped her head toward the microwave clock. "*MIKE!*"

Julie sprang from her chair, her heart pounding as she scrambled for her phone. *7:40 p.m.*—she'd missed Mike's text.

She dug through her bag, hands shaking. No phone. Her eyes darted around the room. Nothing. She raced into the living room, the floor a blur as she searched. The coffee table—empty. The floor under the couch—nothing but crumbs and lint.

Then, finally: "Agh!" She yanked her phone from the gap between the cushions. Her thumb swiped the screen. One inbox message. It was from Mike.

MIKE: Hey! Just checking in to see how your day was going

Julie's eyes flicked to the timestamp. *7:30 p.m.* Guilt crept up her chest as she started typing.

JULIE: Hey! Sorry. Dinner took longer than I thought. I just now picked up my phone. Hope you're doing good!

She hit send and stared at the screen, waiting. The seconds stretched. The silence thickened. Finally, a notification appeared.

MIKE: That's OK. If dinner is more important than me, I understand. I have a lot going on too, and I can still make time for you.

What the fuck?
Julie stared at the message, her grip on the phone tightening.
That's what he chose to say? No "You're such a great mom." No "Sorry your day has been crazy." No trace of compassion, of understanding—just this cold, cutting response. She read it again, her chest knotting with disbelief.
But then doubt crept in. *Maybe he was right.* She had been up late last night, scrolling through that chatroom, losing track of time. She had fallen asleep, dreaming about Cole—dreams that still left her flushed and unsettled. *Maybe I'm not making the time I need for Mike. Maybe I'm not doing enough.*
Her fingers trembled as she typed.

JULIE: I'm *SO* sorry! You're right. I know you work hard, and I really appreciate everything you do. I really need to get my shit together. I'm sorry. Is everything else good with you?

MIKE: It's fine. I'm just tired now. I'm going to get ready for bed. I'll talk to you tomorrow. OK? Love you.

Julie's thumb hovered over the keyboard. She didn't know what to say. She felt the weight of his words pressing down on her. Finally, she typed back.

JULIE: Love you too.

Her stomach churned as she hit send.
She set the phone down and leaned back against the couch.
But this isn't my fault, she thought. *It's NOT my fault. I don't deserve to be treated like this.*
She felt anger rising in her chest, hot and sharp.
This isn't fair, she told herself, the words repeating in her head.
It's not fucking fair.

| 33 |

Julie found herself questioning everything she had ever thought she knew. The truths she had clung to now seemed like illusions, unraveling one by one. Each memory that surfaced sharpened her understanding and left her reeling.

She was still piecing it all together, but one thing was undeniable: she was not happy. Not truly.

Her mind was crowded with recollections she had spent years suppressing—moments she tried to forget, to ignore, or to pretend never happened. Now, they pressed forward with a clarity that was both painful and liberating. She was done living a lie.

Leaving the kitchen as it was, Julie climbed the stairs to her bedroom. The boys were safe in their rooms, blissfully unaware of what was happening. For now, at least. Whatever this was, she knew it would eventually touch them too. But right now, she needed to figure out what she was dealing with.

Julie closed her bedroom door and sat down on the edge of the bed. Her stomach churned, and her eyes burned with unshed tears.

This is the beginning of the end, she thought.

Could she and Mike find a way back from this? Could they rebuild their marriage into something that felt real? Deep down, she already knew the answer: *No.*

Mike would never admit fault. He would never let go of the control he had fought so hard to gain and maintain. Trying to rebuild would require dismantling everything, and she knew he would never do that.

Julie sat motionless, her heart breaking—not for the love she was losing, but for the love that had never truly existed.

She mourned the fantasy she had constructed, the false hopes she had held onto for so long. She grieved for everything she had convinced herself wasn't so bad, for every small lie she told herself to keep going. But the truth refused to stay hidden anymore.

Speaking with Barbara had shattered the silence Julie had maintained for so many years. Saying it out loud—hearing her own story in her own voice—left her feeling hollow and sick.

How had I been so blind, so willing to play along?

As with everything in their relationship, Julie had simply done what she thought she had to do.

Mike had perfected the art of stripping away her choices, stifling her voice whenever it threatened his image, his plans, his power.

And now, for the first time, Julie saw clearly that she had never truly loved him—not in the way love was meant to be.

What she had felt was obligation—appreciation for the role he played as the father of their children. But it wasn't love. Not the kind of love built on mutual respect, trust, and understanding.

Julie's fear swelled. *What now? What would come next?*

The room around her was silent, but her thoughts roared. She couldn't bring herself to move, so she sat still, listening to the battle inside her mind.

She wanted to scream, to release the painful pressure building within her, but she wouldn't frighten the boys. Instead, she drew in the deepest breath she could manage and held it.

Her chest ached as she resisted the urge to exhale, her body crying out for relief. Still, she held it in, as though if she could just keep it bottled up a little longer, she might regain control.

But she couldn't. With a shuddering cry, Julie released it all.

The tears poured out, mingled with the pain, the resentment, the shame, the anguish. She let herself feel every wound, every loss, until the sobs subsided and her breath returned.

After a long moment, she got up and walked to the bathroom.

She stared at her reflection, feeling as though she was seeing herself for the very first time. With steady hands, she wiped away her makeup and turned on the shower. The water streamed down as she took a breath, each one filling her with newfound determination.

It was time to move forward. She was no longer the woman who accepted what was given. She was something new. Something more.

| 34 |

Julie felt better—clearer, lighter. Stepping out of the shower, warmth still clinging to her skin, she exhaled deeply. Finally, calm. At ease.

She pulled on her favorite T-shirt and slid under the covers. The cool sheets sent a ripple of shivers across her body. Glancing at the nightstand, a knowing smile curled at her lips.

Hell yeah.

Leaning over, she opened the top drawer. Right there, waiting, was exactly what she needed.

Sinking back into the mattress, she let it cradle her. Her legs parted, knees bending slightly, the sheets cool and silky against her skin. She could feel the air under the blankets rush by and tickle her exposed skin. She felt free and unbridled. *This is for me. A partner is optional. Pleasure is not. That's what Barbara would say.*

Julie trailed her fingers slowly along the soft skin of her inner thighs, her touch featherlight. She closed her eyes, letting her head sink deeper into the pillow.

With lazy precision, she traced around the neatly trimmed hair at her center, reveling in the slow, teasing sensation. The warmth of her own touch was soothing, unhurried. Anticipation coiled low in her belly, a delicious ache building. She let herself slip—drifting, surrendering—to fantasy.

She imagined Cole's hands on her again—gentle yet firm, soft but commanding. The thought sent a fresh wave of heat through her, the pulse between her legs growing stronger, insistent.

Julie's breathing deepened, each inhale slower than the last as her fingers continued their teasing exploration. She reached lower, sliding a fingertip between her folds, parting the warm, slick heat.

She ran her fingers through her wetness, spreading it languidly, deliberately. Her clit throbbed, aching for attention, but she resisted—drawing out the anticipation, making herself wait.

With aching slowness, she traced delicate circles along her most sensitive edge, teasing just past the threshold. Heat and tension bloomed inside her, a delicious burn.

Cole... She imagined his touch, his fingers teasing, claiming—not just her body, but something deeper. Something more.

Her fingers slid deeper, curling inside herself.

"Ahh—" A sharp gasp escaped her lips. She let herself feel everything—the stretch, the heat, the soft, rippling texture beneath her fingertips. Her breathing hitched as she explored further, her body attuned to every sensation, every tremor of pleasure.

Her palm pressed lightly against her, offering a moment of relief—but not nearly enough.

"Umm... Cole," she murmured into the dark.

With a trembling hand, she reached for the toy, fingers pressing the raised power button. Eyes closed, she felt the subtle jolt as it came to life.

The soft hum of the puffing mechanism filled the quiet, and her anticipation tightened. The cool surface brushed against her skin as she guided it lower, letting it glide over every heated inch.

Shifting the blankets, she felt the rush of cold air sweep past her bare skin, heightening every sensation. *Cole...* She imagined him there, between her legs, his mouth hovering, waiting. She spread herself wider, offering every bit of herself to the pulsing rhythm and her imagination.

The toy found its place, and the instant pleasure sent her arching off the bed, a sharp gasp breaking from her lips. It felt like a thousand kisses, each one perfectly placed, perfectly relentless.

She moved it in slow, deliberate circles, careful to keep the seal unbroken, dragging out the sweet torture.

Cole...

She pictured him—*Cole*—between her legs, his tongue exploring her with perfect precision. Soft, firm. Soft, firm. She matched his imagined rhythm with the slow circles of her touch.

In... and out... In... and out...

The tension built steadily, coiling deep inside her. Her muscles tightened—first in her thighs, then her abdomen. Her breath quickened, coming in short, uneven gasps.

Her body moved with the rhythm, rocking into the sensation. The circles. The pulse.

"*Cole!*" she cried, unable to hold back any longer.

Pleasure ripped through her in waves, her body arching, trembling, releasing. She kept her hand moving, prolonging the pleasure, drawing out every last spasm.

"*Fuck!*" she gasped, her voice breaking.

The intensity became too much. She yanked the toy away, throbbing in oversensitivity.

Panting, her body still quivering, she let herself sink into the moment—weightless, blissful. *Nothing else mattered.*

Her hand fumbled for the toy, switching it off before tossing it onto the pillow beside her.

Mike's pillow.

A laugh bubbled up from her chest. *"Partner optional. Pleasure? Not."*

Sinking deeper into the mattress, she let the last traces of tension fade. The weight of stress, of worry—gone. For the first time in what felt like forever, she felt *free.*

She closed her eyes, surrendering to the afterglow.

And drifted into the best sleep she'd had in a long, long time.

| 35 |

Julie woke up the next morning feeling like she was recovering from an emotional hangover. Her body was rested, but her mind felt hazy, lingering somewhere between last night's release and the reality of the morning.

She smiled as she replayed the events of the night before in her mind. As she pulled back the blankets and swung her legs over the edge of the bed, something caught her eye.

She turned.

There, still resting on the pillow, was the undeniable reminder of last night.

Heat rushed to her cheeks as she grabbed the toy and quickly tucked it away in the top drawer of her nightstand, sealing away both the evidence and the memory.

With a steadying breath, she got dressed and headed downstairs.

By the time she reached the kitchen, Tommy was already at the table, spooning cereal into his mouth.

"You okay, Mom?" he asked, his voice laced with concern.

Julie's stomach tightened. *What did he mean? Did he know? Had he heard her crying last night? Could he see it on her face? Did she have some kind of tell she wasn't aware of?*

"Uh, yeah! Why do you ask?" she asked, trying to sound casual.

"It's just that you fell asleep on the couch yesterday. The kitchen is still a mess from last night. I know you've been really busy. I just wanted to make sure you're feeling okay."

Julie exhaled, relief washing over her. She smiled, warmth filling her chest.

That's definitely not a trait he got from his father, she thought.

She was proud of Tommy—proud of his kindness, his intuition, the way he cared.

"Yeah, I'm fine! Never better, really. I was just a little tired, that's all."

Julie glanced around the kitchen. He was right. It was a mess.

Plates and silverware still cluttered the sink. Crumbs littered the counters. A baking sheet sat abandoned on the stove next to a pot of uneaten potatoes.

"You're right. It *is* a mess!" she admitted. Then, with a shrug, "It can wait till later."

Tommy's eyes flicked to hers, his expression full of quiet curiosity. "Really?" He was still trying to figure out if she was actually *okay.*

"It's fine!" she reassured him with a smile. "Now, get yourself ready and tell that brother of yours we have to leave soon."

She set a pot of coffee to brew, filling her mug while the boys got ready for school.

Should I tell them?

The thought pressed in on her, thick and suffocating.

She *wanted* to. She wanted to tell them the truth. She wanted to tell them she was *sorry*. Sorry that the only life they'd ever known had been built on a lie. Sorry that she had let it go on this long.

She wanted to tell them it was over.

That she *couldn't* do this anymore.

That things were going to change.

But *what* was going to change?

She didn't even know her next move.

But she *did* know one thing—she had to talk to Mike. And the thought of it made her stomach twist.

She felt so sure now—right now. But he had a way of unraveling her, of breaking her down until she doubted herself again. Until he got exactly what he wanted.

Not this time.

No.

This time, she would be the one who wouldn't take no for an answer.

For now, though, the boys would have to wait.

For now, they would have to pick up on the little changes.

Like the kitchen.

| 36 |

The ride to school and work was unintentionally quiet and uneventful. But as Julie found herself stuck behind one bus after another, frustration crept in. When she dropped the boys off at school, she sighed and told them, *"We really need to start leaving earlier. I'm tired of feeling like we're running late every single day."*

The sun was shining earlier and earlier in the morning. And at this time of year, Julie was often deceived by its perceived warmth. Inside her car, it seemed as though the sun had already warmed the air. But the moment she opened the door, the sharp bite of cold reminded her—spring had not yet fully arrived.

Julie stepped through the front doors of Franklin, drawing in a deep breath. She remembered her very first day of teaching—how overwhelming it all had felt. The towering doors, the vast hallways, the sheer weight of all the expectations. Everything had seemed so big, so intimidating.

But now? Now, she finally felt at home. She felt confident. In control.

Julie continued into the building and stopped at the office. It was Friday, after all, and she wanted to pick up her paycheck before things got too crazy.

She remembered how there had been a few weeks when she had forgotten to pick it up because she was running late, and Mike had been furious about it. It seemed like a big deal then. Hell, it seemed like a big deal just a day ago, but right now, she really didn't care what he thought.

Who was he to get mad that she forgot her paycheck? He was the one who always said she didn't have to work. So what concern was it of his, really? It wasn't like before when they really needed the money. *Just another example of him being an ass*, she thought.

"Good morning, Mrs. Tosh!" Mrs. Reed called out, trying to get Julie's attention. From the look of things, she was having quite a morning herself—papers were scattered across her desk, an untouched cup of coffee sat nearby, and she was still holding her phone to her ear while attempting to talk to Julie.

Mrs. Reed managed a smile. "You're all set! Everything went through on Wednesday."

She continued, her eyes focused on Julie. "Monday morning, the buses will be here and ready to leave at 8:30 a.m. Two parents called to say they can't make it, so you're down to twelve chaperones. You'll need to find one more, but Paul mentioned you already had something worked out."

She took a breath. "Just remind the kids they need to bring a lunch or money, and you should have a great field trip!"

Julie smiled and mouthed, *Thank you!* careful not to distract her from the chaos around her desk.

I need to get her a thank-you gift! she thought, making a mental note to do something nice for her later.

After turning her focus to the mailboxes at the back of the office and retrieving her paycheck, she was ready to start her day.

She made her way down the hall, turning left without a second thought. And then—Bam! She collided, full force, with another body.

"*Ugh!*" Julie yelped, stumbling back. "I'm so sorry!" she added quickly, regaining her balance.

She looked up to see Miss Crane, who waved it off with a quick shrug. "Uh, it's fine. I think it was me—I wasn't paying attention. I was looking at my phone. We're good!"

Julie let out a breath, still flustered. "I was rushing, and my head's all over the place," she admitted, trying to take the blame.

Truthfully, she knew it was her fault. She should have been on the other side of the hallway—or at the very least, not taken the corner so tight.

"Hey, since I have you?" Melanie asked. "Have you thought about Saturday night? Did you want to join us for drinks?"

Julie had completely forgotten to get back to her about drinks on Saturday.

"Um?" she muttered, the invitation finally clicking, remembering Mike wouldn't be home until Tuesday or Wednesday.

"It'll just be me, though… if that's okay?" Julie added, glancing up uncertainly.

"That's fine!" Melanie said. "So far, you're the only one who said they can make it. I was starting to think nobody liked me!" Melanie laughed.

Julie couldn't believe she was the only one going. Then again, she thought, a lot of people have plans on Saturday nights—especially those with families.

Maybe it was better that way. Too many people, too much noise—it all made her anxious. If the night felt overwhelming, she wouldn't even have a chance to try and enjoy herself.

"Um…" Julie hesitated, trying to recall the details.

"It's going to be…?" she asked, pressing Melanie for more information.

"The Tap House. Seven-ish," Melanie said with a smile. "It'll be fun to just get together and relax. I'm sure you could use it right about now."

"You have no idea!" Julie said, her excitement bubbling up. The thought of going out felt good—really good. She still wasn't accustomed to having plans she was actually looking forward to.

Mike would hate this, she thought, but for once, she didn't care.

She couldn't believe she'd assumed earlier that Barbara had set her up, that the invitation had been some kind of trick or pity move. Maybe, just maybe, this was exactly what she needed.

"Gotta run! But seven! Tap House!" Melanie said, pointing at Julie as if to make sure she was really going.

"Seven! Tap House!" Julie recited back, pointing at Melanie with a smile.

Julie hurried down the hallway, eager to reach her classroom, but once again, she was stopped.

"Hey, Jules!"

The familiar voice called out from down the hall. It was Mr. Anderson, standing by his classroom door. But this morning, Julie didn't see him as just Mr. Anderson.

No. This morning, all she could see was *Cole*.

Cole. The man who had unknowingly helped her fall asleep last night.

"I see you ran into Melanie," he said with a knowing smile. "Literally," he added with a chuckle, making sure she took the joke in stride.

Julie felt a flush of heat rise to her cheeks. "Yeah... you saw that?" she asked, trying to brush off her embarrassment.

"Oh! Before I forget," she added quickly, eager to change the subject. "I still need one more chaperone for Monday if you're still available. I just talked to Beth, and she said I'm short one parent volunteer." She smiled, hoping he'd say yes.

"Uh—yeah! Of course," Cole said without hesitation. "I'll just check with Paul and get a sub. Anything else I need to know?"

Julie grinned. "Buses leave at 8:30 a.m. Bring a lunch. And I'll bring the coffee." She added a playful smirk.

"Great!" Cole said enthusiastically. "Can't wait! It's a date!"

Julie's smile grew wider.

"Speaking of dates..." Cole teased. "Did Melanie mention anything about Saturday night?"

Julie let out a small laugh. "Yeah, she did."

The thought of going out again made her grin.

"I told her I'd love to go. It sounds like fun, and honestly, I could use a night out. Plus, with Mike out of town, I've got nothing else going on." She scrunched her nose and lifted her shoulders in a casual shrug.

"Too bad you're not going too," she added, a hint of disappointment in her voice.

"Oh! I'm going," said Cole in return.

Julie was confused.

"Wait. Melanie just told me I was the only one who said they were going to make it?" she asked, looking for clarification.

"Yeah," he said. "The only one going to join us for drinks and whatever."

Julie scrambled to put the pieces together.

Join us? US?

"Wait?" she questioned him, shaking her head. "She said drinks with her and her boyfriend? Her boyfriend... CJ?" Julie looked at Cole, questioning if she understood the facts right. Hoping—praying—he wasn't about to say—

"Yeah. That's me. Most of my friends call me that," he continued. "Cole James Anderson."

He tilted his head and smiled. "It's a nickname my dad gave me when I was younger, and just about everyone I know calls me that now. Except you. That kind of makes you special," he added with an even bigger smile.

But Julie didn't feel special.

"I think you might have told me that before," she said, though it was a lie. She had no idea. No idea he went by CJ. No idea he was dating Melanie.

How am I going to get out of this? she wondered. She had already told both Cole and Melanie she was going. And apparently, she was the only one.

Julie took a small step back, motioning toward the door of Room 10. "Seven o'clock," she said with a smile, pointing at him before turning and heading to her classroom.

She didn't know what to think as she sat down at her desk, waiting for the bell to ring. On the edge of her desk sat the coffee cup he had brought her earlier that week.

For some reason, she hadn't been able to throw it away. It felt like a keepsake—something small but meaningful.

Julie reached for it, then hesitated.

With a quiet exhale, she knocked it into the trash can.

For a moment, a sharp sting of grief struck her—an ache for something that had never truly been hers all along. She mourned the possibility, the *what ifs*, the fleeting glimpse of something that would likely never be.

| 37 |

The morning flew by. Julie had purposely planned an easy day, knowing most of her students wouldn't be invested in learning on a Friday before a field trip.

Hell, *she* wasn't all that invested today either. There was too much on her mind, and she could hardly keep her head straight.

Her first two classes worked on pronoun worksheets—more than just busywork, they mimicked the state's standardized tests, helping students practice answering questions in different formats. They didn't need much direction, but grammar assignments always brought up a few questions.

Third period started with their weekly journal entries before moving on to a free writing assignment to eat up the rest of the period. That gave Julie a little time to sit and think.

She still couldn't believe how the morning had played out. She couldn't believe she'd asked Cole to chaperone the field trip. She *definitely* couldn't believe he was dating Melanie.

Oh my God. Melanie.

All those things she'd said about her boyfriend at Barbara's party—*that was Cole!*

Julie just couldn't wrap her head around it. And now, she had to sit across from them for drinks on Saturday night?

Could this get any worse?

Oh yeah. That's right. *My marriage is in a tailspin, and I feel like I'm done with my husband.*

She smirked bitterly to herself. With everything going on, she had almost forgotten about Mike entirely.

Julie leaned back in her chair and glanced at her students, still working away. She had already gone through the field trip materials, packed them neatly in her bag, and triple-checked that nothing was missing. Now, she was just... bored.

"Ugh." She let out a quiet sigh.

Turning to her computer, she clicked through her overflowing inbox.

Delete.

Delete.

Delete.

For someone who prided herself on being organized, her inbox was a disaster—full of junk, spam, and messages she'd never get around to reading.

Her eyes flicked to the screen, and a thought crossed her mind.

That chatroom program Barbara had suggested.

Yesterday, she'd talked to Justin from Florida.

I wonder who else is on?

Julie closed her email window, lowered the volume on her computer, and double-clicked the *CUCME* icon.

The chatroom window opened, displaying hundreds of names and profiles to browse through. Before logging off last time, she had added Justin to her friends list so she'd know if he was online. And there he was—*JustinTime*.

She opened her messages window and found even more messages than before.

Julie couldn't believe she was this popular. *Nobody even knows who I am.* Her profile was plain and boring—nothing like some of the flashy, attention-grabbing ones she had seen.

I'll look at those later, she told herself.

Glancing over the top of her laptop screen, she checked on her students. All of them were still focused on their writing.

Satisfied, she double-clicked Justin's name. His chat window popped up, just like before—her image on the left, a text box on the right. She quickly typed out a greeting.

"Good morning! Hope you're having a great day!"

Send. And wait.

A notification popped up—a new message from Justin.

Click.

His image showed him sitting outside in the sun, possibly on a porch or deck.

"Good morning!" he wrote. *"Nice to see you again. I wasn't sure I would! Thought maybe you'd forget about this old man."*

Julie found the comment odd at first, but the more she thought about it, the more it made sense. With so many people to talk to and so many conversations left hanging, it would be easy to forget about someone until much later.

She could understand how people became missed connections.

She typed her response.

"How could I ever forget? LOL. It looks so nice there. Definitely jealous today."

Send. And wait.

Justin's reply came almost instantly.

"You just made an old man very happy. LOL."

Then he added, *"It's just that I don't see too many people in the Clean Chat room who don't eventually move to the Adult one—and never come back. Most people here seem to be looking for that kind of thing, not just to meet and talk with regular people."*

That's right, Julie remembered. There were multiple rooms to visit.

Glancing to the top of the window, Julie spotted the list of rooms—*including the Adult room.*

She typed out her reply:

"That's OK. I'm just regular people too!"

They messaged back and forth for a little while, with Julie always peeking up over the screen to make sure the students were still distracted and didn't need her help.

As the conversation continued, Julie asked Justin about his late wife. She felt comfortable asking if they ever had problems and if he had ever felt like giving up on their relationship.

He spoke nothing but fondly and lovingly about her, but she was glad to hear they didn't always see eye to eye. Still, he could never even think about leaving her.

"She was the single best and most important decision I ever made," he wrote. *"I can't bring her back. But I could never leave her behind."*

He went on, telling her that he considered himself one of the lucky ones. So many people, he said, make the wrong choice when it comes to marriage. He had seen it happen firsthand—with family, with friends.

He explained, *"Some people take the easy route. The convenient choice. And some... don't really get a choice at all."* He added that for some, *"The best decision they can make in the moment ends up being the worst decision for the rest of their lives."*

"And nobody deserves that," he commented in another message.

Julie followed up by asking him, *"But how do you know when it's over? Time to walk away?"*

His response was quick: *"That's an easy one, Hun. You know!"*

Julie found it so easy talking to Justin. Maybe it was because he reminded her of someone's grandpa. Or the distance. Or the means. But it felt like they had known each other longer than just a day.

Julie appreciated his insight and advice and thanked him before logging off.

Her class was almost over and Julie definitely didn't want to be caught chatting online while she was at work.

| 38 |

The rest of the day flew by after lunch. Julie wasn't sure if everything had simply gone smoothly or if she was so lost in her own thoughts that she had tuned out everything around her.

Either way, she wasn't going to complain.

As the last bell rang, she began gathering her things and packing her bag. The building never emptied faster than on a Friday afternoon.

Walking out to her car, she mentally ran through her plans for the rest of the day and the weekend. She was relieved to see the sun still shining, the air warmer than it had been that morning. Taking a deep breath, she inhaled the crisp, refreshing scent of early spring.

For just that moment, it felt like everything was going to be okay.

First on her mental checklist—dinner. She felt like she had dropped the ball last night and wanted to make it up to the boys. Not that they cared much about *what* they ate, as long as they *got* to eat.

Neither of the twins had a favorite meal. But *she* did.

Chinese.

Ahh, just the thought made her mouth water. Greasy, MSG-laden, utterly satisfying Chinese takeout. And not the fancy sit-down kind either. No, she was craving food from the little mom-and-pop shop on the corner—the place with the best chicken lo mein and spare ribs. The crispiest, most comforting egg rolls. Perfectly fried chicken fingers.

And the *duck sauce*.

Yes, that was it. Julie was going to treat herself and the boys to some of the worst-for-you, absolute *best*-tasting Chinese food in town.

She could hardly wait.

But it was early Friday afternoon, and she wasn't in any kind of rush. So, instead of calling ahead, she decided to drive there, order in person, and wait.

When Julie arrived at the Chinese restaurant and placed her order for her favorite combination platters, the cashier informed her it would take about 20 to 30 minutes.

"No problem!" she said with a smile. "Just give me a call when it's ready—I'll be in my car outside."

Julie settled into her car, turned on the radio, and let the afternoon show play. The on-air personalities bantered back and forth, making jokes and rambling about nothing in particular. But more importantly, they provided a welcome distraction.

She closed her eyes, letting the radio chatter fade into the background of her mind.

The sun beamed through the windshield, heating her face. A cool breeze stirred outside, slipping through the cracked window and replacing the warmth with a crisp bite of cold.

Even with her eyes shut, she could see the sunlight glowing through her lids in shifting shades of orange and red. She breathed deeply, letting herself sink into the rare stillness—the safety and solitude she had carved out for herself.

For the first time in a long time, her mind was blank.

Her phone rang.

Food's done!

Julie sat up, stretching slightly before heading inside to retrieve her dinner.

When she got home, she was greeted by the usual chaos of a lived-in house—the twins' belongings scattered haphazardly across the floor.

"Boys, I'm home!" she called, her voice carrying up the stairs.

The sound of shuffling and clanking erupted from above, followed by the unmistakable pounding of feet on the stairs.

Chad and Tommy burst into the kitchen.

"Chinese! *YES!*" Chad cheered.

Julie laughed as she wrestled the bags of takeout onto the counter.

"Hold on, guys!" she said, half-laughing, half-scolding. "Give me a second! It's barely even dinnertime."

She straightened up and gave them a look.

"Can you grab some plates and glasses and set the table? I want us to eat together tonight."

The boys apparently loved Chinese food just as much as Julie. Or maybe they just loved *food*.

They didn't hesitate for a second—scurrying around the kitchen, grabbing cups, plates, and silverware. They set the table, laid out paper napkins, and moved with the urgency of kids who knew a delicious meal was waiting.

"What else, Mom?" Tommy asked.

"Grab some soda from the fridge and have a seat. I'll bring this in," she said with a smile.

The three of them sat down at the table together. Julie pressed them to share more about their day—something *more* than the usual *It was okay.*

Somehow, that led to reminiscing.

She started telling them stories about when they were younger—like how Chad had refused to use a fork and insisted on eating everything with his hands, or how Tommy couldn't say *chips* and would always ask for *tits* instead.

They laughed. They smiled. They shared.

And Julie *loved* it.

When dinner was over, Chad asked, "What do you want us to do with the plates and stuff? There's still stuff out from yesterday."

Julie smirked at both of them. "Just scrape them into the trash and throw them in the sink. I'll do the dishes tomorrow."

I could get used to this, she joked in her head, smiling.

With the table cleared and the dishes piled in the sink, Julie poured herself a glass of wine. Her routine kicked in as she settled onto the couch and turned on the news.

She had writings to read, worksheets to grade, and none of it was going to do itself.

Might as well get ahead—because the next few days were going to be *more* than busy.

| 39 |

Julie settled onto the couch as she usually did, savoring the quiet moment. She was pouring her second glass of wine when her phone chimed—a text message.

It must be Mike.

She sighed, sat back down, and picked up her phone.

Just as she had guessed, his ever-thoughtful evening check-in:

MIKE: Hey! How was your day?

Julie stared at the screen, debating whether she even wanted to reply.

If I don't, will he call?

Could she get him to have a real conversation for once?

She doubted it. He hadn't called last night when she missed his text—just threw a temper tantrum instead.

Was it worth possibly starting something?

Throughout the day, she had convinced herself—without hesitation—that it was *over*.

Was she trying to make a scene? Set an example?

No.

Not right now.

JULIE: Good thanks!

JULIE: It's been a long day. The weekend looks pretty crazy too. The boys have bowling in the morning, and I have another thing with a few friends tomorrow night.

MIKE: Another one? Really? You know how I feel about that.

Julie thought hard about how to answer.

JULIE: It's not a big deal. It's just a few of us getting drinks later in the evening. But should be fun. When are you expecting to be home?

MIKE: You know how I feel! Right now, Tuesday I think.

JULIE: OK. I have the field trip on Monday. Can't wait to tell you about it.

MIKE: OK. I'm gonna grab a shower and get ready for bed. Love you.

JULIE: Love you too.

Julie exhaled, relieved things hadn't escalated. But did she really expect them to? No. Not over text.

If it's too much effort for him to call, it's too much effort for him to argue.

She sat back on the couch, the news still playing in the background.

She didn't feel bad.

She didn't feel worried.

She didn't feel any of the things she *used* to feel.

She felt *relieved*.

It had been a long day. That much was true.

Julie grabbed her laptop and phone and headed upstairs, calling out to the boys as she passed their rooms. "Goodnight, guys."

As she walked by, she thought about dinner—how much she had *actually* enjoyed it.

She tossed her phone and laptop onto the bed and made her way into the bathroom.

Time to get out of these clothes, she thought, turning on the shower.

She looked in the mirror and once again saw the face of someone she was learning to love—herself.

As the bathroom filled with warm, humid fog, she wiped away her makeup, revealing bare skin that no longer felt like a stranger's. She brushed her teeth, then began to undress, still watching her reflection.

You still got it, she joked to herself, trying to be less critical of her body.

Stepping into the shower, she felt another wave of peace and relaxation. The hot water cascaded over her, wrapping her in a shell of warmth. The steady flow against her skin was soothing, washing away the weight of the day.

She stood there, motionless, savoring the quiet.

When she finally stepped out, she quickly wrapped herself in a towel, shivering as the cold air hit her damp skin. She dried off as fast as she could and rummaged through her drawers for something comfortable.

A pair of soft cotton shorts. A tank top.

Perfect.

She grabbed her phone, plugged it into the charger on her nightstand, and climbed into bed. The blankets formed a familiar cocoon around her as she pulled her laptop closer and powered it on.

Julie's mind drifted back to her conversation with Justin.

He had made her curious about the other chat rooms she hadn't explored yet. She hadn't dared to look while she was at school, but now... now she had the time.

She clicked the *CUCME* icon, and the screen loaded as usual. Moving her mouse over the chat room labels, she paused as small descriptions popped up:

Clean Chat (General Chat, All Ages)

Friends and Family (Share With People You Know)

Meeting Zone (Group or Work Meetings)

Adult Chat (18+ Topics & Conversation)

Her curiosity got the better of her.

She clicked on the last one.

The directory refreshed, repopulating with a new list of names. The layout looked the same, but the users were different now.

Julie scanned the list: *Aceman, Dale, KingKong, Mr.Right.*

Okay... she thought, glancing at the names.

Then, out of the corner of her eye, she noticed the *"Messages"* tab blinking.

That was fast.

She opened her inbox.

Three new messages.

Ramrod. Dusty. Kalvin.

Julie hesitated for half a second before clicking on the first one.

She couldn't believe it. The photo left no room for interpretation—a bold, unmistakable picture of his arousal, paired with a message that read, *"Wanna help?"*

Julie leaned back, her eyes widening as she took in the entire screen.

That's huge!

Six inches? Seven? Eight? She wasn't sure. All she knew was that it looked monstrous—easily the biggest she had ever seen.

She leaned in closer.

"Goddamn!" she blurted out, laughing.

Fuck, why not?

Her pulse quickened as she nervously clicked *Reply.* A chat window popped up.

"What can I do to help?" she typed, attaching an image of herself playfully covering her eyes.

His response came almost instantly.

"Want to watch me cum?"

Julie blinked.

She leaned in, studying his picture again. Another shot of him—this time, gripping himself. The angle gave her a rough idea of just how big he was. And he was *hard.*

Was he serious?

Was *she* serious?

Did she want to watch?

Not really... and maybe?

She hesitated, fingers hovering over the keys before finally typing:

"Really?"

"Fuck yeah. I'm so close already!" he replied.

Julie couldn't take her eyes off the image.

"Fuck it," she muttered under her breath.

"How?" she typed.

A new window popped up.

"Accept Video Call – *Yes/No.*"

Julie stared at the screen, her heart pounding.

Did she *really* want to do this?

She took a deep breath.

Then, with a click, she pressed *Yes.*

The chat window shifted, replaced by two video screens and a chat box beneath them.

One screen filled with *Ramrod's* live feed.

The other—her own.

Julie almost couldn't believe what she was watching.

He leaned back in his chair, unbothered and bold, touching himself with unapologetic confidence. His movements were steady, unhurried, and with his free hand, he reached toward his keyboard.

A message popped up beneath his video window.

"*Thanks! U like?*"

Julie hesitated, unsure what to think.

"*Nice,*" she typed. "*Yes.*"

Ramrod leaned back further, his length standing straight up, thick and glistening with lube. His strokes were slow and deliberate, his fingers wrapping tightly around himself.

Julie watched.

His hand slid from base to tip, pausing briefly before sliding back down. It had to be nearly two full fists long.

"*Wow!*" she typed.

His strokes quickened. His hand worked over himself with practiced ease. He leaned toward the keyboard again.

"*CLOSE. Ready?*"

Julie sat back, unsure what to do—unsure what she *wanted* to do.

She didn't reply. She just watched.

His grip tightened, his movements became urgent, focused. His breath hitched. Then, leaning back even further, his body tensed—

Julie watched as his release pulsed from him, his body tensing with each wave. His abdomen clenched, his breath ragged as the tension unraveled.

His climax coated his hand, his stomach clenching with every contraction. He stroked himself through it, slower now, his fingers gliding over slick skin. His hand, covered in milky white fluid, continued its measured pace as the final tremors worked through him.

A message flashed on the screen.

"*Thanks!*"

And just like that, the window disappeared.

Julie blinked, staring at her inbox, now filled with even more messages.

She couldn't believe what had just happened.

It felt so *weird*—and so *hot*.

She kind of liked it… but she wasn't sure.

Julie clicked on another message.

Another dick.

And another.

And another.

Well, that was definitely fun, she thought, smirking to herself. *That was a HUGE cock. But… is this all there is?*

She clicked through the messages, deleting them as she went. But for every one she removed, another took its place. The inbox seemed endless, filling up as fast as she cleared it.

A new notification flashed.

Another message.

This one from *JimStroker.*

Julie already knew what this was going to be before she even clicked.

And she wasn't wrong.

Another dick pic.

But… it's so small and cute, she thought, amused.

It reminded her a lot of Mike—like a *penis-thumb*, buried in a big belly. It was *anything* but sexy and definitely didn't get her as excited as *Ramrod* had.

His message was short.

"*Wanna watch? Please.*"

He sounded *so* desperate.

Poor little guy.

Julie actually felt *bad.*

"*Fine,*" she typed back.

Almost instantly, the connection window opened.

Jim was *already* going at it.

Julie stared, half in fascination, half in disbelief, as he worked himself over. His fingers pinched and rolled over the peak of his arousal, pressing it against his round stomach.

It reminded her of that kids' game—"Someone's Got Your Nose."

Before either of them could even type, he was already spilling over, the evidence undeniable.

Julie smirked.

Well... that was fast.

The thought was all too familiar.

She watched as his body tensed, his stomach shifting slightly with every shallow thrust into his own fingers.

Then, just like that, the screen closed.

Julie closed her inbox and returned to the directory, scrolling through the endless list of suggestive and downright ridiculous usernames.

Most of the profile pictures, surprisingly, looked normal. She had expected something *way* more risqué. Sure, there were a few six-pack shots from the guys who could pull it off, but other than that? Pretty standard.

The usernames, on the other hand...

HardRick. DickSmith. FunTime88. Mr.Dong.

Julie smirked, shaking her head.

She kept scrolling, clicking on profiles just for fun, amused by the effort—or lack thereof—that some people put into them.

Eventually, she scrolled back to the top, starting over with a more deliberate look at each one. That's when a name caught her eye.

Abercrombie.

That's an interesting choice, she thought, clicking on the profile.

Abercrombie - *United States : Male 20-25 : Single : Let's Talk.*

His profile picture showed a young man with scruff, holding a puppy.

Julie swore it was just the low-quality image messing with her eyes, but at a *quick glance...* it almost looked like *Cole.*

"Agh!" she huffed, exasperated, before clicking *Send a Message.*

She adjusted her posture, tilting her head slightly to one side, exposing her neck, and smiled at the camera.

"Nice," she muttered under her breath.

"Hi! How are you?" she typed. *"Hope to talk sometime!"*

And with that, she hit *Send.*

Julie went back to her inbox, deleting the unread messages that had piled up. All while keeping an eye on her screen, waiting—hoping—*Abercrombie* would respond.

New messages kept rolling in, but none from him.

She either ignored them or deleted them the moment they appeared.

The tension in her chest tightened. Only a few seconds had passed, but it felt like forever.

Then—finally—a new message popped up.

It was from *him.*

"Please don't be a dick, don't be a dick!" she muttered under her breath as she clicked to open it.

Her eyes immediately went to his picture.

No, he wasn't Cole.

But there was *something* familiar about him—the olive skin, deep brown eyes, dark hair, and a bit of cute stubble. He was sitting in bed, just like she was.

And oddly enough, they were both wearing the same color shirt.

His message was lighthearted. Normal.

"Hey, we're twins! I'm great, how about you? My name's Finn. Nice to meet you!"

Julie smirked. After an hour of scrolling past nothing but *wankers,* she had finally found someone who at least seemed halfway normal.

She struck another cute pose and typed back.

"Hi, I'm Julie. I'm kind of new here. What brings you on tonight?"

Finn explained that he was new to the program too—this was only his second night online. He was 24 and worked part-time as an emergency firefighter in a small town in upstate New York. A friend had convinced him to try online chatting, claiming he needed to *get out there* and meet people since dating back home wasn't going so well.

He wasn't necessarily looking for love, just people his age to talk to—maybe even make some new friends. He had tried the General chat room earlier but felt like everyone there was just *too old* to relate to.

And then, he admitted something else.

"You're really, really pretty. Beautiful, you know. And you don't seem like any of the other girls I've talked to tonight... or last night."

Julie felt heat rise to her cheeks.

A *firefighter?* God, that was kind of hot.

And the compliment? That was even better.

She didn't have the heart to tell him she was *way* out of his age range.

She also *very carefully* avoided mentioning that she was married—or had kids.

But she did tell him she was a schoolteacher in Massachusetts.

They chatted back and forth for nearly an hour.

Finn had an absolutely *gorgeous* smile—one that completely disarmed her. Their conversation flowed effortlessly, just like it had with Justin, but *this* was different. There was an *energy* to it, an unspoken pull that made it feel... new. Exciting.

Now, she understood exactly what Justin had meant earlier about people *not going back* to the General chat room.

Still, as easy as their conversation was, Julie kept a careful eye on the clock. When 10:00 p.m. rolled around, she sighed and typed her goodbye.

"I have to sign off, but add me to your friends list. I'd love to talk again."

Finn agreed without hesitation.

Julie shut down her computer and set it on the floor beside her bed. Pulling the covers up, she let out a slow breath, her mind still spinning.

Cole. Finn.

What a *day.*

With that thought lingering, she closed her eyes and drifted into sleep.

| 40 |

The next morning, Julie woke up feeling better than she had in a long time.

Lighter. Clearer.

For the first time in *forever*, she felt *free* to be herself—without guilt, without hesitation.

And more than anything...

She felt *in control.*

As she poured herself a cup of coffee, Julie found herself replaying last night's conversation with Finn.

It had felt almost *magical.*

He was *enchanting*—kind, caring, and, not to mention, *easy on the eyes.*

There was an effortless charm about him, a warmth in his smile that made her forget—if only for a little while—everything that had been weighing on her.

She drifted through the motions of making breakfast, her mind still wrapped up in the memory, while the boys stayed in their rooms, getting ready for bowling practice.

"Breakfast is almost ready!" Julie called up the stairs before setting the plates on the table.

Last night's dinner had been so enjoyable that she figured she'd try for a *family* breakfast too.

Chad and Tommy eventually made their way downstairs, sliding into their seats. In a hurried frenzy, they wolfed down their food, barely pausing between bites.

Julie shook her head, amused. "Thirty minutes to cook and three minutes to eat," she teased, watching them devour the scrambled eggs, bacon, and toast.

"The car is warming up. Get your stuff—we leave in five."

She gathered the plates, stacking them in the sink as the boys rushed off to grab their things.

Every Saturday followed the same routine.

The boys had bowling until about 1:00 p.m., then Julie dropped them off at home before tackling her errands and grocery shopping. Today, she moved through her to-do list quickly, efficiently checking off each task.

It felt like any other Saturday—except for one thing.

Tonight, she was going out.

She was meeting *Cole* and *Melanie* for drinks.

It wasn't a big deal. *Not really.*

At least, that's what she kept telling herself.

But the truth was, she had little experience going out with friends. And to top it off, she wasn't sure how she felt about the *company*.

What was she supposed to *talk* about? What would she *say*? What would she *do*?

Her thoughts spiraled, working her into a minor frenzy.

It's just Cole, she reminded herself. *Just Cole.*

But that wasn't entirely true, was it?

For the last two weeks, *Cole* had been at the center of her thoughts. The fixation she couldn't shake.

He wasn't just the friendly teacher down the hall anymore.

No.

Now, he was *Fucking Cole.*

The monotonous routine of the day bled into an equally uneventful afternoon.

Julie did some light housework, finished grading, and made dinner for the boys.

She was supposed to meet *Melanie* and *Cole* at *The Tap House* at 7:00 p.m.

That gave her a few hours to get ready—plenty of time, yet somehow, *not enough.*

Julie found herself staring into the bathroom mirror again, studying her reflection with a critical eye.

She hated the way time had etched itself onto her face. The wrinkles were more pronounced than they had been a year ago, the weight of age settling into her cheeks.

But then, she thought of *Finn.*

"Beautiful."

That's what he had called her last night.

Had he meant it? Or was it just something he thought she *wanted* to hear?

Either way, she realized—she *had* wanted to hear it.

It had been forever since *Mike* had called her beautiful.

Or told her she looked nice.

Or said *anything* kind at all.

She remembered when they were dating—how effortlessly the cruel words had slipped from his mouth.

"If you ever gain too much weight, I'll break up with you. No one wants a fat girlfriend."

Or the way he'd say, *"You're not really that pretty, but I think you are. That's what makes us special."*

Even now, years later, he never missed an opportunity to criticize her.

Whether she was getting dressed for a wedding or one of the boys' soccer games, his response was always the same.

"You're going to wear that?"

It wasn't a question.

It was a *judgment*.

The truth was, she had grown up with him—spent her entire life with him—never really feeling *pretty*, *attractive*, or *wanted*.

But he *loved* to show her off.

He loved the attention.

Loved the way people responded when he played the role of the *adoring boyfriend*, the *doting husband*, the *devoted father*.

It was never about *her*.

It was always about *him*.

Julie slowly undressed, her gaze never leaving the mirror, searching for the beauty she *knew* was there.

Stepping into the shower, she let the hot water cascade over her, rinsing away the lingering scent of the bowling alley and the weight of the day. By the time she emerged, freshly dried and wrapped in a towel, she felt re-energized—if only slightly.

She pulled open the top drawer of her dresser, fingers sifting through years' worth of bras and panties. Most were practical—comfortable, sensible, safe. Full backs, wide hips, muted shades of black, beige, and white. Perfect for a mom. For a teacher.

But tonight, she wasn't teaching.

Her fingers brushed against something different, something she barely remembered owning.

A flash of red.

Tucked away in the back of the drawer, nearly forgotten, was a matching set so unlike the rest. If not for its bold contrast against the sea of neutrals, she might have overlooked it entirely.

She pulled them out and set them on the dresser, running her fingers over the fabric. So pretty. She picked up the panties—soft, silky, nothing like the cotton granny panties she was used to.

Letting the towel slip from her shoulders, she slowly pulled them on.

The bikinis had a full backside of smooth, shiny satin. The front was mesh lace, delicate and sheer, with a tiny bow at the center. Thin waistbands made them feel almost nonexistent against her skin. The matching bra was the same bold red, its cups adorned with the same lace pattern, set over soft foam padding.

Julie slid her arms through the satin straps and fastened the clasp at the back. It had been years since she'd worn anything like this. Lately, she'd been more of a sports bra woman, so the delicate fabric felt unfamiliar at first—light, almost fragile.

Standing in front of the dresser mirror, a rush of excitement coursed through her. Sexy. Confident. Alive.

She turned slightly, admiring how the lingerie hugged her curves, accentuating her small frame in a way she hadn't noticed in years. The lack of coverage made her a little self-conscious, but the way it made her feel far outweighed the fleeting doubt.

She loved it.

She loved how the soft lace traced over her skin, how the deep red stood out against her body.

Pushing the drawer closed, she pulled open the one below it.

What to wear? What to wear?

Her fingers sifted through neatly folded pants, debating her options before pulling out one of her favorite pairs of jeans.

She loved the way they fit—soft, stretchy, just the right amount of give. They felt as comfortable as leggings but had enough structure to offer a little support.

She glanced at the mirror again, catching the way her damp hair fell over her shoulders. In nothing but her jeans and bra, she felt... sexy.

Twisting to the side, she checked herself out. A turn. A little pose.

If Finn could see me now...

A smirk tugged at her lips, followed by a quiet laugh.

Crossing the room, she ran her fingers along the row of hanging clothes before settling on a maroon sweater.

Though technically a sweater, it felt more like an oversized, lightweight knit tee—soft, effortless, draping just right. The wide neckline slipped off her shoulder, baring just enough skin, while the plunging collar hinted at her cleavage.

It cinched slightly at her waist before falling just below her hips, hugging her shape in all the right places.

Subtle. Flattering. Just enough tease.

She stepped back to the dresser mirror, giving herself one final look.

"Perfect," she murmured, a satisfied smile curling on her lips.

In the bathroom, Julie struggled with her makeup. She had never been much of a *girly-girl* and never really learned how to apply it properly. Day to day, she kept it minimal, but she knew the basics—foundation, concealer, a little blush.

She added some eyeliner, a light coat of mascara, and picked a lipstick that closely matched the color of her bra.

Her own little secret.

That was it. Makeup done.

Julie swept her hair into a messy, low twisted ponytail and took one last look in the mirror.

"Fuck," she murmured, admiring her reflection.

She loved it all.

Grabbing her phone, she snapped a selfie. For a moment, she just stared at the screen—almost not recognizing the woman looking back at her.

Then, out of habit, she sent the picture to Mike.

The second it went through, regret hit her like a slap.

Agh!

Fuck!

Why did I do that?

Heart pounding, she sank onto the edge of the bed, waiting for his reply.

MIKE: What the hell is that? Where are you going? You said you were meeting friends?

She didn't need to hear his voice to know how angry he was.

MIKE: No! You are NOT going! NOT LIKE THAT! NO!

Julie crashed backward onto the bed, the phone still clutched in her hand.
"Fuck!"
The word escaped her lips this time as she stared up at the ceiling, heart pounding.
The phone rang.
Julie shot up to her feet.
Mike. Calling.
"Oh fuck," she whispered under her breath, staring at the screen.
Fuck.
Nervously, she swiped to answer.
"WHAT THE FUCK ARE YOU DOING?" Mike's voice exploded through the speaker. "WHAT is GOING ON!? Why did you send me THAT?"
Julie's heart pounded so hard she thought it might burst from her chest.
"I'm sorry!" she cried. "I thought I looked cute and—"
"CUTE? YOU LOOK LIKE A FUCKING WHORE!" Mike's rage slammed into her like a blow. "WHAT THE FUCK IS

WRONG WITH YOU? WHERE ARE YOU REALLY GOING?"

Her voice cracked as she stammered, "I'm sorry! I thought you'd like it! I'm just meeting two friends for a drink, that's it. I promise! I wanted to look nice. I thought I did. I'm sorry!" She pleaded, her voice shaking. "I'm sorry! Please stop yelling. Please!"

She could hear his heavy breathing, the sharp sound of something being kicked in the background.

"Mike, I'm sorry!" she repeated, gripping the phone tighter.

"Aghh! You know how I feel about this!" His tone was quieter now, but still laced with fury. "You *know*! I don't want you going out. And I *definitely* don't want you going out looking like THAT!"

"Mike!" Julie's voice cracked with desperation. "I already told them I was going. They're probably already there—I *have* to go."

She hesitated, the weight of her own words pressing down on her.

"Mike, I *have* to go. I *have* to! I need to get out of this house. I need to have a life too. Don't you understand?"

Silence.

The only sound was the low hum of the room as they both waited, neither willing to speak first.

Then, finally, Mike's voice came—calm, cutting.

"You don't *have* to," he said, pausing long enough for the words to sink in. "You *want* to. And if that's what you want… then you don't want me."

"That's not fair!" Julie shot back, frustration and desperation clawing at her throat.

"If that's what you want," Mike repeated, his words slow, deliberate, twisting the guilt like a knife.

Julie's thoughts swirled.

Her pulse pounded.

Then, she took a deep breath, steeling herself.

"Fine!" she snapped. And then she hung up.

| 41 |

Julie sat on the edge of the bed, staring at her phone. She carefully wiped her eyes, trying not to smear her makeup. The room felt painfully silent. If she had been uncertain before, there was no doubt now.

She was done.

How had it taken her this long to see the truth? Deep down, she knew she had always seen it. It had just taken her this long to accept it.

Julie stood and made her way back to the bathroom. Again, she found herself in front of the mirror. She took a deep breath, staring into her own reflection.

"Fuck this," she muttered at the image staring back at her.

For the first time, she felt like she was making a decision for herself—one that wasn't influenced by Mike or anyone else.

"He wants me to choose?" she asked her reflection. *"I pick me."*

She wiped her eyes, touched up her makeup, and grabbed her coat before heading downstairs.

Chad and Tommy were sprawled on the couch, watching basketball. As Julie descended the stairs, both turned to look at her.

"Wow! Wow, Mom!" Tommy chuckled. "Look at you!"

They weren't used to seeing her in anything other than her usual "mom clothes." This outfit wasn't flashy, but it was a departure from her norm—especially for a Saturday night.

"Thanks," she said, smiling as she raised her eyebrows nervously.

"I'm heading out for a little while. I won't be late. Think you guys can hold down the fort?" she asked, already knowing the answer.

Chad smirked. "Uh, yeah? We're not exactly going anywhere." He shrugged and turned his attention back to the game.

"Have fun!" Tommy grinned.

Julie slid into her car and headed for the bar. It was nearly 7:00 p.m.

She didn't want to arrive too early—that might seem desperate. But she also didn't want to be too late and have them think she was blowing them off.

Timing was everything.

The drive was short, but long enough for her to steady herself.

She had been looking forward to tonight, and she wasn't going to let Mike ruin it.

Not this time.

Julie stepped inside the bar, her pulse quickening with a mix of nerves and excitement.

It had been forever since she'd been to a bar—especially alone.

The Tap House wasn't the kind of place with dark corners and sticky floors. It had more of a restaurant feel—warm and inviting. A large bar sat in the center of the room, surrounded by stools, the soft hum of conversation filling the air.

The lights were dim, casting a golden glow that made it hard to see all the way across the room. People were everywhere—standing, weaving through the crowd with drinks in hand, talking, laughing.

For a moment, Julie just stood there, taking it all in.

She stepped further inside, nudging the door closed behind her to keep the warm air from spilling out.

The deeper she moved into the bar, the tighter the space became. Bodies pressed against her, voices overlapped, the air thick with movement and conversation. It was far more congested than she was used to, and with every step, she felt smaller—trapped in a restless sea of people.

She peered through the shifting crowd, her movements slow and deliberate as she squeezed through, scanning for a familiar face.

Halfway across the floor, she finally spotted Melanie and Cole sitting at a tall table along the back wall. Relief washed over her as she maneuvered through the last stretch of people, weaving her way toward them.

"Hey, guys!" she said with a laugh. "I made it!"

Julie held out her arms in a playful *ta-da* gesture.

"Hey! Come on, have a seat," Melanie said, motioning toward the chair closest to her.

The tall table had three stools—Melanie and Cole sat across from each other, leaving the middle seat open. Julie slid onto it, straddling the stool before scooting herself closer to the table.

"Glad you could make it!" Melanie added with a warm smile. "We were just about to order. Do you know what you'd like?"

Julie could hardly focus on what she wanted to drink. She was still struggling to believe she was actually out at a bar, having drinks at all. She glanced at Melanie, her mind spinning.

"Right now? Anything," she joked.

Julie had no idea what to order. When it came to drinking, she usually stuck to wine—and that was at home, on her couch. This felt like an entirely new experience.

"Cole and I were going to do shots. We'll get three to start," Melanie answered for Julie. She glanced at Cole and nodded her chin. He got the hint and raised his arm, flagging down the waitress.

"Three shots. Tequila. Gold," he told the waitress, his voice surprisingly firm.

Tequila.

Julie hesitated. She had never had tequila before.

She'd tried whiskey once—and that hadn't gone well.

What have I gotten myself into? she wondered, a flicker of doubt and fear creeping in.

Drinking wasn't the only thing Julie wasn't used to.

Seeing Melanie and Cole like this—outside of school—felt surreal. They looked normal, yet strangely different at the same time, as if stepping into another version of themselves.

Before Julie could say a word, Melanie grabbed her hand.

"You look so cute!" she said, a giddy excitement in her voice. "I'm not used to seeing you like this!"

"Thanks," Julie replied. "I'm not either!" She laughed. "I wasn't sure what to wear, so I just threw this on."

"I love it! You should dress up more often!" Melanie said eagerly. "I'm so glad you could make it."

"Me too," Julie said warmly. She turned toward Cole. "You look great too!"

And he really did.

Cole wore a fitted black long-sleeve button-down, neatly tucked into a pair of heathered gray pants. The shirt hugged him in all the right places, accentuating his broad frame. The deep tones of his outfit complemented his winter-olive skin and dark stubble effortlessly.

Julie swallowed, forcing herself to reset.

"You better not wear that Monday!" she teased, trying to keep things light.

"I know!" he shot back, pulling a playful face.

Then, just as quickly, his expression shifted. "It's supposed to rain tomorrow night. Hopefully, it isn't too wet Monday morning." His tone turned serious, effortlessly shifting gears.

"Rain or shine!" Julie replied. "It's going to happen. Bring an umbrella!" She tried to joke again.

Just in time, the waitress arrived with their drinks, setting them in the center of the table along with three limes.

"Lick! Shoot! Suck!" Melanie called out across the table, grabbing the salt shaker with a mischievous grin.

Julie watched as Melanie dipped her finger into her glass, wiped it across the back of her hand, and sprinkled salt over it.

Cole followed suit, so Julie did the same, mimicking their movements.

With lime wedges in one hand and shot glasses in the other, they were ready.

Cole lifted his shot glass a little higher and cleared his throat. "Everyone should believe in something. I believe I'll have another drink!" He licked the patch of salt on his hand, drank his shot, and bit down on the lime.

"Yeah!" Melanie cheered as she did the same.

Julie glanced at the two of them, then leaned in, licking the patch of salt from her hand. The sharp, briny taste hit her instantly, making her face scrunch in reaction.

She grabbed her glass, hesitating for just a fraction of a second as the harsh, smoky scent of tequila rose to meet her.

Then—down it went.

The liquid burned across her tongue, searing down her throat, and somehow, all the way up into her head.

She bit into the lime, the cool burst of citrus cutting through the fire, washing over her taste buds like relief.

"Whoo!" she shouted, slamming the glass onto the table. "I needed that!"

Laughter filled the air as the night carried on, fueled by shots, mixed drinks and easy conversation.

Julie learned that Melanie and Cole had only started dating after Valentine's Day and that, once upon a time, Cole had considered becoming a veterinarian before going to college.

The more they drank, the more handsy Melanie became.

By the fourth round, she had already shifted her stool closer to Cole, practically draping herself over him. Her head rested in the crook of his neck, only lifting when she had something to say. One arm stayed wrapped around his for support, while the other...

Julie couldn't quite see from where she was sitting, but she knew.

Melanie's hand was in his lap. Every so often, Julie caught the slightest movement—a squeeze to his thigh, a shift of her fingers.

Julie took another sip of her drink, pretending not to notice.

"I'm going to go freshen up," Julie said, feeling the weight of the night settling over her.

"I'll go with you!" Melanie shouted, fumbling to untangle herself from Cole as she tried to steady her balance.

She let out a laugh. "I could probably use the help!"

Julie and Melanie wove through the crowd toward the bathroom, Julie already feeling the effects of the evening starting to kick in.

Once inside, they ducked into separate stalls, meeting up again at the sinks.

Julie gripped the edge of the counter, both hands pressed firmly against the cool surface as she steadied herself. She caught Melanie's gaze in the mirror—her reflection slightly unfocused, but her emotions sharp.

"I'm so glad you invited me!" she blurted out. "You have no idea what kind of afternoon it's been."

She turned fully to face Melanie, her voice dropping to something more serious.

"I'm done."

Melanie's brows lifted. "Done?"

Julie nodded, swallowing hard. "I can't... I can't do it anymore. Me and Mike."

Melanie's face filled with surprise, but Julie pressed on.

"I'm done. This isn't what I want. I want... I want what you have. I want what I *deserve*—love, thoughtfulness, real affection." Her voice trembled under the weight of her own admission.

"I just... I just want to be happy."

"Good for you!" Melanie said supportively. "You *deserve* to be happy!"

Her eyes lit up at Julie's resolve. "I've never really met him, but I can already tell he's an ass. I *know* you can do better—so much better. You shouldn't have to settle."

"You are amazing, and you deserve *amazing*! Good for you!"

She threw her arms around Julie, pulling her into a supportive hug.

Then, lowering her voice to a mischievous whisper, she leaned in. "But shhh!" Her breath was warm against Julie's ear. "You know who else is happy? Or... maybe *not*."

She snickered. "I just left him all bricked up under the table. *Shhh!*"

Julie's eyes widened. "Oh my God! Are you *serious*?"

Melanie put on an innocent face. "I'll take care of him when we get back to my place," she said with a smirk. "But he's so cute, right?"

She smiled dreamily. "He's *so* perfect."

Back at the table, Julie couldn't help but think about Cole sitting there, just a foot or two away from her—excited, waiting. She kept glancing at Melanie, remembering everything she had said about him at Barbara's party. And that tonight, she would be the one going home with him.

Tonight! Julie thought.

"Hold on, guys! I want to remember tonight. Can we take a picture?" Julie said, loud and enthusiastic. "It would be a shame if we didn't. We all look so good!"

She hopped off her stool, lifting her phone and angling the camera toward herself and the couple behind her.

"Say cheese!"

She snapped a few pictures, shifting the angle and adjusting her pose slightly with each shot, capturing the moment from different perspectives.

"This one!" she said, scrolling through the photos and showing them to Cole and Melanie. "You guys look so good together! And I love my smile!"

"Send that one to me," Melanie said, leaning in to glance at the screen.

"First, I need to send it to Mike," Julie said, winking at Melanie vengefully.

Melanie smiled back in support.

"This is what I WANT," Julie typed into her text message.

"And send!" she declared defiantly, flashing a smirk at Melanie.

"I don't have your number," Julie admitted, glancing at Melanie.

"I'll put it in," Melanie said, motioning for Julie to hand over her phone.

She fumbled with it for a moment, tapping and swiping before flashing a satisfied smile. "Sent! Now you have my info."

Then, lifting her empty shot glass, she grinned. "One more?"

Julie hesitated, eyeing the glass. "One more?" she echoed. "I don't know…"

"Come on. Just one! Then we can go!" Melanie insisted, ordering another set of shots for the table.

Leaning closer to Julie, she whispered, "Then we can go. I think Cole is ready to get out of here. Look at this picture again."

Melanie handed Julie back the phone. "I like this one better!" she said with a grin.

Julie stared at her phone, frozen. The picture Melanie had just swiped to and sent herself filled the screen, and Julie's mouth fell open.

"Oh my God!" she gasped, looking at Melanie in disbelief.

When Julie lifted the phone to frame the photo, Melanie had grabbed Cole—her hand gripped over the unmistakable outline in his pants, the tension beneath the fabric impossible to ignore.

Melanie laughed. "Good pic, right?" she said, wide-eyed.

"Oh my God! I can't believe you did that!" Julie said, still in disbelief.

"It's no big deal," Melanie said. "Actually, it kinda is!" she joked, raising her eyebrows again.

The shots arrived, and the three of them settled in to down one last round.

Melanie held her glass in the air and looked at Julie. "Here's to all that wish us well. All the rest can go to hell!" she toasted.

They downed the last shot and cheered.

"Oh my God, what a night!" Julie said, thanking Melanie and Cole for inviting her out again. "Don't forget Monday!" she reminded Cole as they made their way through the parking lot.

"I got it!" he said with a smile. "Are you okay to drive?" he asked.

"Why are you so nice?" Julie blurted out.

"'Cuz he's awesome!" Melanie quickly replied, looking doe-eyed at Cole.

"I'm fine," Julie said. "Really."

Julie watched Cole and Melanie kiss before they got into his car and drove away.

Ugh!

She was so jealous. She loved seeing them together. They made a great couple. But she also hated it.

She sat in her car for a while, wondering if she should really drive home. She hadn't had this much to drink—ever. She turned up the heat and looked at the photos still on her phone.

"Fuck," Julie muttered under her breath.

She zoomed in on Cole.

Wow.

Her eyes traced the way his pants stretched under Melanie's grip, her hand framing the shape beneath—defining every contour. And that devilish smile on her face…

Julie could only imagine what they were up to now.

She sat in the car for another 30 minutes, just thinking, before she felt safe enough to drive home.

She drove slowly and cautiously. It wasn't long before she pulled into the driveway. She gathered her things and went inside. The house was still and quiet.

Julie carefully walked up the stairs. It was much later than she thought she would be home, and she didn't want to wake the boys. She lay down on her bed.

I'll lay here for just a second, she told herself.

Then I'll get ready for bed.

But the weight of the night settled over her, and she wasn't sure if she'd move at all.

| 42 |

Julie woke up still lying in her bed, exactly where she had fallen asleep the night before. Her hair had come loose from her ponytail. Her makeup was smudged across her face. Her head was pounding.

Oh my God, she thought, barely able to move.

This is what dying feels like.

She squinted across the room at the glowing red numbers of her alarm clock.

9:44 a.m.

"Fuucck," she groaned painfully, pulling herself to her feet.

She slowly walked to the bathroom, her body weighed down by exhaustion, her head throbbing with every step.

Looking in the mirror, Julie barely recognized herself. This wasn't the same person who went out last night.

She groaned, reaching for the aspirin in the medicine cabinet. The harsh glow of the vanity lights made her head throb even more, forcing her to switch them off.

Fumbling toward the shower, she turned the water on, hoping the heat would wake her up—or at the very least, wash away the worst of her hangover.

The hot shower provided almost immediate relief. Julie stood beneath the steady stream, eyes closed, letting the water wash over her as her thoughts drifted.

Last night had been incredible. She loved everything about the evening—the laughter, the jokes, the carefree energy. And if this pounding headache was the price she had to pay, well... it was worth it.

Tomorrow is going to be such a busy day, she thought as she turned off the shower. *Today, she had to focus on feeling better—and figuring out what she was going to say to Mike.*

Mike.

Fuck.

Julie's stomach dropped. She grabbed a towel, barely drying off as she bolted for the bed, snatching up her phone.

She pulled up her text messages from the night before.

SENT.

There was no response.

Her fingers hovered over the screen, her mind racing.

What the hell was I thinking sending him this?

But what did it matter? She was having fun.

At least she didn't send the other one.

Julie took her time getting dressed, moving slowly as the remnants of her hangover lingered.

She decided she wasn't going to message Mike. Not unless he reached out first.

Baggy sweatpants and a sweatshirt—that's the kind of day this was.

The rest of the afternoon was spent slowly catching up on housework and laundry, the mundane tasks helping to keep her mind busy and her body moving.

But deep down, she knew exactly what she was doing.

Her instincts had already kicked in—the silent urgency to start cleaning for Mike. He'd be home in a few days, and she expected the week ahead to be nothing short of exhausting.

Julie made the boys lunch before collapsing onto the couch. It was definitely a slow-moving, sweatpants kind of day.

Neither of them mentioned how late she had come home last night or how rough she looked this morning.

They probably figured the nicest thing to do was to say nothing at all.

Julie closed her eyes, letting herself rest for a bit.

She must have dozed off because she woke to the soft pitter-patter of rain against the living room window.

A glance outside told her everything—the crisp blue skies from earlier in the week had vanished, replaced by a blanket of dark, moody gray. The rain looked cold, heavy, the kind that seeped into your bones.

She exhaled and closed her eyes again, sinking into the quiet rhythm of the falling rain.

Julie rested with her eyes closed for a long while, catching herself just before slipping into sleep. Even without fully dozing off, the stillness was restful, rejuvenating.

When she finally opened her eyes, she reached for the remote and turned on the news.

Outside, the soft drizzle had escalated into a steady downpour, raindrops hammering against the windows.

She sighed, remembering what Cole had said—hopefully, it would clear up by morning.

Closing her eyes again, she let the sound of the rain fill the quiet space around her, waiting for the weather report to come on.

"It's a wet one out there today!" the familiar voice of the weatherman announced. "If you're driving tonight, take it slow and be careful. Heavy downpours at times could lead to localized flooding in some areas."

Julie didn't even bother opening her eyes.

Great, she thought. *Just great.*

The voice returned. *"But don't worry too much—the rain looks to taper off early tonight, making way for another sunny week ahead. Tomorrow morning will be damp and cool, with a high of 60 by the afternoon. We'll have the full weekly forecast when we return."*

Julie got up and turned off the TV.

Alright, she thought. *Dinner and back to bed.*

She opened the fridge, scanning the shelves for something easy to make. Too many choices. She had just been grocery shopping, and the options felt overwhelming.

Grinders.

Super easy, super fast, and barely any cleanup.

"Boys! Grinders for dinner!" she called up the stairs, her voice echoing slightly. "Ham, turkey, or roast beef?"

"Roast beef!" Tommy yelled back.

"Yeah! Roast beef!" Chad echoed.

Even easier, Julie thought with a smirk. *Three roast beef grinders, coming right up.*

She grabbed the roast beef, a bag of grinder rolls, shredded lettuce, and a tomato. Within minutes, she had three grinder shop-worthy sandwiches lined up on the counter.

"They're ready!" she called upstairs. "I left them plain, so fix them how you like!"

She sat at the table with her own sandwich, expecting to eat alone.

But to her surprise—and delight—both Chad and Tommy came down right away and joined her.

"Feeling better?" Tommy asked. "Did you have a good time?"

Julie laughed. "Yes! Thank you!" she said with a smile. "It was nice to go out. I'm just not used to being up so late!" She joked, trying to keep things light.

Chad's expression shifted, his voice more cautious. "Was Dad mad?"

Julie exhaled slowly, steadying herself.

"Listen, I'm going to be honest with you guys." She looked at them both, choosing her words carefully. "Yes, Dad was mad. Really mad. We got into a bit of a fight, and... well, I'm not sure what's next."

She hesitated, then pressed on.

"Your dad and I... we haven't been getting along for a very long time now. A *very* long time. And I don't know if I want to live the rest of my life unhappy like this."

She swallowed, her voice soft but firm. "Your dad and I need to talk when he gets home. I don't know what the right thing to do is yet, but I want you to know this—no matter what happens, I will always love you. Always. And nothing will ever change that."

"Dad can be a jerk, Mom!" Tommy blurted out. "I'm sorry, but it's true. He treats you like shit all the time, and he treats us like shit too. I know I shouldn't say it, but..."

"Yeah!" Chad cut in, nodding. "Everybody sees it but you. He's out almost every night with work people or *whoever*, but when he's home, he hardly ever has time for us—or you. That's not fair!"

Julie's posture stiffened.

"Listen!" she said firmly. "You do *not* get to take sides. This is between your dad and me. Do you understand?"

"Yeah, but—" Tommy started, his frustration boiling over. "It's just... it's *so* much better when he's not here! You *know* it."

Julie's tone sharpened. "*Understand.*"

Tommy clamped his mouth shut, but defiance still burned in his eyes.

Julie exhaled, softening her voice. "Eat your dinner, and let me handle this. Okay?"

She looked between them, her expression full of love despite the tension. "I love you guys."

"We love you too," Chad said. "And we just want you to be happy."

Julie looked across the table, her heart aching.

She knew what she was about to put her kids through, and the weight of it was crushing. A small part of her felt relieved by their reaction—they saw the truth. But it also shattered her to realize she hadn't been able to shield them from it.

Had they seen right through Mike's mask so easily?

And yet, *she* was only just now seeing it for the first time.

With dinner finished and the kitchen cleaned, Julie poured herself a large glass of wine, the exhaustion of the day settling deep in her bones.

"I'm heading to bed early," she told the boys. "Don't forget, we have to leave on time in the morning—I need to be at work early for the field trip."

They nodded, then wrapped her in a tight, warm hug.

"We'll be ready, Mom. Promise."

| 43 |

Julie made her way up to her room, closing the door behind her with a quiet click.

She set her glass of wine on the bedside table before heading to her closet, searching for something to wear tomorrow.

Her fingers sifted through the hangers and drawers until she settled on a plain gray sweatshirt and a pair of jeans.

Warm enough, she thought.

Just in case, she also pulled out her boots and a small knit hat.

After brushing her teeth, she turned toward the pile of dirty clothes still on the floor from that morning.

A flash of red peeked through the heap.

Julie paused, her mind flickering back to last night—how cute she had looked, how good she had felt.

Her gaze shifted back to the neatly folded outfit she had just laid on the chair. *Should she dress up a little more?*

Nah. This would do just fine.

But... she smirked at her makeup-less reflection in the mirror.

I'll have to at least do my makeup.

Julie stepped out of her baggy sweats and into the shower.

This morning's shower had been about recovery and survival, not cleanliness, she joked to herself, stepping under the warm spray for the second time today.

Earlier, she hadn't had the energy to wash her hair or shave her legs—both of which desperately needed attention.

As the water cascaded over her, her mind wandered from topic to topic, thoughts spinning in a restless loop.

Ahh.

I wish I had someone to talk to. Anyone.

Maybe she could call Melanie. Or Barbara?

No. They would support her. Defend her. But she knew who she *needed* to talk to.

She was glad she had opened up to the boys, but they didn't need to know *everything*. She could still shield them from the painful details she had kept buried for so long.

But for now—for *right now*—she just wanted to forget the truth. To escape the reality of her situation and find a moment of peace for herself.

Julie took a deep breath, letting the steam envelop her, willing herself to just *relax*.

The soft floral scent of her shower gel filled the air, soothing her senses. She loved the feeling of freshly washed hair, of smooth, clean skin—simple comforts that, for a brief moment, made everything feel lighter.

Her life was surrounded by testosterone and masculinity, and most days, it was hard to appreciate and embrace her femininity. But right now, she felt refreshed—lighter.

She dried off and made her way to the dresser, rummaging through her top drawer for something to wear to bed.

Her fingers brushed over a cute pair of underwear.

I'll wear these tomorrow, she decided with a small smile.

Digging deeper, she pulled out a lacy bra—it didn't match, but that was okay. At least they weren't granny panties and a sports bra, and that was what mattered.

She tossed them onto the chair with the rest of her clothes for the morning.

As she continued searching, something at the bottom of the drawer caught her eye—soft, silky fabric.

Julie pulled out a satin pajama set she had completely forgotten about.

It wasn't sexy in a lace-and-risqué kind of way, but it was still pretty. Feminine. A soft, girly pink with light gray vertical stripes. The short-sleeved, button-down top and slightly oversized matching shorts were loose-fitting, cool, and impossibly comfortable.

She slipped them on, smoothing the fabric against her skin.

A perfect fit.

Julie smiled at her reflection. She had forgotten how much she loved—and missed—feeling pretty.

She made her way toward the bed, only to stumble over her laptop, still lying on the floor.

"Ouch."

She scooped it up and tossed it onto the bed before climbing in herself, sinking into the cool sheets.

Reaching for her wine, she took a long, slow sip, letting the warmth settle in her chest.

I wonder...

She opened the laptop and powered it on, her fingers hovering over the keyboard for a moment before double-clicking the newest icon.

Within seconds, her chat window filled the screen.

She glanced at her friends list.

Abercrombie was online.

Julie hesitated for only a second before typing:

"Hey! How's it going?"

She snapped a cute photo to go with it.

Send.

Taking another generous sip of wine, she exhaled deeply.

Hopefully, this would help calm her nerves.

Hopefully, it would help her sleep.

Julie opened her message window, scrolling through the flood of new messages that had piled up since the last time she logged in.

Delete.

Delete.

She wasn't even interested.

Finishing her glass of wine, she sat there, waiting.

Maybe he's talking to other people?

Maybe he found someone better to talk to?

Younger? Prettier?

Julie wouldn't blame him if he had. She suddenly remembered—her profile still said *"Married."*

Shit.

He must have seen it.

Her stomach twisted, but before she could spiral further, a new message popped into her inbox.

Finn. *"Hey you!"*

She smiled despite herself, clicking on the message.

Attached was a picture of him sitting at his desk. From what she could make out, he was wearing a dark gray T-shirt and thick black suspenders.

God, he looked good.

"Hope you've had a good day so far?" Julie typed, attaching another cute, smiling picture.

She was so glad he had messaged her back.

"What's up?" she added, still smiling as she hit send.

A moment later, his reply popped up.

"Yeah. It was pretty good. Worked all day. Just got home and sat down before changing and jumping in the shower."

Julie noticed it now—the black firefighter patch on his T-shirt.

Then, another message appeared.

"I'm glad you messaged me."

A pause.

"I've been thinking about you since we talked the other night."

Julie blinked at the screen, her heart skipping.

"Really?" she typed back. *"Why?"*

She watched the screen, waiting.

Then, finally—his response.

"I don't know, exactly. I just really like you! You're smart, funny, wicked cute. I mean, just look at you. You're perfect... Except for being married."

Julie's heart sank.

He did look at her profile.

What to say? What to say?

Her fingers hovered over the keyboard before she finally typed:

"Well, that's not entirely true."

She attached a playful photo of herself shrugging, nose wrinkled in amusement.

A second message followed.

"We are currently unofficially separated."

Finn's reply came almost instantly.

"Oh? Really? So... it's okay if we talk?"

Julie didn't hesitate.

"Absolutely."

Last night, if you were here, we would have done more than talk, she thought secretly to herself, biting her lip as she stared at the screen.

Instead, she typed something else.

"Are you wearing a uniform?"

A little flirty. A little bold.

Finn's response came with a grin.

"Uh, yeah! Hold on."

Julie waited, her pulse quickening.

"Better?"

Finn's next message popped up with a new photo—this time, he had pushed his chair back, snapping a shot from the neck down, showing off his tan work pants and sturdy boots.

"I haven't changed yet," he added, sending another picture with a slightly different pose.

Julie smirked at the screen.

"You don't happen to have a calendar, do you?" she teased, adding a playful smile to her message.

"Ha! No. Sorry! LOL." Finn replied.

Julie lingered on his last photo, her pulse skipping as she studied it.

Wow.

Finn was gorgeous. Every inch of him.

Her fingers hovered over the keyboard before she finally typed:

"Damn! I would have liked to see more."

She snapped another picture—this time, a blushing smile tugging at her lips.

A second later, his reply popped up.

"Well, you look pretty dressed up yourself! What's the special occasion?"

Julie hesitated.

How could she explain that there was no special occasion?

How could she explain that she had just endured the craziest two weeks of her life and *desperately* craved to feel wanted—to feel beautiful again?

And that *he* made her feel that... and so much more.

She swallowed, then finally typed her response.

I was hoping to see you!

And hit *send.*

The rhythmic back-and-forth flow of messages seemed to stop. Julie sat in her bed, staring at her screen, holding her breath.

Fuck!

Was that the wrong thing to say?

Did she just scare him away?

Fuck!

A message popped up—it was Finn. Julie let out a deep breath, relief washing over her.

"*Really?*" he wrote. "*Are you serious?*"

His face looked like there was some doubt.

Julie smiled and sat up on her knees, pushing the laptop further down the bed. She framed herself from the neck down and snapped a cute, flirty pose.

"*YES!*" she wrote back. "*Do you like?*"

Julie wasn't sure what she was doing. But what she did know was that she was tired of being afraid. She was tired of playing it safe.

She snapped another picture, this time pulling her shirt collar off her shoulder.

Then another—leaning slightly forward, letting her shirt hang loose, exposing her cleavage.

A moment later, Finn's response appeared.

"*Holy fuck! Wow! OMG! You are breathtaking!*"

Julie smirked at the camera. "*So you like?*" she teased.

"*YES!*" Finn replied. "*But I don't know where you are trying to take this?*"

Julie didn't hesitate.

She posed again on her knees, raising her arms, exposing her midriff.

"*Wherever you want to take it.*" she typed back, hitting send.

No! she thought. *Wherever I want to take it.*

"*Stand up again!*" she wrote. "*I want to see more of you too!*"

"*Seriously?*" Finn replied.

Julie smirked at the screen.

"*Fuck yeah! You're hot as hell!*"

Heart pounding, she started to unbutton her shirt and stopped at the last one, allowing the front to spread open, exposing the center of her chest.

She posed again.

"Your turn!"

A new message popped up.

The first image—him standing just like she asked.

Then another—pulling his shirt loose from his waistband.

Julie couldn't take her eyes off the image. Her gaze drank in every inch of his physique—the defined ridges of his abs, the broad strength of his shoulders, the way his body looked effortlessly sculpted.

A new message—his shirt was off, leaving only his suspenders.

"More!" Julie commanded in her next message, her fingers trembling slightly as she typed.

She could feel the heat rising in her body, her skin flushed, burning.

Fuck!

A new message appeared.

His suspenders were pulled down, no shirt, and his pants unbuttoned.

Oh my God! she thought. *He is fucking perfect.*

Julie's breath came faster as she slipped the last button free, her fingertips grazing the soft fabric as she pulled both sides apart.

Her bare skin was now fully exposed between the open folds of her shirt, the deep valley of her cleavage framed perfectly.

Snap.

She captured the moment, her pulse racing as she hit send.

A beat later, she typed another message, heart pounding.

"Video call me! I want to see it all!"

Julie leaned her back against the headboard and nervously waited for Finn to reply.

A window flashed on her screen.

"Accept Video Call - *Yes/No.*"

Julie's heart was racing. Her fingers trembled.

What the Fuck am I doing?

Her pulse roared in her ears as she moved the mouse cursor over the button.

[YES] *Click.*

The video window popped open.

Julie's breath hitched.

Finn stood just like he had in the last photo—bare-chested, pants unbuttoned at the waist. His body was perfectly sculpted, effortlessly confident.

Her fingers flew across the keyboard.

"OMG! You look amazing."

A moment later, Finn leaned forward, muscles flexing as he typed back.

"So do you! FUCK!"

Julie swallowed hard, her skin flushing under his gaze.

What the hell was she doing?

And why did it feel so damn good?

Julie typed back, *"I want to ;)"* as she squeezed her breast to encourage him some more.

She slowly pulled her shirt over her shoulders and let it fall open across her chest.

She watched as Finn slowly unzipped his pants and pulled them down. Julie could easily make out the bulge of his erection in his boxer briefs.

"Holy fuck!" she typed.

Julie wasn't sure what had gotten into her, but she had gone this far. *Fuck it now!*

Her breath caught again as she watched Finn's fingers hook into the waistband of his boxer briefs.

Slowly—so slowly—he began to pull them down.

Her eyes stayed locked on the screen, her pulse racing as, inch by inch, more of his skin was revealed.

Fuck!!

Julie's breath hitched as her gaze followed the sharp definition of Finn's V-line, that perfect dip leading lower—the kind of thing that universally drove women wild.

And she was no exception.

Julie roughly mirrored his movements, sliding her hand down under her waistband and into her shorts.

She slid her fingers over herself and felt the heat radiating from her core. She couldn't remember the last time she had been this wet, this turned on.

Finn pulled his shorts down a little further.

The waistband caught against his rigid length, the fabric straining.

The harder he pulled, the more resistance he met—until, finally, he freed himself, springing up and out like a giant flesh jack-in-the-box.

Julie watched him intently as her fingers disappeared beneath her touch, a soft gasp escaping as pleasure built. She explored deeper, her other hand teasing over the curve of her breast.

Leaning forward, barely aware of anything but the screen in front of her, her fingers flew across the keyboard.

"*FUCK!!! FUCK!!!*"

Her pulse raced and her body flushed as she watched Finn's hand glide over himself, in front of the camera.

Julie couldn't look away.

Everything about him was perfect.

She wasn't an expert by any means, but judging by the way it filled his hand, she guessed he was around seven inches long and impressively thick—almost like a paper towel tube.

Slightly veined. Rock-hard. *Perfect* in every measure.

Her breath hitched, pulse pounding as she took it all in.

Fuck.

"*OMG CUM WITH ME!*" she wrote before sitting back and pulling off her shorts.

Leaning back, Julie let her knees drift apart, catching the gleam of her own arousal in the screen's reflection.

She watched Finn's steady rhythm, her own fingers following suit as she gave in to the moment.

Fuck! she thought again.

It didn't take long for her to begin to feel the tension building up in her body. Her touch became more insistent, matching the urgency in Finn's strokes as his pace quickened before her eyes.

"Fuck!" she yelled as she watched him take pleasure in her pleasuring herself.

Her body tightened, the pulse of her desire intensifying, building in a steady, relentless thrum of pleasure.

Rhythmic circles and pressure caused it to build heavier and heavier. Her mind exploded as she crossed the point of no return and her primal responses took over.

"Fuck!" she called out as her hips thrust and her body contorted in convulsions.

"Fuck! FUCK!" she screamed as she came harder and harder, her body shaking, entirely out of her control. The sensation ran down her spine and across her entire body.

"FUCK!" she cried out again, her body still trembling as she opened her eyes just in time to see Finn reach his peak, his release spilling across the desk and near the camera.

She watched as his abs tensed with every stroke, the rhythm of his movements unrelenting, his body riding out the last waves of pleasure.

It spread across his hand and the desk, yet he kept going—drawing out every last sensation, letting her savor the moment with him.

Julie reached over to the keyboard.

"OMG! Fuck. That was incredible!" she typed, still trying to catch her breath.

Finn sank into his chair, his arousal still visible at the edge of the frame.

"You're telling me! I can't even stand right now," he wrote. *"I don't know what got into me. I've never done anything like this be-*

fore. It's just... You... You! I couldn't help it. Wow. That was definitely fun though! But I need to clean up now."

Julie smirked. *He's so cute*, she thought to herself.

"*And I need to go to bed. But we should do this again sometime,*" she replied with a devilish grin.

"*Absolutely!*" Finn wrote back. "*I hope we do. And I hope we can talk more too!*"

Julie blew him a kiss before clicking off the connection, the screen fading to black.

She lay back in her bed, her chest rising and falling, still breathing hard.

What the hell did I just do?

She couldn't believe it.

But God—she was so glad she had.

A slow smile curled at her lips as she let the moment settle over her.

No regrets.

Not tonight.

Julie shut down the laptop and set it back on the floor.

Still giddy from the experience, she slid back into her pajama bottoms and buttoned up her shirt, her fingers trembling slightly—not from nerves, but from excitement.

She slipped beneath the heavy blankets, the warmth wrapping around her.

As her head hit the pillow, one final thought pulsed through her mind—

Fuck. What a night.

| 44 |

Julie woke to the sharp sound of her alarm. She opened her eyes to the dim morning light peeking through the pulled shades. The chill in the air caused her to shiver for a moment as she pulled the warm blankets against her body.

Today's the big day, she reminded herself excitedly.

With a deep breath, she turned to get up—then noticed the laptop lying on the floor next to the bed.

Wow. Last night. Last night...

A flush warmed her cheeks as the memory resurfaced. *Finn.* She recalled the events of the previous evening.

She drew in another deep breath, shaking off the thought. There was no time to dwell on that now—she had to stay focused. Today had to go perfectly.

Julie smiled as she got up and started getting dressed. No matter how hard she tried, her mind stubbornly lingered on the night before.

Catching sight of herself in the mirror, she grinned at the soft fabric of her pajamas, a quiet giggle escaping her lips. With a renewed sense of purpose, she reached for the outfit she had laid out the night before—cute panties, a simple bra, and a cozy sweatshirt. The perfect blend of comfort and confidence for a crisp New England spring day.

Julie rushed downstairs to make a pot of coffee, not forgetting to knock on the boys' doors as she passed by.

"Remember, I can't be late!" she reminded them as she hurried down the hall.

The kitchen was still a mess.

I really should clean this up before Mike gets home, she thought, the familiar flicker of obligation creeping in.

But then, just as quickly, she shut it down.

Nope. Actually, I don't.

Julie glanced around, assessing the scattered dishes and cluttered countertops. It wasn't that bad. She could live with it for a few more days—or at least until she felt like dealing with it.

With a small, defiant smile, she reached for the biggest travel mug she could find and filled it to the brim.

"Good morning, Mom!" said Tommy, making his way to the downstairs bathroom. "Don't worry, we got you," he said reassuringly before disappearing behind the bathroom door.

The boys got ready for school in what felt like record time. Before she knew it, they were all dropped off, and she was pulling into the parking lot at Franklin.

Julie made her way across the chilly sea of parked cars, wrapping her arms around herself as the cold bit through her sweatshirt.

Ugh, spring needs to hurry up and act like spring, she thought, quickening her pace toward the building.

The blast of warmth inside was a welcome relief, and she exhaled as the door shut behind her. She made her way down the hall to the front office, her steps steady with purpose.

Inside, Mrs. Reed sat at her desk, the phone pressed to her ear, nodding along to the conversation as Julie stepped in.

"Good morning, Mrs. Tosh!" Beth said, waving to get Julie's attention. She put up a finger, gesturing for her to wait a moment. "Uh-huh!" she said, turning her head down and directly into the phone. "No problem! I'll make a note. Goodbye."

Mrs. Reed turned her gaze back up toward Julie. "You are all set. The buses are waiting behind the building. Anything else you need, just let me know," she said with a proud thumbs-up.

"Thank you so much, Beth! For all your help!" Julie replied. "I'm going to stop at my room for a sec and then meet the kids in the gym. If any of the students or volunteers are looking for me, just send them down there. I think that's it!"

Julie's excitement grew as the clock ticked closer to 8:00 a.m.

"Wish me luck!" Julie said with an anxious grin.

"Good luck!" said Beth. "And HAVE FUN!"

"I will!" Julie said, smiling wider before quickly checking her mailbox and heading to her room.

Julie just needed to unlock the door and throw some things on her desk for Mrs. Martinez. She was covering Julie's classes for the day, and even though the plan was to show a movie, Julie figured she would leave some real English assignments—just in case Maria had a change in plans.

Next stop: the gym to meet up with all the students and volunteers.

7:50 a.m.

Here we go! Julie tried to pump herself up as she headed down the hallway.

The morning gym scene was not something Julie was accustomed to. The gym was large, loud, and chaotic. Every morning before the 8 o'clock bell, students congregated here, filling the space with chatter and restless energy.

Julie knew that once the bell rang, chaos would erupt. Herding a group of excited students while coordinating with volunteers would be no small task. If she had any hope of keeping things under control, she had to act fast. And she knew exactly what to do.

Stepping into the gym, she didn't hesitate. She reached into her pocket, pulled out an old plastic whistle, and brought it to her lips.

The sharp, piercing sound cut through the buzz of conversation.

Instantly, the room quieted. A hush of curiosity settled over the students as all eyes darted toward the gym doors——then locked onto Julie as she strode in, poised and in control.

"Good morning!" Julie's voice rang out, firm and commanding, cutting through the chatter.

"Listen up! I need everyone's attention," she called again, her tone firm but upbeat. "Today is the sixth-grade field trip. When the bell rings—" she paused, taking a steadying breath, "—I need all sixth graders going on the trip to stay here in the gym. Got it?"

She scanned the crowd, making sure they were following. "Volunteers, please meet me by the bleachers so we can get everything squared away before we head out."

Julie's gaze swept over the students, her voice clear and direct. "If you're in sixth grade and staying at school, head to your homeroom as usual. Your day will be a pretty normal Monday." She took another deep breath, checking for any confused expressions.

"Seventh and eighth graders, when the bell rings, you go upstairs. Sixth graders on the trip, stay put. Sixth graders not on the trip, head to your homeroom."

She pointed to the clock. "Four minutes! Thank you!"

Julie looked away from the crowd and around the gym, searching for a space where she could collect her thoughts.

She sat down on the bleachers, placed her bag on the ground, and waited for the bell to ring.

Mr. Anderson sat down next to her, laughing. "Wow, I have never seen you like that before!" he said with a smile. "So in charge! Are you ready for today?" he asked with playful sincerity.

"I think so!" Julie smiled back. "Fingers crossed. We just need to get there and get back!" she laughed nervously.

"Mrs. Tosh?" asked Lisa, who was standing behind Julie. "What do you want Alyssa and me to do? Or where should we go?"

"Good morning, 'L,'" Julie smiled. "You two can stay here too. As far as things go, you are both just sixth graders on the field trip. I have you two in the same group so you can stay together. So when the bell rings, just hang out here."

"Got it!" Lisa smiled. "Can't wait!"

Julie watched and waited until the bell rang. Everyone followed her instructions, and within a few minutes, all that remained were her charges for the day, Mr. Anderson, and a handful of volunteers.

Julie blew her whistle once more to get everyone's attention. The room fell silent again.

"Listen up!" she said in a fun and excited tone. "We have 30 minutes before we leave. I am going to meet with the chaperones and then divide you into groups. Once you are in your groups, you will stay in those groups for the rest of the day. Does everyone understand?"

Julie looked around the room for any questions. "No questions?" she asked again. "Okay. Give us five minutes, and we'll get going."

She corralled all the chaperones, including Mr. Anderson, around her on the bleachers and pulled out her folder of student permission slips.

She explained that she had already divided the students into groups and would be calling out their names to organize them. Each group would then meet their assigned chaperone, ensuring every adult was introduced to the kids they'd be supervising.

At the top of her stack of papers was a roll call sheet for each group. Julie had carefully marked an asterisk next to any student with special notes on their permission slip—food allergies, medical needs, or other important details. While she would collect the permission slips, the chaperones would keep their roll call sheets for reference.

To make things even easier, she had included her cell phone number on every sheet, ensuring the chaperones could reach her at any point during the day if needed.

"Wow!" Cole smiled. "You really have this well-organized! Good for you! I'm taking notes!"

Julie smiled back. She had worked hard putting this together, and it felt nice to get a little recognition.

Methodically, she called out each student's name, directing them to their assigned chaperone. One by one, the groups took shape, each student accounted for and paired with an adult.

Once the final name was checked off, she gave a satisfied nod. Everything was running smoothly. With a quick glance around to ensure no one was left behind, she led the way as the students and chaperones made their way to the buses, just as planned.

| 45 |

Everyone going on the trip made their way out the back door of the gym and loaded onto the buses.

Julie's excitement grew as she watched the students board. The cold air and smell of bus exhaust brought her back to when she was younger and in school.

She took a deep breath as she climbed up the stairs to the lead bus. "We're all set!" she told the driver as she took a seat.

Julie gazed out the window as the buses rolled out of town, merging onto the turnpike. The passing scenery—stretches of dark wooded areas and rugged, stone-faced cliffs—held a quiet beauty she rarely had time to appreciate.

Rain from the night before had left a glistening sheen of ice on the rocky surfaces, catching the pale morning light.

Last night...

The thought slipped in before she could stop it.

Finn.

A slow smile curved her lips as the steady hum of the bus and the rhythmic vibrations beneath her feet lulled her into a wistful daze. Her mind wandered, tracing the electric thrill of teasing him, the way she had unraveled him completely. It had been intoxicating—to be wanted, to feel desired and sexy.

The ride to Old Patriot Village passed in a blur, and all too soon, reality pulled her back. The buses rumbled to a stop in the parking lot of the living museum, breaking the spell and bringing her firmly back to the present.

Julie hopped off the bus to meet the village trip coordinator, who was waiting by the visitor center entrance. She was directed inside to confirm and finalize paperwork, while the coordinator boarded the buses to review rules and park policies with the students and chaperones.

Once Julie was done inside, the buses were parked, and the students assembled around her for further directions.

"Okay, everyone, huddle up so I don't have to yell," Julie called out, motioning for the group to gather closer. As they tightened the circle, she handed maps and schedules to each chaperone.

"Remember, today you represent Franklin," she continued, her tone firm yet encouraging. "I expect you all to be on your best behavior—be polite, cooperative, and respectful. Stay in your groups and with your chaperone at all times."

She glanced around, making sure she had their attention. "Each group has a map and a schedule. What you see and do is entirely up to your chaperone, but the most important thing to remember is that we need to be back here and ready to leave by 1:30 p.m. Chaperones, you can take your lunch whenever you'd like, just make sure you eat in the designated areas."

Julie scanned the crowd, her eyes sweeping over the eager faces. "I'll be checking in with each group throughout the day, so if anything comes up, let me know." She hesitated for a moment, then grinned. "Oh, and one more thing—have fun!"

As the students broke into their smaller groups and wandered off, a deep sense of satisfaction settled over Julie. The sun had finally pushed through the morning chill, warming the air with each passing minute.

She hadn't felt this good in a long time.

All the careful planning, all the hard work—it was paying off. Everything was running smoothly.

With a smile, she watched the students step back in time, disappearing into the world of early 19th-century New England.

Julie spent most of the day wandering the historic grounds, checking in with different groups and soaking in the lively atmosphere. She couldn't help but smile as she watched the students eagerly explore—crowding around the old printing press, marveling at the craftsmanship in the cabinet-making shop, and chatting excitedly about their discoveries.

Time and time again, students rushed up to her, animatedly recounting their experiences at the blacksmith's forge or describing the intricate pottery they had seen being shaped by hand.

Their enthusiasm was infectious, and as Julie listened to their stories, she knew the trip had been a success.

Everyone was learning, exploring, and—most importantly—having a great time.

Julie wandered the grounds, letting the charm of the village wash over her. The worn cobblestone paths, rustic wooden buildings, and the quiet hum of nature made it easy to imagine what life might have been like here centuries ago.

Her steps carried her along the Riverwalk, the gentle ripple of water lulling her deeper into thought. As she strolled, an old covered bridge came into view, its weathered beams standing against the backdrop of the now bright blue sky.

That would make a cute photo, she thought, reaching for her phone.

She snapped a few shots of the bridge before turning the camera on herself, angling for the perfect selfie to send to Finn later.

Agh. She frowned.

The sun was too harsh, the angle all wrong.

Maybe later.

As she lowered her phone, movement caught her eye. Cole and his group were just stepping out of the simple machines exhibit, and for a moment, Julie hesitated, her pulse quickening as she adjusted her grip on her phone.

"How's it going?" Julie asked, stepping toward Cole and his group.

"Fantastic!" Alyssa shouted from the back of the pack, her face lit with excitement. "This place is amazing! I can't believe they lived like this—without electricity!"

"That's right!" Cole added with an easy grin. "They relied on science and engineering to make their lives easier. Pretty impressive, huh?"

Julie laughed at Cole's obvious attempt to tie science into their experience.

"Just have fun!" she teased, shaking her head. "Where are you headed next?"

"I think we're checking out the sawmill before grabbing a quick lunch. You?"

"I'm heading back to the picnic area to meet up with some of the other groups," she replied.

Cole chuckled. "Oh! It looked like you were trying to take a picture." His grin was playful. "Want me to take it for you?"

Julie hesitated for half a second before sighing. "Uh, sure!"

She could already feel the warmth creeping into her cheeks as she handed him her phone.

Leaning casually against the edge of the bridge, she smiled while Cole snapped a few shots.

"Slay it, Mrs. Tosh!" a student called from the back of the group.

Julie burst out laughing, shaking her head. "Mrs. Tosh does not slay it!" she shot back, her voice full of amusement.

"Hold on," Cole said, his expression thoughtful. "Come here."

Before Julie could react, he gently took her hand and led her into the covered bridge's shadowy interior. The scent of aged wood surrounded them as he positioned her near one of the massive beams.

"Yeah, here," he said confidently. "Now you've got the old beams in the background—it'll frame the shot better."

Julie laughed, a little self-conscious, as Cole snapped a few more pictures.

"There's got to be a good one in there," she said, tucking a loose strand of hair behind her ear.

"They're all good ones," Cole replied with an easy smile as he handed her back the phone.

"Thanks," she said, her voice warm as their fingers briefly brushed.

"Wait—hold on!" Cole grinned, pulling his own phone from his pocket. "Let me take one."

Before she could protest, he wrapped an arm around her shoulder and angled the camera. "Smile!" he said, snapping a quick selfie.

He glanced down at the screen and nodded, satisfied. "That one looks great!" He turned the phone toward her.

Julie burst out laughing. "Oh my God. Yeah!" she agreed, shaking her head as she met his gaze.

"I'll send it to you and Melanie. She'd love to see we're having a great time while she's stuck at work," Cole joked as he quickly texted the photo to both of them.

Julie let out a small laugh, though a flicker of jealousy ran through her chest at the mention of Melanie's name. She pushed the feeling aside, forcing herself to focus on the moment.

But before she could say anything, Cole had already turned back to his group. "Alright, guys! Let's go! There's a lot more to see before we head out."

He gave Julie a quick fist bump before leading his group down the road toward the old sawmill.

Julie watched them go, a lingering smile on her lips. With a small sigh, she glanced down at her phone and opened the picture Cole had just sent.

Another smile.

What a day.

Julie spent the rest of the afternoon moving between groups, watching as students eagerly churned butter and tried their hand at milking cows at the old farmstead. At the cobbler's shop, they marveled at the intricate craftsmanship of handmade shoes, while at the tinsmith's workshop, they observed metal being shaped into everyday tools. The herb garden filled the air with the earthy scents of rosemary and thyme, adding to the immersive experience.

There was so much to see, so much to learn, and Julie couldn't have been happier with how the day had unfolded.

All too soon, the trip came to an end. As the students gathered in the parking lot, Julie moved from group to group, double-checking headcounts before guiding everyone onto the buses. Once the last student was seated, she climbed aboard and flashed a grin at the driver.

"Alright," she said with a laugh, "take us home."

She turned to face the bus, scanning the tired but satisfied faces behind her. "I hope everyone had a great time?"

A chorus of mumbled yeses and yeahs rippled through the rows, some students still buzzing with excitement, others already leaning against the windows, ready for the ride home.

Julie let out a deep breath, allowing herself a moment to take it all in.

The trip had been a success. And for the first time in a long while, she felt proud of herself.

"Mrs. Tosh!"

Julie turned at the sound of her name, finding Lisa and Alyssa sitting just behind her, both grinning.

"Thank you for letting us come along!" Lisa said sincerely. "We really had a great time."

"We got so much for the paper!" Alyssa chimed in excitedly. "And we took tons of photos."

"Show her!" Lisa nudged Alyssa, motioning toward her phone.

Alyssa shot her friend a look. "Hold on! I will!" she huffed playfully as she unlocked her phone and began swiping through the pictures.

She paused, tilting the screen toward Julie. "We thought this one looked so cute."

Alyssa turned the phone toward Julie, and the image on the screen made her breath hitch for just a moment.

It was a photo of her and Cole, taken beneath the bridge when he had been helping her get the perfect shot. He was holding her hand, pulling her slightly forward, his face alight with laughter. The sun streamed behind them, casting a golden glow, while the shadows of the aged wooden beams framed them in a way that felt almost... magical.

The picture was innocent—just a captured moment between two friends—but there was something unspoken in the way they looked at each other. Something that, perhaps, neither of them had fully acknowledged.

"Oh my!" Julie laughed in shock, pressing a hand to her mouth. "It is a beautiful photo!" She kept staring at the screen, her smile lingering.

Then, snapping herself back to reality, she added in a more matter-of-fact tone, "But definitely not for the school paper."

Alyssa and Lisa giggled, exchanging a knowing look.

Julie hesitated for a split second before glancing back at the image. "But... can I send it to myself?" she asked, her voice light. "I'm sure Mr. Anderson would like to see it too."

Alyssa nodded and handed Julie her phone, letting her text the photo to herself.

As they continued scrolling through pictures, the girls excitedly pointed out their favorite moments, debating which sights they would highlight in their article. The ride back to Franklin passed quickly as they chatted, their enthusiasm making the trip feel shorter than it was.

As they neared the school, Julie pulled out her phone and called Mrs. Reed. "Hey, could you have one of the custodians meet us at the rear entrance of the gym?" she asked.

Once they arrived, Julie efficiently guided everyone back inside, gathering them in the gym to wait for the dismissal bell. They had made it back with ten minutes to spare.

Standing at the front, Julie blew her whistle one more time to get their attention. "I just want to thank you all for an amazing day!" she said, her voice full of energy. "I hope you had fun and learned a lot."

She turned toward the chaperones and raised her hands in applause. "Let's give a huge thank you to all of our volunteers!" She started clapping, encouraging the students to join in.

"Thank you again," she added sincerely, nodding toward the chaperones. "Students, you can grab a seat on the bleachers. You'll be dismissed when the bell rings."

As the applause faded and the students began settling in, Julie exhaled, a satisfied smile on her face. The trip had been a success.

The students sat on the bleachers, their voices buzzing with lingering excitement as they chatted amongst themselves.

Cole made his way over to Julie, a warm smile on his face. "You did a great job," he said sincerely. "Seriously, what a day. Everything went perfectly. You should be really proud."

Julie met his gaze, her own smile widening. "Thank you! That means a lot coming from you," she said, her voice full of appreciation. Then, with a playful smirk, she added, "And thanks for coming, too. You definitely made it special." She held up a fist, prompting him for a bump.

Cole chuckled and returned the gesture just as the bell rang at 2:30.

In an instant, the gym erupted into motion as students scrambled toward the exits, their excited chatter fading into the halls. Within moments, the large open space was empty, leaving only Julie standing in the quiet echo of the day's success.

She took a deep breath, letting the satisfaction settle in.

After a brief pause, she made her way back to Room 10 to check in with Mrs. Martinez. When she arrived, a small yellow note was waiting for her on the desk.

"Hope you had a great trip! See you tomorrow."

Julie smiled as she picked it up.

I guess that means no issues, she thought as she sank into her chair.

Mondays meant staying after school, though no one had signed up for extra help. Still, she decided to wait, just in case. The silence of the empty classroom wrapped around her, a stark contrast to the whirlwind of the day. It had been amazing—but she was exhausted.

Fifteen quiet minutes passed before Mr. Anderson walked in.

"Hey! Good, you're still here," he said with a smile. "I wanted to give you this before I lost it or forgot."

Julie watched as he reached into his pocket and pulled out a small, flattened metal object.

"I made this for you today," he said, setting it on her desk. "It's not much, but... the gift shop had one of those penny presses, and I thought you'd like it."

Julie picked up the warm, smoothed-out coin, turning it over in her fingers. It was an imprinted penny from Patriot Village, embossed with the image of the Old Meeting House. Around the edges, the words *Old Patriot Village* curved neatly in raised letters.

"Oh my God. Cole, you—" She stopped, momentarily at a loss for words. "You didn't have to do this!" She looked closer, a genuine smile spreading across her face. "Thank you! I love it."

"You deserve it," he said simply. "You did great today."

He held up a fist, and Julie bumped it with a grateful laugh.

"What would I do without you?" she teased.

Cole grinned. "Well, you don't have to worry about that—because I'm not going anywhere."

And with that, he turned toward the door. "Have a great night! See you in the morning!"

Julie watched him go, the penny still resting in her palm.

I better go too, she thought, gathering her things.

The day had been long enough. It was time to head home.

| 46 |

On the drive home, Julie's thoughts drifted back to the night before. She couldn't wait to tell Finn all about her day—about the success of the trip, the little moments that made it special. And just as much, she couldn't wait to hear about his day.

Excitement buzzed under her skin, a warmth she hadn't felt in a long time.

But beneath that anticipation lurked something heavier.

Mike comes home tomorrow.

The thought settled over her like a storm cloud, darkening the edges of her excitement. She gripped the wheel a little tighter, her stomach twisting at the uncertainty of how things would unfold.

She pushed the thought aside—for now. She wanted to hold onto the good parts of the day just a little longer.

When Julie got home, she called upstairs. "Tom! Chad! Come down for a minute!"

A moment later, the boys trudged downstairs, their footsteps heavy with curiosity—and maybe reluctance.

"I'm making spaghetti for dinner," she said, meeting their eyes, "but before that, I need you both to help me clean up a little before Dad gets home tomorrow." Her voice was calm, without its usual edge of urgency.

"Can you at least pick up your rooms and make sure the bathrooms are clean?" She hesitated, then softened her tone. "You guys know what's going on. I'm not going to pretend. But if we can make things a little better than they are now, I'm sure it'll go a long way. Okay?"

"Of course!" Chad agreed. "I'll finish my homework before dinner, then I'll get on it."

"You got it, Mom," Tommy added. "Don't worry about it!" Then, with a grin, he asked, "By the way, how was the field trip?"

Julie beamed at them, warmth filling her chest. "It was so good! SO good! Everyone had a great time—no catastrophes, no disasters. I really think it went super well." She let out a breath, still riding the high of a successful day. "I can't wait to talk to Mr. Dryer tomorrow and hear what feedback he's gotten."

She paused, looking between her boys, her heart swelling with gratitude. "Thank you," she said, exhaling deeply. "I love you guys. So much. Seriously, thank you."

"We love you too!" Tommy replied with an easy smile.

Julie clapped her hands together. "Alright, get your homework done—dinner will be ready in thirty minutes!"

The boys dashed back upstairs, and Julie turned her attention to the kitchen, prepping for dinner. She loved that Mondays were Pasta Nights—a small tradition that made her late days so much easier.

Before she knew it, dinner was ready and on the table. The boys joined her, and soon, their usual chatter filled the room.

Julie had the most to share. Of course, she told them all about the field trip and how relieved she was that everything had gone smoothly. But she also dove into the details—the exhibits, the demonstrations, the little moments that made the day special. She showed them the pictures she had taken and pulled out the pressed penny Mr. Anderson had given her, rolling it between her fingers as she explained its significance.

"And now that I actually know what I'm doing," she added with a grin, "I would definitely volunteer to do it again next year."

She let out a satisfied sigh, twirling her fork in her spaghetti. "But I won't lie—I'm so glad it's over."

Julie knew she couldn't avoid the conversation about Mike. As much as she wished she could shield her boys from the uncertainty of tomorrow, she also knew she needed to be honest—at least as much as they could handle.

She set her fork down and took a steadying breath. "Guys," she said gently, looking between them. "I can't tell you exactly what's going to happen when your dad gets home. But what I can tell you is that I can't keep living like this anymore."

She paused, choosing her words carefully. "That's what I plan on telling him. I'm not happy. I'm not happy with him. I'm not happy with the way things are between us. And I really think something has to change."

She exhaled, her gaze softening. "I'm so sorry you have to be involved in this at all. And honestly, I don't want you to be. At least not right now. This is between your dad and me."

Julie reached for their hands, giving each a gentle squeeze. "But no matter what happens, I love you. Okay?"

Julie watched the expressions on her boys' faces shift as she spoke. The sadness in their eyes was unmistakable. They were upset—of course they were. And it broke her heart.

"I don't know what else to say," she admitted softly. "But if either of you needs to talk, I'm here. Just let me know, okay?" She took a breath, forcing herself to stay steady. "For now, we can't assume anything until your dad gets home."

She was trying to reassure them as best she could. But in truth, she was trying to reassure herself, too.

She had no idea what to expect.

Mike still hadn't called or texted since Saturday, and she didn't expect him to tonight, either.

With dinner finished, Julie threw herself into cleaning. She scrubbed the kitchen, wiped down the counters, and swept the floors. The living room got the same treatment—vacuuming, dusting, straightening up. The boys pitched in, tackling their own spaces without complaint.

At least that was done.

He can't be too mad at the house.

She hoped.

Julie made her way upstairs, pausing by each doorway to wish the boys goodnight.

I am exhausted, she thought as she flicked on the bathroom light.

Stepping inside, she caught her reflection in the mirror and studied herself for a moment. There was something different about her today—something she liked. Maybe it was the confidence from pulling off a successful trip, or maybe it was just the way she felt in her own skin.

A smirk tugged at her lips. *Maybe I should trade in the granny panties and sports bra more often.*

Julie wiped off her makeup and brushed her teeth, her body already craving the warmth of a hot shower.

The moment she stepped under the spray, the tension of the day began to melt away. She let the water cascade over her shoulders, releasing a deep, audible sigh.

"Ahhhh," she murmured, closing her eyes.

It had been such a long day, and this—*this*—was exactly what she needed.

She stayed there for a while, savoring the comfort until exhaustion began to creep in. Finally, she shut off the water, wrapped herself in a towel, and padded over to her dresser. Pulling out her favorite t-shirt, she slipped it on, relishing the familiar softness before climbing into bed.

Lying on her back, she stared up at the ceiling, her mind still buzzing despite the weight of fatigue settling over her.

She should sleep—she needed to sleep.

But all she could think about was Finn.

She wanted to tell him everything.

I have no idea if he's even on, Julie thought, biting her lip.

Oh, why not?

She reached down, grabbed her laptop from the floor, and pulled it onto the bed. With a few familiar keystrokes, she powered it up and launched the chat program. At this point, navigating the interface felt second nature—like she had been using it for years.

A quick glance at her friends list confirmed it—*Finn wasn't online.*

It's still early. I'll wait a little, she decided, hoping he might pop on soon.

As the familiar chime of new messages filled the room, she ignored them, only interested in one name appearing on her screen. To pass the time, she aimlessly scrolled through the directory, skimming usernames and profiles. Some were mildly amusing, others downright ridiculous.

Richard The Big, she read with a smirk. *Subtle.*

Jake The Snake, she chuckled.

She absentmindedly resorted the list alphabetically, starting from the bottom.

Her scrolling stopped cold.

The last username— *Waltz&Tango*—caught her eye.

Julie gasped quietly as she stared at the small profile image. She blinked, then leaned in closer, her pulse picking up speed.

It was a picture of *Barbara and Harold.*

Barbara, wearing a pink bra. Harold, shirtless.

Julie hesitated before double-clicking the profile, a sinking feeling settling in her stomach.

Waltz&Tango : Married 45–55 : Fun-loving couple always looking for another to join.

Her eyes widened.

"What?!" she blurted out, the word escaping before she could stop it.

Her pulse pounded as she read further.

3Somes / Swapping / We Like To Have Fun.

Her stomach flipped.

Barbara?

Barbara!

Really?

But the more she thought about it, the more it made sense. *Of course* Barbara would be on here—she was the one who told Julie about the program in the first place. She had been so eager to introduce her to the chat, to invite her and the other women to her party.

Julie's hands hovered over the keyboard, her mind racing.

Holy fuck.

Julie logged off and shut down her computer, exhaling as she tried to process everything.

Wow.

Laying back against the pillows, she gently lowered the laptop to the floor. Her mind raced, but her body felt heavy with exhaustion. Staring up at the ceiling, she let the whirlwind of thoughts settle.

After a moment, she reached for her phone, instinctively checking her alarm for the next morning. Her thumb hovered over her messages.

Maybe Mike finally texted me.

Nope.

Not that she was surprised.

Her gaze drifted down her message history, pausing on the one she had sent herself from Alyssa's phone. She tapped it open, and the image filled her screen.

She and Cole, walking under the bridge. The way he was pulling her forward, the way they were looking at each other, laughing.

Julie traced the edge of the screen with her thumb.

"*Cole,*" she whispered, as if he might hear it in his thoughts—or as if saying his name might somehow bring him closer.

She pulled up the text. The one he had sent—the photo of the two of them under the bridge.

Her eyes lingered on his face, studying the way the corners of his mouth lifted, the slight creases around his eyes as he smiled.

That smile.

Warmth spread through her chest.

That smile defines his amazing personality.

It was effortless, genuine—so him.

Julie let out a slow breath, her fingers brushing the screen. For a moment, she let herself get lost in the image, in the way it made her feel.

She closed her eyes, letting herself drift back to the feeling of his arm around her—the quiet strength in the way he held her. She had felt small in his grasp, but not fragile. *Safe. Warm. Wanted.*

A soft smile touched her lips as she gazed at the picture again.

"*Ahh, Cole,*" she murmured, her voice barely above a whisper.

Her hand instinctively reached for the nightstand, fingers sliding into the top drawer.

Why not? she thought as she traced the familiar shape, pulling her favorite toy into her grasp.

Settling deeper into the mattress, she shimmied her legs beneath the blankets, loosening them from one another. She bent her knees slightly, parting them just enough to invite the cool air against her skin. A shiver rippled through her—slow, electric, exhilarating.

She let out a breath, anticipation curling through her like a slow burn.

Laying the toy across her chest, she slid a hand under the blankets, tugging at her t-shirt, exposing more of her abdomen to the cool touch of the bedsheets.

Julie glanced at the picture of her and Cole, her fingers drifting further down, skimming along the soft curve of her inner thigh. Her breath deepened with each gentle caress.

In her mind, she was back at the bridge. Just her and Cole. No one else.

She imagined the solid warmth of his body, the way her arms would fit around his neck, her head resting against his chest. So close she could feel the steady rise and fall of his breath, hear the rhythmic beat of his heart.

She let herself sink deeper into the fantasy—his hands sliding down her back, his arms tightening, pulling her impossibly close. The press of his body against hers, the heat between them.

His head dipped lower, their lips just a breath apart.

Julie traced her fingernails over the soft curls between her legs, teasing herself with feather-light strokes. She imagined his hands gripping her waist, his fingers splayed across her hips, anchoring her against him.

Her hands sliding down his chest, finding the waistband of his jeans. The press of his erection against the fabric, the way he would ache to be touched.

Julie exhaled, her fingers dipping lower, parting herself slightly. Warmth seeped from her core as she spread herself open, then closed again, squeezing her fingers around the growing pulse at her center.

A quiet gasp escaped her lips, her breath quickening. She imagined Cole's fingers trailing beneath the hem of her jeans, pressing into her, exploring her.

She reached for her phone, opening the text from Melanie—the one of her hand gripping Cole through his pants.

Oh my God.

The thought pulsed through her mind as the fantasy deepened, as if it were her fingers wrapped around him, feeling the heat, the hardness beneath her touch.

Her hand trembled as she grabbed the toy from her chest and flicked it on.

The low hum filled the quiet room, the vibration sending an immediate rush through her body.

Her anticipation built as she maneuvered it beneath the sheets, carefully positioning the head of the toy exactly where she needed it.

The cool silicone soothed her burning flesh for just an instant before settling into the familiar rhythm Julie loved.

She let her eyes flutter shut, sinking completely into the moment.

In her mind, Cole was between her legs, his tongue teasing her, licking slowly, deliberately.

Julie's grip on the phone faltered, and it slipped from her hand, forgotten. With her free hand, she reached down, sliding two fingers deep inside herself. The sensation of penetration sent a new wave of pleasure surging through her, the combination overwhelming.

She matched the rhythm, thrusting in time with the toy.

Fuck!

The word echoed in her mind as she clenched her teeth, her body tightening. The pressure was building—higher, deeper, insistent.

Her instincts told her to hold back, to resist the overwhelming sensation.

But she didn't stop.

She *couldn't* stop.

She kept going, chasing the pleasure, the deep, rhythmic pace driving her higher.

Faster.

Until she was completely lost in it.

Julie felt her muscles tighten—her abdomen clenching, her thighs quivering. Her breathing grew quick and shallow as the pleasure built deep inside her, a pressure swelling, relentless, consuming.

She focused all her attention on the toy—the pulsing, the throbbing beat against her clit.

"*Aghhhh!*" she cried out as her knees buckled, her body writhing in orgasmic convulsions.

She kept going, prolonging the pleasure, her body twisting with every pulse.

"Fuck!" she gasped, her back arching. *"Fuck! Cole!"*

Her breath came in erratic waves, gasping uncontrollably for air. The sensations were too much—too overwhelming. She couldn't take it anymore. With a final shudder, she pulled her fingers and the toy away, letting them fall to the bed beside her.

Julie lay there, panting, her chest rising and falling as she tried to catch her breath.

A slow warmth spread through her limbs, her muscles melting into the mattress, completely spent.

She let out a deep, steadying sigh, the aftershocks still rippling through her, satisfaction humming beneath her skin.

Fuck.

The word echoed in her mind again as she reached for her phone, lifting it from where it had rested against her chest.

The screen lit up, revealing the selfie—her, Cole, and Melanie.

Julie smiled.

She set the phone down on the nightstand, her fingers lingering for just a moment before leaning over and tucking the toy away in the back of the drawer.

With a contented sigh, she sank back into her pillows, pulling the blankets up to her chin.

Her eyes fluttered closed, exhaustion finally taking hold.

| 47 |

The next morning, Julie woke up excited to start her day. She couldn't wait to hear what everyone thought of the field trip.

The morning followed her usual pattern—getting up, getting dressed, and heading downstairs to make a pot of coffee while the boys showered and got ready for school.

As she waited for them, she busied herself tidying up the house. When they were finally ready, they all headed out the door.

Julie dropped the boys off at school and kept driving toward Franklin, gripping the wheel a little tighter than usual.

She tried—*really* tried—to push the thought away.

Mike comes home today.

Ugh.

Her stomach twisted as the weight of it settled over her. No matter how hard she tried to focus on the road, on the day ahead, her mind kept circling back.

How is this going to go?
What am I supposed to say?
What is he going to say?

She already knew these questions would be lingering in the back of her mind all day, no matter how much she tried to push them aside.

But for now, she forced herself to focus on the drive. On work. On anything *other* than what was waiting for her at home.

When she got to Franklin, Julie made her regular stop at the office. Mrs. Reed was on the phone—*as usual.* Julie nodded as she walked by before checking her mailbox.

Nothing, she thought. *No surprise.*

"I heard things went well yesterday!" Mrs. Reed called out as Julie stepped away from the mailbox. "Some of the sixth graders were talking about it this morning."

Julie looked over and smiled. Mrs. Reed was still on the phone, but she clearly wanted Julie to know she'd heard positive feedback.

"Yes! We had a great time," Julie said. "I'm looking forward to doing it again next year."

The clock caught her eye.

"I have to run, but I'll tell you all about it later."

With a quick wave, she turned toward the door and made her way to Room 10.

Julie pushed open the door and strode inside, tossing her bag onto the desk with a frustrated sigh.

"Fuck!" she blurted into the empty room.

Her laptop.

It was still on the floor in her bedroom.

Not that she *couldn't* get through the day without it, but she liked having it—checking emails, catching up on paperwork between classes. Now, she'd have to manage without.

With a resigned exhale, she sank into her chair, drumming her fingers on the desk as she waited for the bell to ring.

The morning flew by in a blur of conversation and reflection.

Julie spent the day discussing the field trip with her classes, guiding them through thoughtful discussions. She had them write short summaries about what they had learned and their favorite moments, encouraging them to relive the experience through their own words.

She also had her students list things they saw and learned that connected to their other classes.

"What was a science takeaway?" she asked. "Social studies? How about math?"

Each class dove into the exercise, making connections she hadn't even considered. The discussions were lively, thoughtful, and engaging.

A deep sense of satisfaction settled in Julie's chest. The trip had been everything she had hoped for—and more.

The day continued to run smoothly, the morning slipping seamlessly into the afternoon.

Julie's last period was her prep, giving her time to sort through the paperwork from the trip. She carefully organized and filed everything away, making sure to note any details she might need for the future.

Once that was done, she made her way down to the office, stopping to chat with Mrs. Reed as she had promised. After a quick conversation, she headed to the teachers' lounge, craving a much-needed cup of coffee.

The day may have gone off without a hitch, but exhaustion from both yesterday's trip and last night's restless thoughts still clung to her.

She filled her cup, inhaling the rich aroma before making her way back to Room 10, ready for dismissal and the final bell.

The drive home was nerve-wracking.

Julie hadn't heard from Mike since Saturday night, and the silence gnawed at her. As the miles passed, doubt crept in, winding its way through her thoughts.

Maybe she shouldn't have gone out with Cole and Melanie.

He had been so against it—maybe he was right. Maybe she was being selfish. Maybe she owed him more respect for everything he'd done for her.

Maybe... this entire situation was her fault.

The thoughts circled relentlessly, but deep down, she knew the truth.

It *wasn't* her fault.

For years, Mike had controlled everything—his way, his rules. She had spent so long trying to keep the peace that she had almost forgotten what peace even felt like. And now, she was caught between the two.

But his ultimatum... *that* was the real gift.

Mike had always been skilled at manipulating her, at making her feel like she had a choice when, in reality, he had already taken it away. *Shot or stabbed?* That wasn't a real choice. The end result was the same—*dead.*

One thing was certain: Mike never actually expected her to go through with it. He never thought she'd *really* go out—especially without his approval.

And now, Julie wasn't sure what upset him more—*that she went out... or that she had finally stopped obeying.*

Julie kept driving, her thoughts tangled in a relentless loop. She had no idea when Mike would be home.

Or worse—if he was already there.

Agh. I'm so scared. So confused.

She knew what she wanted. What she deserved.

But actually going after it? *That* was terrifying.

As she pulled onto Cabot Lane and parked in her usual spot, she scanned the house for any sign of him.

Nothing.

Relief washed over her as she stepped inside. The boys had hung up their coats and taken their bags upstairs—small victories.

"I'm home!" she called out, forcing her voice to sound normal. "I'm going to start dinner."

Muffled replies drifted down from upstairs.

Julie exhaled and turned toward the kitchen. She hadn't even thought about what to make.

She opened the fridge, scanning the shelves until her eyes landed on a head of lettuce, a few vegetables, and some chicken breasts.

Grilled chicken salads it is, she decided, pulling everything out and setting it on the island.

She worked methodically—grilling the chicken, cutting it into bite-sized cubes, then setting it on paper towels to drain.

She washed and chopped the lettuce and vegetables, tossing everything together in a large bowl. Once the chicken had cooled, she mixed it in, covered the salad with plastic wrap, and slid it into the fridge.

Dinner was done.

With a quiet sigh, Julie poured herself a glass of wine and settled onto the couch. She flicked on the TV, trying—*really trying*—to relax.

The news had just started when she heard it.

The deep, mechanical groan of the garage door opening.

Her stomach tightened.

Mike.

She took a steadying breath, set her wine glass down, and pushed herself up from the couch.

Time to face him.

She walked to the kitchen, forcing her shoulders to stay straight, her breath even.

Then she stood by the door, waiting.

The door opened, and there he was.

Mike stood in the doorway, his expression unreadable—until he shook his head.

"I'm sorry," he said, his tone oddly casual. "I may have overreacted."

Julie blinked. *An apology?* She hadn't expected that.

But then—

"But why do you have to act so stupid and piss me off?"

There it is, she thought bitterly. *Yup. It's my fault.*

His voice took on that familiar edge, laced with condescension. "Why can't you just listen to me? Why can't you just respect what I want?"

He stepped further into the kitchen, closing the space between them.

"Listen. I'm sorry I didn't text or call, but that's on you." His eyes locked onto hers, his tone dripping with self-righteousness. "You pissed me off so much I didn't know what to do. So let's just pretend this never happened and agree you're never going to do it again. Because I don't think this is what you really want."

He tilted his head. "You don't really want me mad. *Right?*"

Julie's stomach clenched.

How could he not hear himself?

How could he not see how twisted his words were?

She took another steadying breath.

"I'm sorry," she said, her voice eerily calm. "But that's not going to happen."

Mike's expression flickered.

Julie inhaled deeply, her heart pounding, but she refused to break.

"I *am* going to go out again. I *am* going to have friends. And I am going to do what makes me happy."

She threw her arms out, motioning to the space around them.

"This—" her voice rose, her conviction unwavering, "*THIS* is not happy. This is *hell* Mike.. And you are not going to stop me from being happy."

Mike's entire body went rigid. His eyes narrowed, locking onto her like a predator.

Then—like the flip of a switch—his face twisted with rage.

"FUCK YOU!" he roared. "You can't tell *me* what to do! That's not how it fucking works!"

His voice thundered through the kitchen, his breath coming fast and hard.

"This is my house! *My* house! All you have to do is keep it clean and take care of the boys. That's it! And you can't even fucking do that right!"

He slammed his hand against the counter.

"This is fucking bullshit! I do everything! I do everything for you! I do everything for the kids! Everything! And this is how you treat me? FUCK YOU!"

His voice kept rising, his body shaking with rage.

"Is this what you want? Is THIS what you FUCKING WANT?"

He was inches from her now, screaming directly into her face.

"You want me this fucking mad? Do you? What the fuck is *wrong* with you?"

Julie stood her ground, but she could feel the heat of his breath and see the beads of sweat forming on his reddening forehead.

"FUCK YOU!" he kept shouting, his words cutting like a blade. "I have done nothing but be a good husband and father! I have done EVERYTHING for you! And you can't do just ONE fucking thing for *me*—just listen?"

She said nothing.

Because she had nothing left to say.

Mike raged on, pacing the hallway, spewing accusations—calling her lazy, ungrateful. Even accusing her of turning the boys against him.

That everything—the house, her car, her entire life—was because of him.

Reminding her, over and over again, that without him, she was nothing.

But Julie knew the truth.

She knew exactly what he was doing. And she was tired of it.

She had tried. God, she had tried. But she was done.

Her gaze followed him as he stalked back and forth, yelling. Screaming.

Pure hatred poured from his mouth.

She felt small. Cornered.

Her heart pounded. Fear surged through her veins, cold and paralyzing.

For a moment, it was as if she were outside her own body, watching it all unfold.

And then, she saw it.

He was unraveling.

His fists clenched in rage, his body trembling. In his anger, he had ripped away the mask that had so carefully hidden his true nature.

And for the first time, Julie saw him for exactly what he was.

For who he really was all along.

Julie wanted to speak her mind—desperately. She wanted to scream, to yell, to match him word for word, blow for blow.

It took every ounce of restraint to hold it in, not to lower herself to his level.

Because she knew.

She knew that if she broke—if she uttered just one single word—what would happen.

She knew that if she argued, he'd twist her words, distort the truth and leave her doubting herself all over again.

So she stayed silent.

And her silence cut deeper than anything she could have said.

The more he yelled, the clearer everything became.

She had spent years afraid. Forced into complicit silence. Fearful submission. Reluctant obligation.

He had stripped her of her voice. Stripped her of her self-worth. Stripped her of who she was—*and who she could have been.*

But now.

Now, she *chose* to be silent.

Not out of obedience, but out of defiance.

In her silence, she found her voice. And it was deafening.

Mike's voice thundered through the house.

"Talk to me, or I'm leaving!"

Julie didn't flinch. Didn't move. Didn't speak.

Her silence was her answer.

His face contorted with fury.

"YOU FUCKING BITCH!" he roared, the words lashing out like a whip.

"FUCK YOU!"

His voice was so loud it physically hurt.

Julie still didn't respond.

With an angry snarl, Mike grabbed his bag and stormed toward the garage.

"FUCK YOU!" he bellowed again, the sound echoing through the house as he slammed the door behind him.

Julie heard his car engine roar to life and the mechanical groan of the garage door lifting.

And then—he was *gone.*

A flood of emotions surged through her, swelling in her chest until she thought she might burst.

"AGHHH!"

She let out a raw, guttural scream—years of frustration, of exhaustion, of *pent-up everything* pouring out of her at once.

Her breaths came fast and hard, her body shaking with adrenaline.

Slowly, she walked toward the garage, her steps deliberate, measured.

She took a deep breath—then opened the door.

Julie stood in the open doorway, between the garage and the tiled hallway leading towards the kitchen, her eyes fixed on the garage door as she watched it slowly close.

www.ingramcontent.com/pod-product-compliance
Lightning Source LLC
LaVergne TN
LVHW091622070526
838199LV00044B/901